The Fourth Book of Five

R. P. Poe

"I can wade grief
Whole pools of it,-
I'm used to that.
But the least push of joy
Breaks up my feet"

-Emily Dickinson

"But whatever I am and Truth is, I
Have stood on a high place, yearning
To know what logic of years, and of
Whatever stride, clamber, climb,
Had brought me here to be what I am"

-Robert Penn Warren

For my mother

Chapter One

The boy eased his bedroom window open inch by inch, trying to avoid a midway squeak he had come to know well. Cool night air spilled over his fingers. He paused as the counterweight thumped inside the wooden frame like a dying clock, stopping and starting and stopping again, as if it knew the rhythm of his life.

With the pane half open, he released his grip and turned, reaching for his backpack. That instant the counterweight slipped, dropping the window with a squeal before he could stop it. He froze. Holding his breath, he strained to listen for any sound, dreading the wrath of his foster parents. Nothing stirred in the house.

He again lifted the window, this time with his free hand, tossing out the backpack and scrambling after it. Then he lowered the window back into place just as the roar of an approaching car echoed over the surrounding hills, mingling with the distant bark of a dog. Careful to avoid the streetlight, Nicolai Tate glanced back at the house one last time before hurrying down the gravel driveway and disappearing into the night.

An hour later he crouched beneath the span of a wrought iron gate, the blue and white sign atop it reading 'Manville State Hospital'. A narrow drive curved away from him, disappearing between a cluster of brick buildings. Steel mesh darkened the windows. Fluorescent light from a nearby open door pooled in the dew-dampened grass.

Doubting his luck, he scampered from shadow to shadow, dodging the streetlight glow while making for the open door. Moments later he slipped through. Stepping into a hallway that stretched before him in empty silence, the lights dim due to the late hour, he hurried inside. The murmur of voices arose in the distance, stopping him. He backtracked and started down an adjacent corridor, trying to recall the way, hoping for a familiar landmark.

He had begun to fear he had entered the wrong building when a nurses' station appeared midway down the hall, the sign over it reading 'Ward C'. A single nurse sat beneath a dim circle of light. He pressed himself into a doorway.

After what seemed hours, she stood and disappeared around the corner. He slipped from his hiding place. Hurrying down the hall and past the nurses' station, he moved along the wall, pausing at each room, straining to see the numbers. Coming to an entrance that seemed familiar, he took a chance and stepped inside.

A lamp covered by a red scarf glowed in the far corner. He glanced at the bed, finding it empty. Fearing he had entered the wrong room and would be caught, he glanced back toward the doorway. Then a familiar voice whispered from the shadows.

"Who's there?"

He peered into the darkness. "It's me, Nicolai."

"Do I know you?"

"Mama, it's me, it's your son." He tried to slick down his cowlick as he moved toward the sound.

"My son?"

Her form appeared beneath the red glow of the lamp. Sitting on the bare floor, her back against the wall, she held her knees to her chest. Her unwashed hair stuck to the side of her head in clumps. He knelt beside her.

"Don't you recognize me?"

She stared at him without expression, her gray eyes dull and glassy. "I... I don't know."

"I'm your son, Nicolai."

She blinked, running a hand through her stringy hair. "Yes, I think... yes, I did have a son once."

"I've come to see you, mom, to talk to you." He leaned in and studied her gaunt features.

"You're a handsome boy." She reached out, tracing the side of his face. "Were you really my son?"

"Mama, what's happened to you?"

2

"I had a son once but the dark people came and took him from me."

"But I'm here now."

"No, only Jesus can bring him back." She looked around the room as if searching for something. "I haven't seen Jesus in a long time. Only the devil comes anymore."

He touched her shoulder and she turned back to face him.

"Mother, I'm here to take you away from this place. I can't stay in that home any longer. All they care about is making money off me."

She leaned in, her face inches from his. "Why do you call me mother?"

Nicolai stood and held out his hand, trying his best to sound older than his age. "I'm your son and you have to come with me. I've run away and I won't go back. Come with me and I'll find us someplace to live."

"You want me to leave here?"

"Of course I do. Look what they've done to you."

She pointed toward the door. "The dark people are out there. They're ghosts, you know. They can hear your thoughts and walk through walls. I've seen them. But the steel window screens keep them out."

"Stand up, mother." He bent, grabbing her hand.

"They took my son."

"I'm here and we need to get moving."

"But I can't leave. They're out there."

"It'll be fine, you'll see." He tried to raise her from the floor. "Come on."

Her eyes grew wide as she struggled to pull away, her voice rising with each word.

"Let me go! Who are you? What are you doing?"

"Keep quiet, mama." He started for the doorway, sliding her across the slick floor. "Your son is taking you away from here."

"But the dark people are out there!"

3

She grabbed the bedrail, her shrieks echoing off the walls. In a flash of light the door flew open and two men rushed into the room. Nicolai released his grip, running between the bed and the wall. An instant later he was out the door. Rounding the nearest corner, he backtracked down the unlighted corridors, ducking into doorways at the sound of passing footsteps. His mother's cries faded as he burst through an exit and slipped into the night.

An hour later he struggled to rid his mind of his mother's cries as he stumbled along the edge of a narrow blacktop, keeping to the shadows as much as possible. He looked behind him, dismayed by the sight. After all his walking the hospital glow still lit the horizon. A roll of thunder moved over the hills.

All at once the flashing lights of a patrol car topped the rise, slicing the highway into shards. He jumped from the roadside, sliding down the shoulder and splashing across a shallow creek before scrambling beneath a low bridge. The car slowed as it reached the crossing. Then a spotlight pierced the brush, its beam jerking from side to side.

He listened to the footsteps passing above him. Moments later a radio crackled to life and the spotlight vanished as the car's engine roared to life. The cruiser strained to climb the sloping roadway, its flashing lights fading into the night. Nicolai huddled against the hard cement, shivering in his wet clothes but afraid to venture out. Time slipped past.

The night seemed to engulf him, dense, silent, water-like. He held up his hand but saw nothing, no reflection, no silhouette. In the blackness his mother appeared before him, her face twisted with fear, her eyes wild, staring at him without recognition, without affection. Struggling to free herself, she opened her mouth but no scream shattered the silence.

Instead a car sounded in the distance. He sat up, trying to shake off the image as the roar grew louder. Scanning the tree line, he could find no sign of flashing lights. He started toward the road then stopped, fear again gripping him, the thought of returning to the foster home too much to bear. He turned and scurried behind the cement columns.

The creaking car slowed, pulling onto the shoulder and stopping. He listened as a door opened and footsteps again sounded on the bridge directly above him. Lightning slit the darkness. Seconds later a man's voice called out.

"You'd be needing a warm spot to hide and I know a place. Them that run trust no one, but trust you must or be lost. I offer small help and want nothing in return.

"A bad time is coming, boy. We must do what we can. There's no good to be had for a young feller on his own when the evil times come. Will you go with me then? We best get moving. The deputy has a bad wheel bearing and I hear his car over that ridge and coming fast."

Nicolai clutched his knees to his chest, wrestling with himself at the thought of the man's offer and puzzling over how he had known he was there. He wanted nothing more than to leave and be warm. Yet he trusted no one, just as the voice said.

Then he realized morning would soon break and in the light of day he would be spotted immediately. The thought of many more hours under the bridge seemed as bad as getting caught so he took a breath and stood, backtracking away from the culvert. A figure with a halo of white hair peered down at him. The old man looked as if he could have just crawled from beneath a bridge himself.

He motioned Nicolai up the slope and minutes later they were bumping down the highway in a rattling pickup, the dashboard casting the old man's gnarled hands in a green glow. Nicolai watched as the flashing lights of the deputy's cruiser appeared briefly behind them before fading into the night. He glanced at the man's stubble-strewn face, wondering where he would take him and if it would be better or worse than where he had been.

He turned his eyes to the windshield. Above the road, thin fingers of light pierced the black horizon, signaling the approach of dawn. He again thought of his mother, wishing she could be like other mothers, fixing his breakfast and sending him off to school on a morning like this. But such hopes belonged to the child he was no longer. He stared into the distance as the broken hills came into focus beneath the dim light of morning, birthed from flat silhouette to substance and form, solid and without ambiguity. He locked his gaze on the roughhewn scene, trying not to think of the future.

Chapter Two

Truman Birdsong peered through the windshield of his creaking camper van, the land before him dense with wood, thick, impenetrable. Brush crowded the narrow road. Only the brief appearance of a pump jack or stock tank served to break the monotony. He cared little. The dark scene seemed to match his mood.

That he had returned to this remote place, a land forgotten by all but misfits and castoffs, the malcontent and reactionary, seemed a just reward for his many failures. At least he would have a job and, in time, a place to live. The van would have to suffice until then.

Rounding a low bluff, the road began a slow descent toward a broad valley. Azure hills spilled onto themselves, the swales and arroyos between them dark with juniper. Knots of cloud, torn and smoke-like, drifted over the horizon.

A memory came to him of the same stretch of highway. Wedged between his mother and father, he peered through the windshield with a child's eyes, finding pleasure in the wide land, comfort even. He had once felt a kinship with the place. Staring at the scene, he tried to conjure the feeling again but found only the shame of his returning.

The van topped a rise and a building came into view, the green metal sides melding with the trees beyond. Pickup trucks crowded the gravel lot. He parked and moments later stood before an office door. Rapping twice on the frosted glass, he turned the knob and stepped through, immediately chafing at the smallness of the cramped space. A man looked up from behind a surplus metal desk, his face veiled by a cloud of blue smoke, his skin like leather.

The man took a long pull on his cigarette, studying him, no welcome in his eyes. Thin arms poked from his shirtsleeves taut and bonelike. Without a word of greeting, he motioned Truman to a chair. Then he pulled a second cigarette from a pack, lighting it with the first. The dry paper crackled to life. He plucked a file from the desktop and held it up.

"Too bad you got the name you do instead of Jones or Smith."

"You know who I am?"

"Of course I do, Mr. Birdsong. We small town folks aren't as stupid as you city people think."

"What does that have to do with Smith or Jones?"

"Well, I'd have to say you came all this way for nothing."

"What do you mean?" he said, sitting up. "I was promised a job."

"That was before we found out about you and your disgusting past."

"You did what?"

"You haven't heard of the internet, Mr. Birdsong? With a name like yours it was just too easy to find out you have a fondness for young girls."

"How did… there wasn't any… he stammered. "I was cleared of those charges."

"The Weeks brothers, owners of this plant, may be millionaires but they're still God-fearing country folk that have no toleration for the abomination of child abuse."

"My wife lied to the police. She wanted me gone so she could carry on with her boyfriend. I cared more about my step-daughter than she did."

"Is that what you call what you did?"

"I've already told you…"

"Everyone knows," he interrupted, "criminals are compulsive liars."

"You don't know what you're…"

He pointed a finger in Truman's face.

"The assault and public disturbance record didn't help either, although we do have our share of rough men here. I suppose you're going to deny that too."

8

"But my ex-wife…" Truman stopped and sighed, his sense of failure again crowding in. "No."

"That explains all the drifting from town to town, job to job."

"Something like that."

"Then I believe we're done here, Mr. Birdsong."

"But what am I supposed to do now?" He stood, his anger rising. "I have no work, no place to live."

"I'm told you have family from around here. Why don't you go home to your mother? Isn't that what child molesters do?"

"She died when I was twelve."

The man sneered at him. "Am I supposed to feel sorry for you?"

"Listen, you little twerp…" he yelled, grabbing a handful of the man's collar.

In a flash the door flew open and a thick-necked man appeared beside him. Truman released his grip. The little man straightened his shirt and pointed his cigarette toward the door.

"Like I said, Mr. Birdsong, we're done here."

He followed the narrow highway across the county line, turning onto the main street of a nearby town, the closest with a bar. He needed a drink. Pulling to the curb outside a barn-like building that had once served as the town ice house, he climbed from the van and followed a gravel sidewalk to the back entrance. A short set of stairs led to an open room with a high, rough-beamed ceiling topping its limestone walls.

Taking a seat at the bar, he ordered a beer. Other than a couple in the far corner, the place appeared empty. He took a breath. He was in no mood for a familiar face. Though he and his father had moved away after his mother's death, he still remembered a few of the locals. Unable to free themselves from family obligations and small town mores, most of them had never left the area.

He glanced at the bar mirror then looked away, disgusted by the sight of himself. As much as he hated to admit it, there was truth in the little man's words. He was far from blameless. His bad decisions and latent anger had led him back to this place.

A shadow falling over his shoulder pulled him from his thoughts. Then an old man appeared to his left, a haze of white stubble crossing his jaw. He stared at Truman without speaking, his watery eyes holding a strange and disturbing wildness. After a moment, he waved his hand through the air as if tracing the outline of an invisible object. Then he tapped the bar with his middle finger.

"You'd be looking for work." His voice held no question. "And I'm the one to tell you where to find it."

Truman studied the man's wizened face, puzzling over his words.

"How could you...?"

He tapped the bar again. "But first, you'd be buying me a drink. Just one is all."

Truman considered how little he had left in his savings, but something about the man made him want to hear what he had to say. He hailed the bartender over. The old man held his thumb and forefinger apart.

"Whiskey, a double shot."

He waited for the glass, emptying it in one swallow. Then he turned back to Truman. His red-rimmed eyes flashed as he spoke.

"There are bad times coming to this place. Dark times they are, too. We best steel ourselves for the darkness. But some need the help of a willing hand, them that don't have the blessings of folks like you and me. Do you follow?"

Truman began regretting his decision.

"I don't know."

"Them they call special are who I mean and special they are, make no mistake. They need a willing man to do their work, to fight against what's coming, a hired hand maybe but no matter. A hand is a hand long as it's willing.

And in time their truth will reveal itself and the hand will understand, hired or no."

"What sort of work do you mean?"

"That too will reveal itself in time."

"But it's a paying job we're talking about?"

"You'd be good with your hands then?"

"I know my way around a hammer and saw, if that's what you mean."

The man waved his hand through the air again and pointed toward the highway. "You take yourself the main road there back to the town of Mohan, and on from there to Clayton. Past a tall brick building once owned by the oil company that built the town, you turn. At the top of the hill stands the old house, a tall Victorian, forest green and white with a curved porch across the front."

"It's someone's home?"

"The name is Mercer."

"Mercer? That name is familiar."

"Well, it would be wouldn't it?"

"But how so?"

The man ignored his question.

"He owns the boarding house but no ordinary house it is."

"That's where I'd find a job?"

"The old man is too fat and lazy to keep up the place anymore. He needs a hired hand. But beware the greedy bastard."

The man stood and started toward the door. Truman turned, calling out to him.

"What's your name?"

"Parfit's the name, just Parfit."

"What about the darkness?"

He yelled over his shoulder. "A man must steel himself, hired or no."

He slowed as the road dropped into a brush-choked arroyo, passing through a seemingly endless stretch of scrub oak and cedar, close and lightless. All at once he found himself gulping for air, his heart racing, his pulse pounding in his ears. He thought he had beaten the claustrophobia. Gripping the steering wheel, he kept his eyes to the road, taking each breath slow and biting back his shame.

Tattered clouds hugged the horizon. In the occasional clearings, mobile homes stood alongside crumbling shacks gray with neglect, their yards cluttered with castoff furniture and rusted farm machinery. Truman turned from the familiar sight, trying to avoid thoughts of his childhood, his ruined father, his dying mother. In the years since he had scarcely allowed himself to think of the place.

The trees fell away all at once as Clayton appeared in a broad swale below him. He remembered little of the town except for its sense of decay. Beyond a railway crossing, the road opened onto a wide street flanked by a line of ramshackle buildings, many of them empty. The entire town seemed to be made of red brick, even the streets. Truman slowed as he approached a four-story building, the collapsed roof visible through its broken windows. A sign hanging above the doorway read 'Clayton Oil and Gas'.

Turning onto a rutted side-street, he passed between an abandoned hotel and train station before climbing a steep incline. Vacant lots littered the unpaved road. He crested a rise and a house appeared on the hilltop, its curved porch deep in shadow. Green shutters stood dark against the dull white of the house. He angled the van beneath a sprawling live oak and climbed out.

A dim remembrance arose in the back of his mind and he again recalled his parents, realizing with a tinge of remorse they rarely crossed his thoughts anymore. Something about the house had stirred his memory. Straining to recall, he could find no foothold for the thought.

He turned toward the jagged horizon and surveyed the maze of hills stretching below him. The scene seemed vaguely familiar, like an image from a long-forgotten dream. Standing in the shade of the massive tree, he puzzled over how he had been drawn back into this forgotten place, a place he never wished to see again, his mind already seeking escape, unwilling to think beyond the moment.

Chapter Three

Julius Rose looked up, pausing from his work as the sound of an approaching car drifted up the hill. At four feet ten inches tall, with a curved spine that bent his face toward the ground, he looked up at much of the world. Early on he had formed a habit of cocking his head to one side for a better view.

As if to compensate for his ill-shaped form, Julius owned a deceptively engaging manner, attentive to every gesture, every intonation. He observed without seeming to, his thin and angular face revealing little. His green eyes belied a keen mind for those who dared a second look. Few did. He had no illusions about ability outweighing appearance.

A rust-marked camper van bumped up the hill, coming to a stop below the porch. He turned his eyes from the van, wondering who might have reason to come all the way up a road leading nowhere but the old house where he now stood. Only those lost or wanting something ventured there willingly. He decided he must know. Returning to his work, he acted as if he had seen nothing, stealing glances where he could.

A man with close-cropped hair stepped away from the van. He had the self-contained look of a loner, a man apart, a man without friends. Julius considered what personal history could have led him to such a life, what misfortune could have caused him to retreat, to close himself off from the world.

The man's deep-set eyes seemed to reflect the world back on itself, as if to avoid contact, to maintain an impartial distance. Julius' skeptical mind would not accept the man's appearance of neutrality. Everyone has their passions, their weaknesses. This man no doubt had his share.

He stole another glance as the man turned to study the house. Julius imagined his view, the cracked and peeling shiplap, the shutters off their hinges. Above him roof tiles sat at odd angles, some chipped or missing, others covered with green-gray moss. Tapered posts supporting the balcony leaned to one side. Yet the brass lamps and windows framing the front door gleamed beneath the tree-scattered sunlight, showing some care was still given the old place.

Julius turned away, visualizing himself from the man's perspective, his bent and misshapen back, his tilted head. He listened to the rhythmic scratch of his broom across the porch floorboards. Then all at once he pivoted, disappearing around the corner. Moments later he stood before the living room windows, watching the man from behind a veil of lace curtains.

The man started for the house, climbing the wide set of stairs to the porch landing before pausing to catch his breath. He considered for a moment his broken reflection in the door's cut glass. Then a voice sounded to his right.

"Truman Birdsong is standing at the brink, and he is, he is!"

Truman flinched at the high-pitched twang. Below him a man lay stretched out on the floor, his cloudy eyes staring at the porch ceiling, a white, foldable cane clutched to the middle of his chest. Framed by the wooden planks, his lanky form resembled the tomb of a fallen knight. Truman peered at him, puzzled by his words.

"How do you know my name?"

"Your friend, Parfit, he knows things, and he does, he does."

"But I never told him my name."

"He just knows things and there it is, no other way to put it, no two ways about it, he knows. Some of us are just that way, just born that way and that's how we stay, day in and day out, day out and day in, just that way. We've been wondering when you'd get here and here you are. We must welcome those who are lost. Carlisle said it and Carlisle knows, yes he does."

"Carlisle?

"Carlisle from the protected tower, the walled city, he comes, he comes."

"Who is he? Does he live here?"

"Names have meaning, they do you know, they do. Are you a man true, Truman Birdsong? That you must know or find out, you must. Ask me mine, then."

"And who are you?"

"I wasn't always blind, Truman Birdsong, no not blind. I can still remember stretching out in the grass, much like I am now, and looking up at the sky and wondering if the blue went on forever, and what it must be like to float in it like a bird, yes like a bird. And I can see my mother's African violets on the windowsill with their green, round leaves and purple petals, and I can. And sometimes it seems as if I saw them just yesterday, just yesterday and no longer, not a bit."

Truman glanced at the doorway, wondering what strange sort of place he had come to.

"What happened?"

"I was ten on that day, ten and not a day less, ten and no more. We had a party under the trees for my birthday. And my mother sent me up to the house for more lemonade, and she did. She never knew there was a gas leak, no never, not ever. When I switched on the light the house exploded into a giant fireball and I flew like a bird, like I always dreamed of, dreamed and did, yes did. Hit the back of my head, the place that controls sight, all sight, every bit. I see different now, Truman Birdsong, different and not the same, no not."

"You were burned as well?"

"You see true, Truman Birdsong. My Irish father said I was born of fire and so I was that day, born into what I am now, not before but right then, born and born again. The name stayed true, Truman Birdsong, and true it was."

"The name? What name do you mean?"

"Why, my own name, of course. Aiden Burns it is, born of fire and of fire born, yes of fire. Aiden means 'little fire' and it does. Not to forget my last name, not at all, no. Some would laugh to hear it and laugh they do. But laugh or not, Aiden Burns is my name, and it is."

The door swung open and the little man Truman had seen earlier stepped through, slipping sideways along the porch, one shoulder dipped below the other, his head bent forward and tilted to one side. Julius stopped before him, squinting up at him across his sharp nose.

"Ah, yes, and you must be the hired man we've been expecting."

"No one has offered me a job yet."

Julius studied him, again wondering what sort of trouble had led him there. Only a desperate man would willingly seek work in such a place.

"Oh, but Mercer will make the offer. He has little choice. Time the avenger has him in its inevitable grip. But why come work here of all places?"

Truman ignored the question, hoping to avoid the humiliation of an answer.

"Who is this Mercer?"

Julius snorted, thinking of all the words he could use to describe their landlord. "He is the warden of our exile. As you can see, he takes great care of the old place."

Truman glanced at the flaking paint. "The house needs some work but it must have been beautiful once."

"Yes, and you are her savior."

"How can you be so sure, Mister…?"

"I am Julius, as in Caesar. But I am emperor of nothing, nothing but myself and my own thoughts. Therein resides freedom, Truman Birdsong, that and several pints of good beer. Remember those words and you will never despair, or at least not overly so."

"You've been talking to this Parfit character too." Truman squinted at him, wondering what game the two men were playing.

17

"Not at all, Truman Birdsong. I do not share Aiden's fondness for the supernatural. But neither do I deny it. I simply observe the world as it is." He waved his hand before his chest as if it belonged to someone else. "Fate gave me this to live in but left me with my senses, so I enjoy what the world offers up whether for learning or for pleasure. In your case, I overheard your conversation with Aiden the Verbose. His voice carries like the wind, impossible to avoid."

Aiden slapped his leg. "And like the wind, I move where I will, and I do, I do!"

He jumped to his feet and disappeared through the door. Seeing the suspicion on Truman's face, Julius gestured down the porch.

"You are, no doubt, wondering what sort of house you have come upon, Truman Birdsong. I can see the doubt in your eyes. You're wondering if you should seek employment elsewhere."

"No, I…"

He held up a bony hand. "I deal in truth and truth only, Truman Birdsong, nothing more, nothing less. Unless, of course, untruth trumps truth, which as it happens is not uncommon in my experience. In any event, you are having second thoughts, are you not?"

"I am, maybe a little."

"Then truth it is. What would you like to ask?"

"I'd like to know more about this place."

"My spine pains me, Truman Birdsong." Julius rubbed the small of his back. "I must sit."

He moved to a chair, wincing as he climbed in. Then he peered up at Truman, a grim smile on his lips.

"Now, please continue."

"So this is a boarding house?"

"We the unwanted and dispossessed have been sentenced to this lovely resort, our own little slice of purgatory. Or is it inferno? I have yet to decide. Those among the living would call it a house of freaks and gimps.

18

Others, the hypocrites who want to appear compassionate, would say we're a disability halfway house. Halfway to where, you ask? All the way to nowhere is my answer."

"You sound bitter."

"I am merely a realist, Truman Birdsong."

Truman guessed he was lying but said nothing. "What sort of disabilities?"

"We come in all shapes and sizes, some obvious like Aiden and yours truly, others who seem normal enough but have their own not-so-obvious flaws. But remember this, Truman Birdsong, things are not always as they seem. Then again, we all have our share of defects, don't we?"

"More than we'd like to admit." Truman took a breath, reminded of his own.

Noticing his discomfort, Julius leaned forward. "Care to elaborate?"

"No." Truman squinted at him, again wondering at his game. "How many of you are living here?"

"Peace and quiet are hard to come by, if that tells you anything." Julius sat back. "Besides Aiden and me, there is Carlisle, our resident saint. He came to us after a bout of encephalitis. The experience left him, you might say, a bit mystical. Before he became ill, he was a professor of comparative religion at a large university."

"There are just three of you, then?"

"We had another but lost the Friar Tuck to our merry band a week ago yesterday. Simon provided a dose of much-needed levity to this dismal land. Sadly, I closed his book only this morning."

"Book? What book do you mean?"

"When one of us passes to a higher plane, or a lesser hell - take your pick - I write their story. I'm sorry to say this was my third. But don't get the wrong idea, Truman Birdsong, I tolerate no sentimentality. I write merely to keep my sanity. Besides, life is about to march on and I fear we will soon be joined by an urchin, to my considerable annoyance."

"You have children living here too?

"Therein resides the problem, Truman Birdsong. Taking in child tenants is yet another of the Mercer money-making schemes. This one is a waif, a stray without a home."

"The owner is taking on an orphan?"

"He is a foster child to be precise, a ward of the state."

"How old is the kid?"

"He has been on this earth a mere ten years, far too short a time to be anything close to civilized. I dread his arrival with each passing hour."

"How does this Mercer fellow get away with putting a kid with a bunch of adults?"

"I doubt the authorities know of his plans. Mercer has little concern for the rules when money is at stake. Besides, the authorities are so desperate for foster parents they'll approve just about anyone with a pulse."

Truman disliked the idea of working in such a place. He wanted no ties. But his savings were nearly gone and he could see few alternatives. He needed the work.

"Where is Mercer?"

"He has an office in town where he does his scheming." Julius nodded down the hill. "Shall I show you the way, Truman Birdsong?"

Truman hesitated, considering the offer but still unsure of the little man's intentions. Deciding that keeping him nearby seemed the wiser move, he stood and pointed toward the van.

"The old truck is battered and not much to look at but she keeps on going."

Julius groaned as he climbed from the chair. "I know how she feels."

Chapter Four

Truman glanced at his passenger, trying to piece together a picture of the boarding house as they bounced down the rutted street. According to Julius, the owner cared for little other than making a profit. And though Julius seemed to have his wits about him, Truman was less sure about Aiden and the others. He again wondered what he had gotten himself into.

The so-called job remained a mystery. Parfit had asked him about working with his hands, so he assumed the owner needed help of that sort. Now he was less sure. But he was certain he had no interest in babysitting a bunch of 'freaks and gimps', as Julius called them.

They turned onto the main road, passing between crumbling buildings and resale shops crammed with the detritus of a dying land. Those able to had left long before, taking only the necessary with them, selling off the rest for next to nothing. Yet there remained a tattered beauty to the place, the stately elegance of a once-grand bank, the still-palpable pride captured in the broad streets. For a moment he could almost feel the heady optimism of an oil boom now long forgotten.

Julius pointed to a wooden building flanked by a vacant lot and car wash. A sign hanging over the door read 'Mercer Land and Realty'. Truman pulled to the curb, waiting as Julius climbed with difficulty from the cab. Truman followed him to the door. They were about to push through when Julius turned his head, whispering from the side of his mouth.

"It will be to your advantage if you let me take the lead."

Surprised by the offer, Truman gave a quick nod as they stepped into a wood-paneled room, the walls littered with black velvet paintings of Mexican bullfighters and senoritas. A layer of cigarette smoke drifted just below the ceiling. Peering out from a row of black and white photographs, oil-smeared roughnecks and mustachioed men in fedoras stood smiling before a forest of wooden oil rigs.

A stocky man in a loose-fitting shirt glanced up from a stack of papers, his discolored nose like a misshapen lump of clay. Although bald, hair sprouted from his nose and ears in dark clumps. A dim memory stirred in the back of Truman's mind, as if they had once crossed paths, but he could find no foothold of recognition. Setting aside a half-eaten candy bar, the man shuffled through the papers then sighed and turned his eyes on them. He studied Truman a moment before turning to Julius.

"You're about to make trouble again, aren't you, Rose? I'll bet this is one of your bleeding hearts here to tell me I should take better care of those poor retards you live with."

"Your propensity for sticking your foot in your mouth is astounding, Mercer."

"What are you saying, Julius?" The man's jowls quivered as he spoke.

"I'm saying you should take better care of the house we poor retards live in, and I've brought just the man for the job."

He squinted at Truman. "You know carpentry and plumbing, that sort of thing?"

"I know enough. I used to be an architect."

"Why'd you get out of the business? It pays well enough."

"Let's just say things didn't work out."

"Where was that?"

"San Antonio."

"A man can make a boatload more money in the city. Why come to this hellhole?"

"I had enough and got out."

"Is that all there is to it?"

"I needed a new start."

"Is that right? Well, going from San Antonio to here is more like a bad end if you ask me. But it's your life to waste if you want to. Besides, I need the help so I guess you'll do. I can't pay much but I'll give you a place to live, all bills included, so you should make out alright. Are you interested, uh... what did you say your name was?"

Julius snorted. "He never said because you never asked, Mercer."

"Alright, Miss Manners, so what's his name then?" Before he could answer, Mercer raised a hand to stop him. "On second thought, I don't want to know. Getting cozy with the hired help is bad for business."

He turned to Truman. "Do you want the job or not?"

Truman stepped to the desk and held out his hand. "I'll take it."

Mercer ignored his hand and instead popped the candy bar in his mouth. Then he turned to Julius, chewing as he spoke.

"Now, don't you let the inmates fill him full of their nonsense about disability rights and all that other mumbo-jumbo." He turned his eyes back to Truman. "All you need to know is that things are just fine the way they are. You're best leaving well enough alone. In fact, that goes for this whole godforsaken place. It's getting downright dangerous out there."

Parfit's strange words of warning came to Truman again.

"How do you mean?"

"There are some real nut-balls hiding out around here and you have no idea what they're capable of. Some say a bad business is on the way. Well, I hope not because bad business is bad for business. I got land to sell and deals to make. If what they say about this new oil technology is true, I'll make a bundle before I can work up a good spit. Maybe I'll even get back into wildcatting. Then I can get the hell out for good. You know what I'm saying?"

Truman could make little sense of it but nodded anyway as more immediate concerns crowded his thoughts.

"You said something about a place to live."

Mercer pulled open a drawer, lifting out a key ring and tossing it onto the desktop. "That's the keys to everything there is. You can live in the cabin out back. Fix what needs fixing. There's plenty of work to do. First off, better make tracks to the hardware store in Albany. Right away would be best. Julius can show you where it is."

"You want me to go *now*?"

"They'll have some paint and wood trim waiting for pickup. Just put it on my tab. The guest house is out back of the boarding house. It's yours now. I'm a busy man, so don't bother me and we'll get along fine."

They followed a narrow highway between canyons choked with cedar, passing over rock-strewn washes and creeks, their reddish soil like an open wound. Metal gates bearing crosses and kneeling cowboys in silhouette appeared along the roadside then vanished from view as if never seen. Faded Confederate flags twisted in the wind.

Truman glanced at Julius, wondering what he might make of Mercer's advice to leave well enough alone. Had he heard it before? Though memory told him parts of the area could be ignorant and backward, Mercer's words seemed to hold something more, something sinister. He had seen the fear in the man's eyes.

A crossroads appeared ahead, a gas station and general store on one corner. Pulling next to a pump, Truman climbed out and filled the van's tank. Then he started toward the store, a narrow wooden building faded to a dull red. Julius' followed, his halting shuffle matching Truman's footsteps. At their approach a three-legged dog let out a bark and vanished beneath the steps.

They pushed through the screen door and into the crowded space. A short man in a grimy ball cap frowned at them from a corner stool before turning his eyes. Behind the counter, a stout, bearded man in a pair of denim overalls and a yellow t-shirt reading 'Send 'em All Back' stood thumbing through a thick magazine.

A state flag emblazoned with 'Border Militia' hung from the rafters above him. He looked up, eying Julius with disapproval. The black handle of a pistol poked from his bib pocket. He fished a dollar bill from his pocket and turned toward the man in the cap, leaning across the counter.

"You see this here foreign currency, Cecil? If you ask me, it's not worth the paper it's printed on. A damn peso will be worth more before long."

The man in the cap grinned, his teeth peppered with snuff. "Then I better get myself down to Mexico and bring back a mess of them."

The heavyset man nodded toward Julius, his eyes still on the man across from him.

"Soon enough the welfare queens and them that don't pull their weight will have to find someone else to leach off. They got the government in their pockets, sure enough, but not for long. Changes are on the way. Then we'll take back what's ours."

"It won't be long, sure enough." The man in the cap chuckled.

"You can bet your last peso on it, Cecil."

The men flinched as Truman slapped a twenty dollar bill on the counter. Frowning, the larger man turned to face him.

"What's the matter with you?"

Truman leaned across the counter, his face within inches of the man. "Is this good enough for you or should I take my foreign currency elsewhere?"

The man reached for the bill, mumbling under his breath. "No, I'll take it."

Truman grabbed his wrist and held it, locking eyes with him. "You wouldn't get a dime off me if I hadn't already filled up."

The man jerked his hand free and took a step back. "No need to get worked up, mister."

"My friend and I have real work to do. We can't afford to stand around looking at magazines and talking nonsense about foreign currency and welfare queens."

Shocked, Julius stared at him. Then he faced the two men, grinning at each in turn.

"Have any snappy comebacks, gentlemen? Please tell me you do, something, anything. This is too good not to continue."

Truman grabbed him by the arm, pushing him out the door while keeping an eye out for the black pistol. Moments later they were back on the highway, again passing between thick stands of mesquite and cedar.

Julius leaned against the seatback, considering all he'd just seen. What lay behind Truman's temper and, more important, how might he use it to his advantage? He knew how easily the well-meaning are led. Yet he was touched by Truman's words. He shifted in the seat, facing him.

"Are you always so quick to anger, Truman Birdsong?"

"Sometimes I am. What I did back there was not smart."

"Oh, but it was so satisfying. I have few opportunities to see bullies put in their place. What made you do it?"

"I have no toleration for a man who tries to make himself look important at someone else's expense. Beneath the big talk his type are always cowards. Still, even a coward can pull a trigger."

Julius cringed as he considered the possibility. "Being shot at would have made it somewhat less satisfying, I must admit. But I believe you put a scare in him. You looked like you were about to climb over the counter."

"Keeping a lid on my temper has been a problem for me."

"And why is that?"

Truman stared into the distance, again thinking of his failed marriage and the events that had led him to this place. He had no answer to Julius' question.

"I don't know why, it just has."

"How do you mean? What does your quick temper have to do with coming here?"

"Everything and nothing, I suppose."

"You sound like a politician."

Truman glanced at him, looking for a way to change the subject.

"What was that foreign currency business back there about?"

Julius decided to abandon his inquiry for the time being. He considered Truman's question and all the many ways he might answer. Then by chance a tattered flag reading 'Don't Tread on Me' appeared along the roadside. A primitive rendering of a coiled rattlesnake fluttered beneath the words. He pointed through the windshield.

"You see that yellow flag? That's the Gadsden flag, named after the general who designed it during the American Revolution. You may ask yourself why a person would fly such a flag nearly two hundred and forty years after its creation."

"I have a feeling you're about to tell me."

"Nothing gets past you, Truman Birdsong."

Truman ignored the jibe. "Does this have anything to do with the bad business Mercer mentioned?"

For a moment Julius stared into the distance, lost in thought.

"Mercer is the lowest form of humanity, a bottom feeder you might say. All he cares about is counting his gold and finding his next meal."

"That's the impression I had."

"On the other hand, he does have a point. The denizens of these hinterlands, or at least a portion of them, believe the government has become a sham, an intruder, and the law, any law, no longer applies to them. You hear

27

little about it but in some places they've effectively taken the law into their own hands, a disturbing thought when you're of the minority persuasion. You've seen how they treat those of us who are a bit different."

"But that sort of complaining has always been around, especially among the uneducated and willingly ignorant. It doesn't amount to much."

"History would agree. But I fear we've reached a tipping point and the first domino is close to falling."

"How do you mean?"

"These people are well-organized and determined to have their way."

"And you know this how?"

"I've seen it myself."

"How did you manage that? Paranoid types such as our friend back at the store don't usually tolerate much snooping around."

"An odd paradox exists for unbeautiful people like me and Aiden and the others." A bitter smile crossed his lips. "Our very strangeness, what gets us noticed, also gives us a sort of invisibility. Did you see the man in the cap look away? People are disturbed by our appearance, as if we're a reminder of what could happen to them at any moment. So they avoid looking at us or speaking to us or even thinking of us. It's as if we disappear altogether and in a way, to them, we do. We can be places they would never allow a so-called normal person."

"What exactly have you seen, Julius?"

"Enough to frighten me, Truman Birdsong, and I don't frighten easily. People like me don't fare well if they can't stare down a threat. But as poor and ignorant as these people may seem from the outside, they mean business. You must keep your eyes open."

The van topped a rise and the land opened below them, the jagged hills stretching toward the horizon. Shreds of gray clouds raced overhead. Truman peered into the distance, a deep unease settling over him as he puzzled over Julius' words - and what he had left unsaid.

Chapter Five

Securing the remaining shutter to the window frame, Truman started down the ladder, pausing halfway to again survey the broad expanse of land that fell away from the hilltop in diminishing shades of blue. A line of hills stretched into the distance, undulating and wavelike. Dense stands of juniper stained the narrow valley in dark clumps. After a week of climbing over the old house, he had yet to tire of the view.

He studied a steel-gray wall of clouds rising above the horizon in stark contrast to the sundrenched land below. A brisk wind buffeted the looming oak. He started again and then stopped at the repeated pop of an automatic weapon echoing through the hills, followed by the chest-thumping boom of a large bore rifle. He studied the landscape. Unable to deny its beauty, he tried without success to reconcile the peaceful scene with Julius' words of warning. Then Aiden's voice sounded from the porch, pulling him from his thoughts.

"Truman Birdsong is a lightning rod, and he is, he is!"

He lifted his eyes to the sky. "I don't see any lightning."

"The lightning sees, the lightning knows, Truman Birdsong."

He stepped off the ladder and rounded the house.

"Aiden, you sure love the sound of your own voice."

"We must be ready, we must." Standing on the top step, Aiden held his cane like a scepter. "A storm is on the way, yes, on the way."

Truman climbed the stairs and faced the horizon. "The only clouds I see are way off in the distance. Besides, I don't hear any thunder. Are you talking about a real storm or something else?"

"Aiden hears, Aiden knows, and he does, like the lightning, he does. We must be ready, Truman Birdsong."

"Yes, your eminence." Truman bowed.

Aiden raised his hand. "Truman Birdsong need not bow, no he need not."

He pivoted and disappeared inside the house just as Julius stepped onto the porch, a smirk on his lips.

"Truman, you ridicule Aiden's predictive powers at your own risk."

"I'll stick to what's real and leave it at that."

"Ah, but who's to say what is real and what is not?"

"Do you see any lightning or hear any thunder?"

"Of course I don't."

"I believe in what I experience, what I can see or touch or hear, not some mystical mumbo-jumbo."

"Truman, you're a realist, an experiential realist. That explains a lot."

"What do you mean?"

"Never mind. Speaking of experience, everyone knows that when a person loses their sight they develop their other senses to compensate. How did you miss that lesson?"

"I must've cut class that day."

"Jest if you wish but Aiden's predictive abilities are not a joke. He has an uncanny sense of changes in the weather, of whose car is coming up the hill, of how much a bag of apples weighs, to name only a few. I've seen them myself. Are they mystical? Perhaps in a way they are, in the same way the talent of a gifted artist or musician is mystical. But make no mistake, they are real. For the truly mystical, we must turn to Carlisle."

"Who is this Carlisle I keep hearing about?"

"Like I mentioned earlier, he came to us after a terrible illness that left him…"

Truman interrupted, impatient with his banter. "I know, a bit mystical."

"True, but mystical in what way is the…"

Julius stopped in mid-sentence, turning as a white sedan appeared down the road. Truman followed his gaze.

The car angled onto the driveway, pulling to a stop beneath the sprawling oak.

Moments later, a young woman climbed out. Black hair swirled about her face, thick, satin-like. Downturned eyes and a thin, slightly crooked nose gave her a flawed yet striking look that Truman found mesmerizing. He struggled to keep from staring as she approached the porch. Stopping at the foot of the stairs, she looked up at him.

"I'm Kennis McDuff with the juvenile court. Is this the Mercer home?"

Julius nudged Truman with his foot, talking under his breath. "Tell her the place was located across town and burned down months ago."

"Why would I do that?" Truman whispered.

"Tell her you're a serial killer out on parole."

"What?"

"Tell her anything you like as long as it will make her go away."

Truman faced the woman again, a strained smile on his lips. "Will you excuse us for a moment?"

She nodded as he took Julius by the arm, half-dragging him down the porch. He leaned in close.

"What the devil are you talking about, Julius?"

"Don't you see? She means to bring the urchin here."

"Where else is he going to go? He has no home."

"Truman, please, I can't stand the thought of a child running underfoot day in and day out. I'll go mad."

"What are you so afraid of?" Seeing the dread in Julius' eyes, he relaxed his grip. "He's just a kid."

Julius sighed, disgusted with having to revisit his childhood miseries. "What do you think life was like for me at that age? Well, I can tell you. My deplorable existence was an endless series of degradations, indignities and the occasional beating, all at the hands of my so-called peers. They loved nothing better that to taunt me, thinking up humiliating names on a daily basis. That and tripping me, mimicking me, making up lewd songs about me and blaming me for something one of them had done.

"So, you can see why I'd rather not have such barbarian company in close proximity. Whether said barbarian happens to be homeless is of no concern of mine."

"Look, I won't lie to her just because you're afraid of some kid you've never even met." Julius moaned.

"I'm doomed." Julius moaned. "Dante was right. Of his nine circles of hell, I'll soon descend to the sixth for my child-hating heresy. And I have no Virgil to guide me."

Truman bent down, trying to make eye contact. "Get a grip on yourself, Julius."

"How can I?" Dejected, he stared at the floor. "You're throwing me to the child-wolf."

"I didn't say I wouldn't help. I said I wouldn't lie. We need to convince her that this is no place for a kid."

Julius grabbed his arm, glancing at the woman as he spoke.

"Oh, you're appealingly devious, Truman Birdsong. We *could* convince her of that, now couldn't we? But she'll be suspicious of me. Strangers always are. You must be the one to speak. I'll stand by and try to appear agreeable to whatever you say."

They walked back down the porch together and Truman nodded to her, smiling.

"Sorry to make you wait. I'm Truman Birdsong and my partner here is Julius Rose. I assume you've come about the foster placement. I have to tell you, a house full of adults doesn't seem like an appropriate home for a ten year old child. You might want to think again before..."

She raised her hand to stop him. "There has been a change in plans, Mr. Birdsong."

"Please call me Truman.

"Then I'm Kennis. The boy protective services had hoped to place here was unexpectedly adopted by his aunt. I came to let you know and because I wanted to see the place for myself. I will no doubt have another child on my caseload that needs a home." She looked to her right and left. "I had no idea the house was so big."

"Not only is it a big house but, as I was saying, the residents are all adults, adults with, uh, uh... conditions."

"Do you mean disabilities, Truman?"

"You'd be right there, Kennis."

"That might be a consideration but it wouldn't rule out the option entirely. Foster homes are very hard to come by in some places, so the child services people have to get creative when the judge says the child must stay nearby. That's especially true for problem children."

"Would it be right to put a problem child here?"

"That depends on the problem."

"What sort of problem would be okay?"

She eyed him with interest as she considered his question.

"Well, we have children whose primary problem behavior is repeatedly running away from their foster homes. After enough running away the available foster homes refuse to take them so we are forced to find an alternative. Regardless of the problem, we want to avoid having children in institutions if at all possible."

Julius cleared his throat, nudging him again with the toe of his shoe. Truman forced a smile.

"I can understand why you'd want to do that. A real home is best."

Julius again cleared his throat, louder than before. Truman glared at him before continuing.

"As I was saying, a child needs a home. That I can agree with, but..."

Julius leapt in front of him, the words racing from his mouth. "I can assure your there is no more institutional abode than the one before you now! Why, we rise at dawn for a meager breakfast before starting the daily grind of cleaning, washing, calisthenics, memorizing Bible verses, polishing the china and a litany of other chores, distasteful all.

"Put us in uniform and we'd be like any army, all spit and polish and strict discipline. And those who fall out of line pay dearly. We're an institutions' institution here, Kennis, no question about it. As a protective services employee, I'm sure you agree."

He ended with a salute. She peered at him for a moment.

"Actually, as I said, I work for the juvenile court. I'm a probation officer."

He waved off the comment. "And we don't want a child in such prison-like conditions, now do we?"

"I see." She looked from one to the other. "Well, this has been an enlightening visit. Thank you, gentlemen."

A gusting wind coursed through the big oak, followed by the thump of distant thunder. She turned and started toward her car. Truman surprised himself by starting after her.

"Are you leaving? I mean, will you be coming back?"

Julius grabbed his wrist, hissing under his breath. "Say nothing, Truman! Let her go."

She stopped and faced them. "As I said, the child we had in mind no longer needs a home."

Truman shook him off, stumbling over his words as he searched for a way to postpone her leaving. For reasons he could not explain, he wanted her to stay.

"What I mean is… I hope we weren't too frank. I wouldn't want you to leave here thinking we tried to run you off."

The hint of a smile crossed her lips. "I'm not run off that easily, Truman Birdsong."

Julius groaned. Truman ignored him and moved down the porch steps.

"Then you'll be coming back?"

A crack of thunder split the sky above them, followed by the first drops of rain. Giving him a quick wave, she disappeared inside her car. Truman watched the taillights vanish down the hill, wondering if he'd ever see her again. Then he caught himself. "Make no ties," he murmured under his breath. "You won't be here long."

Chapter Six

Early morning sunlight splattered the porch in gold. Nicolai Tate watched the old man move through the tree-filtered light, his joints creaking as he stooped over the weathered table and set down a plate of scrambled eggs. Pouring coffee from a battered pot into two mugs, he took the chair opposite Nicolai without a word, motioning him to eat.

The eggs seemed to vanish almost before he started so the old man spooned out another mound, setting the heavy skillet back on the tabletop. Nicolai had never known food to taste so good. The old man watched him, sipping his coffee, eating nothing.

Nicolai could see through a screen door into the unpainted house. Beyond the threshold a spare low-ceilinged living room opened onto a small kitchen, the door to a bedroom off to one side. Shelves crowded with bird nests, animal skulls, snake skins and insect-filled shadow boxes lined the opposite wall. A dozen empty bottles stood on a nearby table.

Puzzling over the odd collection, Nicolai turned his gaze to the yard. Below the porch two spotted pigs, one red, the other black, wandered about aimlessly, pausing now and then to look up at them and sniff the air. Sloping away from the house, the cleared land ended in a dense thicket of cedar bisected by a curving gravel driveway that met the highway a quarter mile beyond.

Between the thicket and the porch a pole filled with colored bottles on sticks, all pointing downward, gleamed in the morning light. The glass rattled before a steady breeze. He studied the contraption, wondering what it must be. Then he pushed away his plate, his curiosity finally winning out. He motioned toward the pole.

"Is that supposed to do something?"

The old man sipped his coffee a moment before answering.

"Nicolai Tate, you believe in spirits, do you?"

"You know my name?" Nicolai glanced toward the stairs, ready to bolt if the old man had found him out.

"And mine's Parfit, just Parfit and no more."

He peered at the man, trying to guess his intention. "Are you going to turn me in?"

Parfit ignored the question and waved his hand over the table. "Do you believe or no, Nicolai Tate?"

"You mean ghosts?"

"Ghosts, spooks, spirits, apparitions, take your pick."

"Those are just stories someone made up a long time ago. They're not real."

Parfit frowned in disapproval, shaking a finger at him. "No, boy, real they are and real they'll stay, some good, some bad, some a little of both."

"You sound like my mother," he said, at once feeling guilty for saying it.

"Your mother knows." He nodded, his face solemn. "She has felt their power."

Nicolai imagined his mother again, distraught and fearful, her eyes wild. "She calls them the dark people. She says they took me from her."

"And that they did, boy. She lost you when the bad spirits got hold of her."

"She's mental, is all. She talks crazy and sees things that aren't there. The doctors said so."

"There's more to this world than doctors and such know of, Nicolai Tate. You feel it, don't you, boy?"

He did feel something though he tried to deny it, worried he would end as his mother had.

"I don't know."

"And what if they're real, these spirits and all?"

"What if?"

"Then you need a bottle tree to protect you from the bad ones, the evil spirits." Parfit nodded down the hill.

"How does it do that?"

"In the evening time a spirit wants to move a little. If there's any colored glass about, they'll take a shine to it, like a bee to a flower. But only the evil spirits, the mean and greedy ones, go into a bottle and can't find their way out. When the morning comes along the sun does them in."

"The sun kills them?"

"Sends them to their proper place is more the way I'd put it. Anyway you want to say it, there are ways to deal with evil."

Recalling Parfit's words at the bridge, Nicolai peered into the old man's face. "What did you mean about a bad time coming?"

Parfit stood and walked to the porch steps. The pigs looked up at him, again sniffing the air.

"You pigs go out back and take a rest. I'll bring a bag of apples out later. First, me and the boy have some talking to do."

Nicolai watched with surprise as the animals turned and disappeared around the corner. Parfit sat again. Nicolai looked at the old man, unsure what to think.

"They acted like they understood you."

"Of course they understood me, boy. Pigs are not stupid. But they can't be trusted. Their tongues will wag and before you know it something you said is spread across the land to be known by one and all."

Nicolai snorted, scoffing at the idea. "You're just joshing me."

"Believe or no but the world is as it is."

He peered at Parfit again, seeing the conviction in his eyes. "Do you really believe in spirits and talking pigs?"

"I believe in the coming evil and that which helps fight it."

Nicolai felt the hair on the back of his neck rise. "Why do you keep saying that?"

"Listen to me, boy." Parfit leaned across the table, tapping the tabletop with his finger. "Trouble is brewing, bad trouble, and you'll need the help of those you can trust.

39

Mark my word, them that are will be hard to find. But there are ways, old ways. Believe them or no, they are real."

He stood and motioned for Nicolai to follow. Stepping into the dimly lighted house, Parfit headed for a stack of wooden crates in the far corner. He knelt alongside the boxes, lifting the top off one, then another and rummaging through their contents. The odor of straw and mildew filled the room.

Moments later, he raised his head and motioned Nicolai over. Resting on a bed of straw was what looked like a yard-long stone in the shape of a bird's foot. Parfit lifted the branchlike rock gingerly, holding it to the light.

"You know what this is, do you, Nicolai Tate?"

Nicolai shook his head.

"Why, it's captured lightning, son. This here is the same lightning bolt that struck me down twelve year ago."

"You were hit by lightning?" Nicolai stared at him, unsure if he'd heard right.

"That I was, boy. I was out to the lake for some pearling. You could make good money pearling back then. I had just finished hauling my boat up on the beach when I saw a flash and the next thing I knew I was flat on my back, steam coming off my clothes.

"You see this here mother of pearl?" He pulled a clam shell from his shirt pocket. "I had a bag of them in my hand when I was hit. The bolt cooked the lot and probably saved my skin. I always keep one with me for luck."

"But how did you capture the lightning?"

"I didn't capture it, the earth did. You see, this here is sand turned to glass. That's what the lightning did, turned the sand to glass when the bolt hit the ground. Here, hold it for yourself. They call it fulgurite."

Nicolai took the strange object from him, surprised at the weight. Light glinted off its rough surface.

"I thought it would be heavy."

"It weighs little because the fulgurite is a hollow tube. Inside was the lightning and the outside sand turned to glass."

He studied Parfit's grizzled face. "But I thought you died if you got hit by lightning."

"In a way I suppose I did, Nicolai." Parfit scratched at the white stubble lining his jaw. "Yet here I am, no different than before or so you might think. No different to look at anyway. Strange to think on, isn't it? Stranger still is what the lightning *did* do to me. Believe or no, afterwards I started knowing things, things I shouldn't ought to know but did in spite of myself."

"What sorts of things?"

"At first I wouldn't accept them. But there was no denying the truth once it came clear to me. You see, I knew you were under that bridge and why, and your name, and the whereabouts of your poor mother and what brought her to that place. I can't say how but such comes to me whether I want or no, torments me you might say, and will do until I answer the call. I had to stop for you, so stop I did."

"The sheriff was after me. You could've heard all that on the radio." Nicolai handed back the stone, his mind refusing to believe. "Or maybe you talked to the deputy yourself."

"I know it's hard to understand but my lot is to know things, believe or no."

Nicolai tried but could find no reason for the old man to lie. Suddenly, he found himself wanting to hear of his own fate but dreading the answer. In spite of his worry, he forced himself to ask.

"Do you know anything else, Parfit, anything about me?"

"That I do, boy."

"Will you tell me?"

"Grab your things, son."

Nicolai tensed and stepped back, again fearing a return to the foster home. He glanced toward the door, ready to run.

"You're turning me in after all, aren't you, you dang…?"

Parfit stood and passed his gnarled hand through the air in an elaborate gesture, as if to banish his words.

"Calm yourself, boy. The two of us are going to meet your future, is all."

Chapter Seven

"What do you mean, you won't ask him. Why on earth not, Aiden?"

Julius paced beside the kitchen table, squinting now and then in Aiden's direction, barely able to contain his frustration. Aiden sat clutching his cane, his eyes darting about as he spoke.

"Truman Birdsong is a man true, and he is, he is! He will not break the law for you or for me, no, not now, not ever."

"What law are you talking about?"

"You want to go on private property without permission, without any at all, no, none."

He dismissed the thought with a quick wave. "It's only trespassing, Aiden, not murder."

"It is what it is, no more, no less."

"How will anyone know we're trespassing? We could simply be lost."

"Aiden knows, he does, yes, he does."

"You won't help me?"

"You can ask for yourself if you must, yes you can."

"But if I ask him, he'll surely suspect I'm up to something. I've made no effort to hide my irritation with the way he handled that probation officer."

"You *are* up to something, Julius, no two ways about it, you are."

"It's only a little something. Besides, that property was in Truman's family for years before the bank stole it from them." Julius stopped pacing, realizing he had an angle to work. "Is that fair, I ask you? I think not!"

"The land belonged to Truman's family, to them only, just them?" Aiden took the bait. "Who told you, Julius, who?"

"I have my sources."

"You said they stole it from him, yes, you did."

"What sort of law does that, Aiden? An unfair law, I say. By all rights he should be able to visit the family homestead, for sentimental reasons if nothing else. He deserves that much. Besides, it isn't as if he wants to steal it back. A brief visit is all we're taking."

"A brief visit is all, nothing more, no, not a thing." He murmured under his breath. "Truman deserves it, yes, he does."

"Then you'll ask him? We must go today."

"Ask and you shall receive. Carlisle said it and Carlisle knows, and he does."

Julius put a hand on his shoulder. "But you must say nothing of the land to Truman. Losing it was an embarrassment to his family, no doubt. We would not want to cause him shame."

Truman ran the paintbrush along a final stretch of porch railing and stepped back to survey his work. After a moment the scene beyond the house drew his gaze. Shadows pooled beneath the sprawling oak. Below the hilltop, sundrenched hills glowed in shades of taupe and ochre. Gray clouds rose above the ragged horizon, wall-like and imposing. He guessed they were in for another round of rain.

The view again stirred his memory. Mercer's meaty face flashed through his mind, pulling at the back of his thoughts, familiar yet strange, as if once known but long forgotten. He puzzled over a vague reminiscence just beyond reach.

Seconds later footsteps sounded behind him. Giving up on the image, he turned to find Aiden standing before him, cane in hand. His eyes darted about as if surveying an invisible world, finally settling on a spot just above Truman's head.

"Truman Birdsong, we need your help, we do, yes we do. Will you take us to a place?"

"What place is that, Aiden?" He gathered up the paint and brushes, starting for the door.

Aiden turned to follow. "A place not far away, a place we need to visit, just visit and no more."

"You and who else?"

"Julius will go too, yes he will."

"And what is the purpose of this trip?"

"A visit is all, nothing more, no, not a thing. Truman deserves it, yes, he does.

Truman paused at the doorway and faced him, Aiden's words piquing his interest. "I deserve this visit?"

"A visit, yes, a deserved visit."

"Why do I deserve it?"

Aiden stiffened, his eyes darting about as if searching for an answer. Truman leaned close to him.

"What are you and Julius up to?"

"Julius and me… up to…? No, nothing, not one thing. I need…*we* need your help to go on a visit, just a visit."

"I see." Truman smiled, catching him in the lie. "And where is this place?"

"Close and not far, no, not far."

"Alright, Aiden, I'll take you. In return I want you to introduce me to Carlisle."

Aiden slapped his thigh. "Carlisle, yes, Carlisle of the protected tower, the walled city, I will take you."

Pushing through the door, he moved across the main room in long strides, stepping to the repetitive tap of his cane. Truman paused halfway. Before that moment, he had been too busy to notice the beauty of the grand room.

Blue light filtered through lace-covered windows that stretched from the floor to well over his head. Above him, stamped tin tiles covered the high ceiling in gold filigree. Landscapes and still life paintings hung among a scattering of antique furniture. The room felt like an abandoned museum.

He started again, finding Aiden waiting at the end of a long hallway. Truman stepped past him into a cramped room littered with books and stacks of paper. A reading lamp and upholstered chair sat next to an open window. In the far corner, a man sat hunched over a massive oak desk, scribbling onto a yellow legal pad. He raised the fingers of his free hand into the air as if holding something unseen but delicate. Moments later, he lowered his pen.

"You've brought someone to see me, Aiden?"

"I did bring someone, Carlisle. I brought Truman Birdsong, a true man and a man true."

The man swiveled in his chair to face them, brushing aside a shock of white hair that fell across his forehead like cut straw.

"That would be a refreshing change. Thank you, Aiden."

"A car is coming, and it is, so I will go now."

Aiden vanished down the hallway. Truman strained to listen but heard nothing other than wind whistling through the porch window. Carlisle grabbed a bentwood cane and stood, shaking Truman's hand before motioning him to sit.

"Forgive me for not welcoming you before now but I've been under the weather and getting around is a bit difficult for me. Several years ago I contracted encephalitis while conducting research at the Nag Hammadi library in Cairo. I had this idea to compare Gnosticism with the work of William James. But that was another life and I won't bore you with it."

He waved his hand through the air as if to brush aside the memory. Truman sat and nodded toward the hallway.

"You don't seem to bore Aiden. Nearly every time he says your name he mentions something about a protected tower."

"Aiden believes in the power of names," he said, easing back into his chair.

Truman chuckled. "As he has reminded me more than once."

"You're a skeptic?"

"Let's just say I like more in the way of proof."

46

"Ah, but perhaps belief and proof are two sides of the same coin. Which of them comes first, Truman? That is the question."

"How did you come by your name then?"

"My mother was born in England near Carlisle, a walled city with a castle and tower, and she named me for the place thinking it would protect me as the tower and wall protected the city. Though we left when I was a child, I've always shared her feeling.

"I felt that protection even when I was very ill. I truly believed I would recover, at least for the most part. I know it may sound daft but I can't deny it. There's nothing like your own death to concentrate the mind."

"But you came through it alright?"

"Other than some paralysis in my right leg and a little vertigo, I have no remaining physical effect of the illness. The non-physical is another matter."

"Then why are you here, Carlisle, in a boarding house, a boarding house like this?"

He tapped his cane against the floor as he considered the question.

"Truman, have you ever contemplated your place in the spin of time, how you got here and where you're going, and if what you do matters in any way whatsoever?"

Truman took a breath, trying to ignore the knot of failures filling his throat. "I suppose I have."

Carlisle looked about the room before turning back to him. "This house used to be mine, you know, mine and my wife's."

"You lived here?" Truman peered at him as a vague memory again stirred in the back of his mind.

"We had many happy years before she got sick with a rare illness. I spent everything we had saved, first to fight the disease, then to make her as comfortable as possible. I even arranged a reverse mortgage when our money ran out."

"That's how Mercer got hold of the place?"

"He promised never to foreclose but went back on his word. No surprise, of course." He stood and moved to a nearby table. "Would you like some tea? It's already made. I had nearly forgotten."

Truman nodded and Carlisle filled two cups from a porcelain teapot, handing one to him and setting the other on the desk before returning to his chair. He lifted his cup, for a moment lost in thought. Then he focused his gaze back on Truman.

"I almost started to believe I'd been cursed by some disgruntled Gnostic ghost after my wife died and then I lost the house. It seemed my world was falling in on me and I had control of nothing, could anticipate nothing. I was certain Mercer would sell but instead he moved in."

"Mercer lived here too?" Truman leaned forward, surprised by the news. "When was that?"

"To tell the truth, I find the elasticity of time disconcerting, Truman. Over twenty years have passed since I lost the house but it seems we lived here only a short time ago. Then again it feels an eternity when I'm missing my wife. I still do, you know. In any event, after she died I moved to the city so I could be closer to my work."

"But you returned here. Why?"

"I had only just recovered from my illness, you see, when I was forced from my position at the university by a young up and coming dean who had no use for a musty old professor of religion. When I discovered Mercer had plans to make this place a boarding house, I decided to move here if I was able. This was once my home after all. My pension is meager but sufficient to cover the rent if I'm careful."

Truman peered at him, reminded of his own troubled circumstances. "That's a lot to deal with Carlisle."

"Yet I consider myself lucky."

"But, how can you?"

"Out of strife comes opportunity, Truman. I've returned to the house I loved, a house I never intended to leave, a house of memories." He pointed out the window. "There is a deceptive beauty to this place, much like the beauty of life itself. The land can be harsh and unforgiving yet sublime, even majestic in its changing moods, the fierce thunderstorm, the first stirrings of dawn. It's all there if you allow yourself to see it.

"Though my wife is gone, I have a new family of sorts here. And I just signed a contract to write a book on the early mystics. All of that is my good fortune. How can I feel anything other than lucky?

The rhythmic tapping of Aiden's cane echoed down the hallway. Truman turned to find him standing in the doorway. He pointed toward the porch, his high voice raised in excitement.

"Parfit is driving up the hill, and he is, he is!"

Truman peered down the hallway. "He's coming here, now?"

"Parfit comes only if he has reason to." Carlisle set aside his cup, turning toward the window. "I wonder what it could be."

"Parfit has a reason, yes he has." Aiden pointed his cane into the room. "You must come to the porch with me, Truman Birdsong, and you must."

Truman started for the door. A vague thought tugged at the back of his mind, something Carlisle had said, something important, something he should remember.

Chapter Eight

The rattling din of empty bottles and discarded cans filled the cab of Parfit's truck as he angled up the steep road, bumping between ruts and potholes. Blocking out the sun, the abandoned Clayton Hotel passed to their left. Moments later they emerged from the shadow. Parfit pointed out the window to a small rectangle of fence in the center of an overgrown lot.

"This here is known as karst land, full with sinkhole and fissure."

"What's a karst?" Nicolai said, peering out the window.

"Karst is a place of mystery and wonder, where caves and caverns live out their lives. You see, when rain falls it makes acid that eats away at the rock. Bit by bit the earth gives way and caves are formed, some deep in the ground and full with all manner of amazing sights, hidden lakes and mountains of water-made stone."

"What does that fence have to do with it?"

"That there's the opening to Throckmorton Hole, a famous cave in these parts, hiding place to outlaw and robber, even a murderous woman by the name Eugenia Pike. No telling what spirits roam there still.

"But the fence is there to keep out boys too curious for their own good. There's danger in caves, bottomless pits and quicksand. You keep yourself away."

Nicolai turned as the truck crested a rise and the fence disappeared from view. Beyond the windshield a green shuttered house rose above the hilltop, looking as if it could be home to more than a few ghosts or spirits. Steps from the porch, a huge oak groaned in the coursing wind.

The thought of living in yet another foster home sent a shiver down his spine. He glanced down the bluff, thinking how he could bolt from the truck and be out of sight before the old man realized he was gone. But he had no idea where he was or where he might go.

An image of his mother came to him and for an instant he imagined she might have left the hospital with him if only he had given her more time. Could it be worth another try? The vision evaporated in an instant. He sighed, recognizing the idea as nothing more than a boy's wishful thinking. Parfit waved his hand through the air as if to banish all such thought, pointing at the house.

"You'll be thinking of leaving before you even set a foot in there but the old mansion is a sight more homey than she looks from the outside. Give yourself some time to get used to the place and the people."

He pulled to a stop beneath the sprawling tree. Nicolai leaned on the dashboard to get a better view.

"Are there spirits here too?"

"The good and the bad are all about us, but this is no evil place, son. This here spot was sacred to the native people. They'd be gone now but the hill is still here, still with its powers and ancient knowledge of the spirit world. Now, come and meet your new friends."

Truman waited at the top of the stairs, Aiden next to him. Julius stood behind, peeking around them for a view. A sense of dread moved over him as he watched Parfit climb out of the truck. He searched his mind for a reason why the old man would pay them a visit. He was not one for making social calls.

The boy was even more of a puzzle. He looked as if he might turn and run at any moment. The probation officer's promise of a return dogged his thoughts as Parfit led the boy toward the porch. Stopping at the foot of the stairs, he looked up at Truman and traced the air with his fingers.

"You'd be needing the help of this here boy, Truman Birdsong."

Truman squinted at him, trying to guess the real reason for his visit. "What makes you think I need help?"

Aiden rapped the floor with his cane. "Parfit knows things, and he does, he does!"

Truman placed a hand on Aiden's shoulder to quiet him.

"What brings you here, Parfit?"

He pushed Nicolai a step forward. "This here lad would be Nicolai Tate. He has a curious and quick mind for a young one."

"What's he doing here, then?" Truman gestured toward the town. "He ought to be in school."

"School will come in time but he'd be needing a steady hand to guide him first, not to mention a roof over his head and a bed to sleep in. He'll be no trouble to you and help out where he can."

Truman stared at him, trying to believe what he'd heard. "You expect him to live here? You can't just bring kids up here and leave them, Parfit. Where does he belong? Where are his parents?"

Nicolai glanced to either side of the porch looking for an escape. Parfit clasped his shoulder, sweeping the palm of his free hand over the ground in a broad arc.

"In all the world he has no home, Truman Birdsong. You know the darkness that can bring to a young mind."

The truth of his words caught in Truman's throat, taking his voice. Julius forced his way past him, stopping at the top step.

"This is no place for a boy, Parfit! Take him away or I'll call the sheriff."

Hearing the sheriff mentioned sent Nicolai into a panic and he wrenched free of Parfit's grip, darting around the corner. Parfit made no effort to follow, instead pointing a finger at Julius.

"The boy is a special one. You know the life of such a boy when parents aren't around to protect him, the world being the cruel place it is. Though you may not want him, Julius Rose, here he'll be, want or no."

Julius moaned as Parfit turned and began making his way toward his truck. Aiden slapped his leg and turned for the door.

"Nicolai Tate, here he'll be. Parfit says it and he knows, yes he does."

"Parfit, wait, don't leave him here." Julius started down the steps. "You must take him!"

Parfit ignored him, cranking the truck engine to life. Turning a half-circle, he angled back onto the road, soon disappearing in a cloud of dust. Julius turned to Truman, his expression a mixture of hope and defeat.

"Perhaps David Copperfield has left the premises never to return. What do you think?"

"I don't know what to think." Truman squinted at him, still troubled by Parfit's words.

"Should we try to find him? I hate to think of the little urchin lurking around after what I said about him. There's no telling what he might do. He could be one of those budding sociopaths you read about in the newspaper and decide to burn the house down around us."

Truman gave him a disapproving glance. "And if we find him, then what?"

Julius thought for a moment and then a wry smile crossed his lips.

"What are we worrying about? Either he runs off, never to be seen again, perhaps eaten by a rogue tiger escaped from some zoo. Or, we turn him in and he ends up wherever all the other homeless urchins go." His eyes brightened as he pointed toward the distant hills. "Besides, Aiden and I have your pledge to take us on an adventure. We must go now or risk unwanted complications. I promise you'll not be disappointed."

Nicolai crouched below the porch, peeking through a clutch of low trees as Julius climbed into the van, followed by Aiden. Moments later they were bumping down the rutted street. Careful to stay hidden, he watched the van wind down around the base of the hill, turning west onto a gravel drive that passed through a stone gate flanked by three wooden crosses. Following the narrow road, the van cast a vast plume of dust into the sky before disappearing behind a rock-strewn ridge.

The sun perched above the horizon, washing the hills in shades of blue. Nicolai absently watched the dust cloud drift on the breeze, puzzling over Julius' promise of adventure. The huge oak above him groaned before the wind. A hollowed out space big enough for a man to stand stood dark above its tangle of roots.

The clack of leather-soled boots sounded above him. Without thinking, he leapt toward the house and pressed himself against the wall, looking for a way of escape. Neither direction offered any cover. Holding his breath, he listened to the creak of floorboards over his head. Then three taps sounded on the porch, followed by a voice.

"The ancient druids believed oaks to be sacred and contain much power. I believe our old tree fits that description, don't you?" Without waiting for an answer, he continued. "The trunk offers a boy an excellent place to hide. Why did you choose the shrubbery instead?"

Nicolai kept still, unsure whether to answer. The voice came again, this time closer.

"Would you like to see a Celtic dagger? Given the chance, most boys would like to see a real dagger."

Nicolai said nothing. The three taps sounded above him again.

"I can see you, you know."

Nicolai looked up and an old man's face appeared above him. He leaned over the porch rail.

"I have to be careful not to touch the railing. It was just painted, you see." He pointed a finger at him, the tip green. "My name is Carlisle. Will you join me for some tea? I imagine you're tired of fleeing from one place to the next."

Nicolai hesitated, unsure what to do yet sensing the truth of the man's words. The old oak groaned again. For a moment he imagined the tree talking to him, telling him it was time to stop running and face his future. He stood and stepped away from the house. Carlisle waved him to the stairs and turned, starting for the far end of the porch and the entrance to his room.

By the time Nicolai rounded the corner, Carlisle had reached the doorway. He leaned on his cane and pulled open the screen door, nodding Nicolai inside. The room smelled of books and tobacco, reminding him of a grandfather he could barely remember.

Carlisle lifted a silver dagger from the bookshelf and handed it to him. Wrapping his fingers around the bronze handle, he waved the blade through the air, watching the light glint off the smooth metal. Carlisle put the teapot on and sat with a groan.

"That dagger was a given to me by Oxford University when I was there researching druid culture. It's a replica, of course, but still quite beautiful. Other than being Celtic in design, it has little to do with them, the druids I mean."

Nicolai carefully replaced the dagger and faced him. "What are druids?"

"That's a very good question, Nicolai." He stood, talking while he prepared the tea. "We're not entirely sure who they were, the reason being they left nothing in writing so we have little to go on. Most of what we do know comes from writings of others, mainly the Greeks and Romans who had contact with them. Even the great Roman emperor, Julius Caesar, wrote of the druids.

"We think they were probably religious leaders, well-educated for their time. And there is some evidence they believed in reincarnation. On the darker side, they may have carried out human sacrifice by wrapping people in straw and setting them on fire, although I'm skeptical of that theory. I believe they limited sacrifice to animals."

Nicolai lifted a carved pipe from a rack of four, holding it to the light. "How'd you get to know so much?"

"Why, from books, of course. Do you like to read?"

Carlisle handed him a brimming cup and pointed him toward a plate of cookies. Nicolai shook his head, the bitter thought of his school failures catching in his throat. He returned the pipe to its place, hoping to change the subject.

"My grandfather smoked a pipe. I don't remember him that much. He died when I was still small."

Carlisle tapped his cane against the floorboards as if considering his words carefully. "I heard Parfit through the window, Nicolai. Do you have no family?"

Nicolai set down the cup and glanced out the doorway, already planning his escape. Carlisle raised a hand as if to stop him.

"There's no need to start running again."

Nicolai stared at him, surprised by the guess. "I won't go back. Even if you turn me in, I won't ever go back."

Carlisle waved off his concern. "I have no intention of turning you in."

"The others would." Nicolai looked at him askance. "Why wouldn't you? You heard what they told Parfit. That dang little one said he hoped a tiger would eat me."

"Pay no attention to Julius. He means half of what he says."

"I think he hates kids."

"Julius wants control over his life, as most of us do. He's afraid of change, of what it might mean for him." Carlisle peered into his face. "Nicolai, I have no intention of handing you over to the authorities. Will you believe me?"

He turned his eyes. "I don't know. People act all nice and then they turn on you."

The doorbell rang and Nicolai jumped from his chair, ducking below the window. He peeked through the curtains, speaking under his breath.

"There's someone here."

"There's no reason to worry." Carlisle turned toward the window. "We do get visitors now and then."

The bell rang again, followed by a woman's voice. Nicolai leapt next to him, grabbing his arm, his eyes wide with fear.

"Carlisle, that's my probation officer. She's come to get me. Please, don't answer the door."

Carlisle put a hand on his shoulder. "I have to answer it, Nicolai."

"But why do you have to?"

"With the windows open she no doubt heard our voices. She'll become suspicious if no one answers the door." He stood. "Will you trust me?"

Nicolai nodded and crouched beneath the window, his back to the wall. Carlisle's footsteps disappeared down the hallway. A moment later the front door opened and he stepped onto the porch. The murmur of voices drifted through the window, just out of hearing.

Nicolai leaned his head on his knees, recalling the truth of Carlisle's words. He *was* tired of running, of never feeling he had a home, of never having a normal life, a life like other kids. He took a breath, blinking back tears.

Then a car door closed and an engine roared to life, slowly fading down the hill. Moments later Carlisle appeared in the doorway. Leaning on his cane, he studied Nicolai's face.

"So, you hate school, do you?"

Nicolai stared at him. "You told her I'm here?"

"No, I told her I was alone. Ms. McDuff came to see Truman. I managed to get out of her that the boy she had hoped to bring here had run away and would probably have to be placed elsewhere due to his behavior. She felt obligated to let us know."

"What else did she say?"

"Do you know how many famous people had dyslexia, Nicolai?"

"She told you?" He jumped to his feet, the shame of his failure mixed with anger.

Carlisle ignored him. "Alexander Graham Bell, inventor of the telephone, had it, and Lewis Carroll, who wrote *Alice's Adventures in Wonderland*, and even the artist Pablo Picasso. They all found their talent in spite of a difficulty with reading. You can as well."

"Why should you care?" he snapped.

"I've lived my life surrounded by books, Nicolai, reading books, writing books. A single book can take you to places you've never dreamed of. Wouldn't you like to go on that sort of adventure?"

"No."

"But why not? Boys love adventures."

"I hate reading."

"But if you could, what then?"

"I'll never be able to."

"Miss McDuff believes you can. I think she's right."

"What does *she* know?" he sneered, trying to hide his fear of never measuring up. "She's not a dang teacher."

"Listen to me, Nicolai, you must never give up." Carlisle leaned on his cane and peered into his face. "Did you know that after my illness I could barely speak? I was like a baby."

Nicolai stared at him, trying to imagine it. "You couldn't talk?"

"No more than a word or two, and very slowly. But look at me now. I had to work hard but it paid off. You can get better too, Nicolai. I understand you may never share my love of books but I'll help you improve your reading if you'll let me. What do you say?"

Nicolai glanced at the books lining the walls, wondering what tales of adventure they held. He gestured to the shelves.

"If I did I could find out what's in those?"

"Sit down, Nicolai." Carlisle pulled a book from his desk and handed it to him. "You have in your hands the story of Jean Valjean, a thief and convict, a man with tremendous strength, a man who overcomes great difficulty and learns to return kindness with kindness."

Nicolai turned the book over in his hands, trying to imagine reading as anything other than torture. He surveyed the shelves again, sounding out the titles beneath his breath, trying to picture the stories behind them. Then he turned his eyes back to the book and nodded, deciding he had to know.

Chapter Nine

Following directions called out by Julius, Truman left the road and drove forty yards cross-country before angling the van behind a thicket of cedar. The reddish hue of a brick building peeked through the trees. He leaned out the window for a better view. Beyond the building a steep incline led to the crest of a rock-strewn ridge where a two-story mansion sat perched like a massive boulder, its honey-colored stone bright beneath the noonday sun.

Truman puzzled over the scene. The area felt remote yet familiar, like the image of a lost postcard. Though the presence of the house and outbuilding clouded the memory, he was almost sure he had been there before.

Without a word Julius hopped from the van and began making for the building with haste. Truman watched him, wondering what motive he had for being there. Although he claimed a friend had left him a gift, Truman sensed he was skirting the truth. He had managed to sidestep any details about the friend or the gift or the place itself. Now that they had arrived, Truman was certain there was more to the story.

He offered Aiden his arm and they rounded the thicket, following a winding path that led to the outbuilding. Moments later they stood before the entrance. Tall and narrow, the building's roof and walls disappeared into the grass-covered slope twenty yards beyond. A massive wooden door marked the entrance.

Julius knelt beside the doorway, pulled a loose brick from the wall and lifted out a key. Aiden waited nearby, rapping his cane on the concrete in some undecipherable code. Truman laid a hand on his fist, silencing the cane. Aiden turned toward him, speaking under his breath.

"Truman Birdsong deserved a visit and he got one, he did."

Truman bent close to his ear. "You don't know why we're here either, do you Aiden?"

Julius held up the key. "Stop whispering if you want to see what's behind door number one."

He slipped the key into the door and pushed through. A rush of cool air flowed past them as Truman led Aiden into an open room with a high, arched ceiling. A single light bulb hung above the doorway. Beyond the entrance, the red brick of the walls gave way to blasted stone before vanishing into the dark interior.

Dancing his way inside, Julius flipped a switch, filling the room with light. Racks of wine bottles stretched along both walls. Stacked wooden barrels filled the center of the room, creating an aisle on each side. The air smelled of yeast and vinegar. Aiden slapped his thigh.

"Julius brought us to visit a cave, a wine cave, and he did!"

"Right you are, Aiden." Julius pulled a bottle from the nearest rack. "Now, fold up your cane and stick it in your pocket. I'll need both of your hands."

Truman surveyed the room. "Who owns all this, Julius?"

"The brothers Weeks are the owners and sometimes residents. Fortunately for us, this is not sometime so we have the place to ourselves."

Truman snorted, recalling the withdrawn job offer. "They're supposed to be religious. What are they doing with all this wine?"

"You've heard of the brothers?"

"They promised me a job and then reneged on the offer without bothering to tell me."

"So that's what brought you to our little slice of hell." Julius peered at him, intrigued by the thought. "What happened?"

"Never mind, it's over and done."

Left to guess at the reason, he sighed. "Truman, you are the ever-secretive one."

"What are we doing here, Julius?"

"I'm collecting my gift, of course, just as I said." He held up the bottle. "Do you doubt me?"

Truman looked at him askance, trying to guess at the real story. "Who gave you this so-called gift?"

"I can see you're a born skeptic. I suppose I'll have to tell the whole truth and nothing but the truth, as much as I would rather avoid it."

Truman smirked, unconvinced of his sincerity. "Is this the real truth or Julius' version of the truth?"

Julius ignored him and replaced the bottle before reaching behind an empty barrel and pulling out two canvas sacks. The clinking of bottles echoed down the walls.

"You are right in wondering why devout men like the Weeks brothers have their very own wine cellar, one blasted out of sheer limestone so as to keep the bottles at a perfect temperature. They spared no expense, though that's hardly surprising considering the millions they've made in the oil industry.

"You see, this is a business investment, pure and simple. Though they disapprove of alcohol, they know that a visiting businessman from, say, Norway will be more agreeable when suitably inebriated. So, they built this place as a way of impressing visitors and getting what they want."

"And they just decided to share it with you out of the goodness of their hearts?"

"Ah, well, that's not exactly the case. My friend is a caretaker here and this gift is in payment for a sort of debt."

Aiden slapped his leg. "Julius is a liar, and he is!"

Julius feigned offense. "What on earth could you mean, Aiden?"

"We were going on a visit, a deserved visit and nothing more, no, nothing."

"We made the visit and I retrieved my gift. I see no harm in doing both."

Truman studied him, wondering what he was leaving out. "Why does this friend owe you?"

"Let's just say I know something and he wanted it kept quiet. In return he offered what you might call an incentive."

"He left the key and the wine, and told you when the coast would be clear."

A self-satisfied smirk crossed his face. "A little extortion is a beautiful thing."

"Some friend you are."

"One must take whatever opportunity life offers up."

"You're stealing from a pair of rich brothers. Do you think they're just going to stand by and let that happen?"

He waved off the concern. "Relax, Truman, they'll never miss it."

"If you're lucky enough."

"Besides, I'm going to share." He rattled a bag before thrusting it in Aiden's hands. "After all, you're driving the getaway car."

"I'll get you back to the house but I want nothing to do with this." Truman turned toward the door. "I'll wait for you outside."

He grabbed Truman's arm, doing his best to sound sorry. "Truman, wait. I know I should have been more forthcoming."

"Are you ever even close?"

"I was afraid if I told you everything you wouldn't help."

"You were probably right. People around here shoot trespassers."

"But we've come this far and good wine should never go to waste." He bent and slid a wooden crate from behind the barrel. "Can't you carry this one box to the van for me? I could never manage it myself. While you're doing that, I'll check to see if my friend left any other goodies."

Julius hurried off down the aisle. Truman watched him disappear and wondered what other surprises he might have in store. Lifting the crate, he turned for the door. Before taking a step, he paused to again puzzle over the feeling he had been there before.

"Come on, Aiden." He offered his arm. "We're going to drop off Julius' contraband and take a look around."

Truman loaded the wine into the truck and offered Aiden his elbow. Within minutes they stood before the honey-colored mansion. A cottage of the same stone sat between the house and a rock-rimmed lily pond. Above them a shortwave antenna vibrated in the gusting wind.

Truman left Aiden standing on the cobblestone sidewalk and moved into the covered entryway. Massive doors of copper and bronze rose above the threshold, their cross-shaped centers etched with Bible verses. Two broad windows flanked the doorway. He leaned toward the nearest pane and peered inside.

On the wall opposite him a tattered Gadsden flag in an expensive frame hung above a gun rack lined with dozens of automatic weapons and other armaments. A shortwave radio filled the far corner. Scattered maps and diagrams, impossible to make out, covered a long conference table in the center of the room.

He stepped back, puzzling over the scene. What would two wealthy brothers want with such weaponry? Leaning in for another look, he spotted the glow of the radio dial reflected in the polished tabletop. He squinted into the glare. Tucked next to the radio and a coffee-stained mug, a half-smoked cigarette balanced on the edge of an ash tray. He pivoted, grabbing Aiden's arm.

"We need to go."

Aiden's high twang pierced the silence. "Truman Birdsong is in a hurry, and he is!"

"Keep your voice down, Aiden." Truman glanced at the doorway. "We might have company."

They hurried back along the walkway. Every few steps Truman cast an eye toward the house but spotted no movement. They were halfway to the outbuilding when

Aiden stiffened and pulled free, tilting his head toward the sky.

"A car is coming, and it is." His eyes darted about as he turned one way then the other. "No, two cars and a truck, two and one."

Truman scanned the ridgeline, straining to listen but hearing nothing.

"Where, Aiden, where are they coming from?"

He pointed past the wine cellar. "On the same road, the road we took, the same one and no other."

"We'll be trapped if we don't get moving. Hang on."

He reached for Aiden's wrist, half-dragging him along the path. Just as they rounded the cellar entrance Julius stepped through the door. Two more canvas bags sat at his feet. Grabbing one, Truman started for the van with Aiden in tow, calling back over his shoulder.

"We have three cars coming up the road. You best get moving."

Julius scurried after him. "I don't hear any cars."

"Neither do I but I'm going to trust Aiden's word on this one."

Aiden slapped his leg. "Aiden's word is good, and it is."

Julius spoke between breaths. "But I was assured the owners would be gone."

Truman tossed the bags on the floor as Julius scrambled into the passenger seat, Aiden close behind.

"You can't be surprised your so-called friend, someone you blackmailed, turned on you." He started the engine. "Someone as devious as you should've seen it coming."

"Devious, you say?" Julius scoffed at the idea. "I merely make use of the resources at hand."

"I hope those resources include getting us out of here." Truman put the van into gear and then jerked to a stop. "What am I doing? We can't outrun anyone in this old heap."

Aiden tilted his head toward the windshield. "Two cars and a truck, they are closer, yes closer."

A faint but growing roar rose above the engine clatter. Truman searched the ridgeline for a way out but found nothing. He began running through a list of possible escape scenarios, all of them unpleasant. He was at a loss as to what to do when Julius pointed up the hill.

"Drive to the mansion."

Truman squinted through the windshield, guessing he might hand them over to the Weeks in order to save his own skin. Anger rose into his throat as he turned. Seeing his face, Julius pressed himself against the door.

"Stay calm, Truman, I have a plan."

"You mean like trading Aiden and me for a ticket out of here?"

Aiden slapped the seatback. "Julius is a traitor, and he is!"

Julius ignored him, never taking his eyes off Truman. "We must not delay. You have to trust me."

"Trusting you is exactly what worries me, you little…"

Julius raised a hand to silence him. "Listen to me, Truman. There's a road on the far side of the main house that runs below a rock ledge and from there to a stock gate. It's rough but drivable… I think. The property past the gate belongs to someone other than the Weeks so I'm not sure what to expect, but the way will take us to the highway."

"Why should I believe you?"

"You probably shouldn't. But consider your options. We can sit here arguing until we're cornered or you can take a chance. Which do you choose?"

Truman glared at him before jamming the van into gear, throwing up a spray of rocks as he wheeled a half-circle and rejoined the road. Moments later they rounded the main house, passing the lily pond before cresting the boulder-strewn ridge. He slowed for a look. The way ahead, more path than road, followed a steep incline that disappeared over the slope. Deep ruts etched the roadway.

Angling onto the drop-off, he started down. The van lurched forward as the tires skipped along the rocks, tossing the cab one way then the other and sending Aiden crashing into the side windows. He reached for the front seat, struggling to hang on. Truman glanced at the precipice, nothing but air and sky beyond, and then pressed on.

Suddenly the van dropped into a pothole, wrenching the steering wheel from his grip. The earth tilted beneath them. For an instant he was sure they would tumble over the edge. Then he regained his hold, jerking the van back into line. They landed with a metallic thud.

Thirty yards further, the road leveled out as it passed beneath a thick rock ledge. Truman aimed for the shade, pulling beneath the cliff and stopping. He loosened his grip with difficulty. Julius leaned out for a view of the cliff, calling back over his shoulder.

"I knew I brought you along for a reason, Truman Birdsong."

Truman took a breath, trying to calm his racing heart. Aiden still gripped the seatback.

"Truman drives like a madman, and he does!"

"He may drive like a madman," Julius said, turning to face them. "But that driving spared us a grisly fate."

"We have a ways to go yet."

He surveyed the smooth rock of the overhang, hoping they we're out of sight and might even escape without the Weeks ever spotting them. He winced at the thought of his own foolishness as he jammed the van into gear, vowing to never again involve himself in one of Julius' schemes.

Chapter Ten

Easing past the cliff, Truman repeated his hope of escape under his breath. He paused at the crest of the hill. The road before them wound down a series of jagged bluffs before descending into a wooded valley. Although difficult, the road appeared drivable. His relief at seeing a way ahead was quickly tempered by the glint of barbwire running along the far side. Unless there was an open gate somewhere along that fence, they would be trapped.

They had just come off the steepest section of road when a boom echoed over the valley. The van lurched to one side. Truman slowed for a moment, unsure of what had happened, then all at once recognized the sound as gunfire, a large-bore rifle.

Slamming the accelerator to the floor, he downshifted just as another blast rumbled and the side window shattered, spraying Aiden with glass. Careening between dips and drop-offs, the van hurtled along the rugged track, bouncing between the deep ruts. Truman cringed at the rattling din, expecting the axel to break at any moment. Another shot roared past.

Seconds later they vaulted over a low bluff, dropping into a tree-filled swale. The road became little more than a grass-lined path. He sped along the smooth track, trying to put distance between them and the rifle. A black gate marked with a large 'W' came into view, blocking the road. Without hesitating he jammed the petal to the floor, smashing through it, sending the twisted metal into the air.

Moments later a brush-choked creek bisected by a cement slab appeared, a shallow layer of water sluicing over the top and creating a small waterfall on the downstream side. Truman stopped in the middle and cut the engine. He turned to Aiden.

"Are they following us?"

Brushing bits of glass from his sleeves, he tilted toward the shattered window. "There is no car, no truck, no, not at all."

"Let me know if you hear anything." He eyed his shaking hands. "That was way too close."

He took a breath and restarted the engine, easing the van across the stream. Within minutes they had entered the dim confines of a cedar thicket. The road narrowed into a tunnel scarcely wide enough for them to pass.

All at once fear that his claustrophobia would return gripped him, matched only by a dread of embarrassing himself. Shadows consumed the roadway. Cedar branches scraped along the van, filling the air with rodent-like squeals. He gritted his teeth and focused on the road ahead.

They had just rounded a curve when a green metal gate came into view. A hand-painted sign bolted to the center and riddled with bullet holes read 'No Damn Trespassing'. The road beyond disappeared into the trees. Julius moaned. Truman pulled to a stop, turning to face him.

"What's wrong now?"

He pointed out the windshield. "The rings of hell are ever-widening."

"What the devil are you talking about, Julius? For once, speak plain English."

"God is torturing me for my lack of faith. He, or perhaps she, has made our freedom close but unattainable."

Truman followed his gaze. Partially hidden behind a crossbar, a padlocked chain reached from the gate to the nearest fencepost. He mumbled curses to himself as he checked to either side. The fence vanished into the dense underbrush in both directions, offering no avenue of escape.

He gripped the steering wheel, trying to fight the feeling his entire life was captured in the moment, his path blocked, his future on hold. Julius leaned toward the windshield and studied the barbwire. Then he pivoted in his seat, peering into the van interior.

"Surely you have tools in this home on wheels? Could there be wire cutters or a crowbar or even a chainsaw hidden back there? I feel a need to fashion a new exit for the Weeks family, purely as a favor, of course."

"First you rope me into breaking into a wine cellar and now you want me to vandalize someone's fence? What gives us the right to destroy property that belongs to someone who did us no harm? They could lose valuable livestock."

Julius squinted at him, tired of his righteous morality. "You have a better idea, I take it?"

"I didn't ask to be put in this situation."

"I'll take that as a 'no'. Now, do we have the proper tools?"

Truman threw open the door and jumped out without another word, making his way to the rear of the van and jerking open the door. The clatter of a metal toolbox filled the cab. Moments later he rounded the van, glaring at Julius as he made his way toward the gate.

Julius hurried after him, followed by Aiden. Truman knelt before the fence, taking the lowest strand of barbwire between his fingers. His other hand held a pair of wire cutters. They watched as he gripped the wire with the tool and then paused, his dislike of the business stopping him. He peered down the fence line, trying to figure another way out. After a moment he turned to face them.

"We're sure we want to do this?"

Aiden bent toward him. "No, we're not sure, not at all, no not."

"Once barbwire is cut it's a big job to repair it." Truman studied Julius' narrow face, trying to gauge his reaction. "You can't just stick another strand in there and expect it to hold livestock. Even something as small as a goat can…"

Truman stopped in mid-sentence as Aiden stood upright and slapped his thigh, tilting his head toward the sky.

"Someone is coming, coming fast, and they are!"

Truman jumped to his feet and surveyed the ridgeline above them. "I don't see them. How far away are they?"

Aiden gave his head a shake and pointed to the gate. "They come from there, no truck, no car, not either."

Seconds later, the whine of a small engine rose above the thicket. Truman stepped away from the fence. Julius looked up at him and nodded toward the wire cutters.

"Try not to look so guilty."

He crammed the tool into his pocket just as a four-wheeler rounded the corner, raising a cloud of dust as it raced toward them. A man in a camouflage cap and t-shirt bounced along behind the steering wheel, a huge white dog in the seat next to him. The four-wheeler slid to a stop feet from the gate. Truman spotted an automatic pistol wedged beneath the windshield. Recalling his previous clash with the locals, he hoped this encounter would prove friendlier.

The man studied them as the dust drifted past. With his cap pulled low and his eyes in shadow, his meaty face was impossible to read. Pulling a tin of snuff from his back pocket, he tapped it on the steering wheel before stuffing a wad under his lip. He spit and then craned his neck to look past them.

"I see you boys got the toolbox out, so you must be doing some work for those no-good Weeks brothers. Sort of a strange-looking crew, if you ask me." He let his gaze drift along the fence line before turning to Truman. "Now I have to ask myself what sort of work needs doing right here in front of my gate. Whatever it is, it can't be good, I'll bet the farm on it."

The man took a handkerchief from his pocket and mopped the sweat from his face, waiting for a response.

"Well, what do you have to say then?"

71

Truman shook his head, searching his thoughts for a plausible explanation. "We, uh… we don't, uh… we're not exactly…"

Julius stepped in front of him. "What he means to say is that the situation is… well, we, uh… there are extenuating…"

"We don't like the Weeks brothers either," Aiden's high-pitched twang cut the still air, "no we don't, no, not at all. So we took their wine and nearly got caught. Now we need to make a getaway, a getaway right through your gate, there and only there, no other place, no, not any."

The man squinted at him. "You sure talk funny."

"I talk as I do and no other way, no, none at all."

"So how were you planning on getting through a padlocked gate, seeing as how you… well, you know, can't see a damn thing?"

"Oh, but I do see, I do, just not in the usual way, no. Give me a penknife and a screwdriver and I can see my way past any lock, any at all, yes any."

"You break into stuff? Is that what you're saying?"

"I hear a lock like you hear a bird, but a lock is not a bird, no, not any bird, not one."

"Sounds like you boys don't mind trespassing or burgling if the mood strikes." The man looked them over. "But since you all share a dislike for those unscrupulous Weeks brothers I'm willing to overlook it."

He climbed from the seat and pulled a ring crammed with keys from his pants pocket, slipping one into the padlock. The lock clicked and an instant later the chain clattered to the ground. He motioned them through. Raising its massive head, the dog followed Julius with its yellow eyes. He moved beside Aiden, making a wide path around the four-wheeler.

Moments later, Truman eased the van past the gate and cut the engine, joining Julius and Aiden where they stood in the shade of a small oak. Closing the gate, the man approached them, removed his cap and mopped the sweat from his broad face before offering Truman his hand.

"The name's Hollister Stokes. People around here call me Hollis."

Truman gestured toward the others. "My friends here, Aiden and Julius, call me Truman, Truman Birdsong."

As Hollis shook their hands the big dog lumbered out of the four-wheeler. Stopping nearby, he eyed them warily. Julius took a step back, imagining a hungry look in those yellow eyes. Hollis let out a chuckle.

"No reason to worry about old Sam."

"When did he last eat? I fear I'm a little too close to meal size."

"He's bred to protect livestock not eat them. He acts funny because he's used to living with goats instead of people."

Truman snorted. "Julius does bear a resemblance."

"I'm beginning to wish I'd given you up to the Weeks brothers after all." Julius glared at him, only half-jesting.

At the mention of the brothers Hollis spit into the dirt. "Those rich S.O.B.'s are a thorn in my side, shooting off their weapons and parading around like a bunch of idiots. They have some sort of delusion that owning a gun makes you a patriot."

Truman recalled the room he had seen. "I took a peek inside their house and saw plenty. What are they up to, Hollis?"

He glanced at the sky and blew out his cheeks. "It's too dad-burn hot to be hobnobbing out here. You boys follow me to the house where we can get something cold to drink."

He called to Sam before starting for the four-wheeler. Julius hurried after him, hoping for a quick return home.

"We wouldn't want to trouble you, Hollis. Truman is only mildly curious about the Weeks brothers. He has a preoccupation with the rich and famous. Isn't that right, Truman?"

Truman locked eyes with him, wondering what game he was playing this time. "After the arsenal I saw in that mansion, I'd say I'm more than curious."

Hollis motioned Sam into the seat, calling over his shoulder as he climbed in. "It's no trouble at all, Julius."

Julius tried to think, searching his mind for an excuse to leave. "But the wine can't be exposed to the elements. This sort of heat will ruin it in no time."

"You sure like to worry, Julius." A look of puzzlement crossed Hollis's face. "Is that because you're on the small side?"

Aiden slapped his thigh. "Julius can't help but worry, no, not at all!"

"I didn't risk my neck only to see the fruits of my labor lost."

Truman snorted. "And you didn't have any help in that labor of yours, did you?"

"You girls stop arguing and relax." Hollis started the engine. "I've got a big icebox on the back porch that can hold a whole side of beef. We'll stick your precious grape juice in there while we discuss the Weeks boys."

Julius sighed, seeing he was beaten. Minutes later they pulled next to a low-slung house made of river rock. Truman climbed from the van and studied the house, feeling the sting of regret for never having lived in such a place though it had long been a dream.

He stood lost in thought until Sam's bearlike head slipped under his hand, pulling him back into the moment. Scratching the dog's thick neck, he let the dream slip away, determined to force such pointless musings from his mind. Better to travel light, he said beneath his breath, though he felt little conviction.

Hollis appeared at the back of the house and waved him over to a deep porch overlooking a maze of tree-studded hills. The unbroken landscape reached to the horizon. Studying the view, Truman wondered what

74

evildoings might occur beneath the dense cover of those woods.

Hollis disappeared before returning with two bottles of beer and a plate full of fried chicken. Julius and Aiden had already taken seats at a wrought iron table. An open bottle of wine and two glasses sat on the table between them. Hollis set the plate down and handed Truman a bottle.

Midway down the porch a black rooster stood atop the railing, pecking at a weathered knothole. An orange cat eyed the bird from a nearby bench. Hollis bent toward the cat.

"Now, Clem, I can see you're giving Langhorn the evil eye. You know what happened the last time you pestered him. It took me an hour to patch you up."

The cat squinted at Hollis before turning its gaze back on the rooster. An instant later, Aiden slapped the tabletop.

"Hollis Stokes reads Mark Twain, and he does!"

Still annoyed about being outvoted, Julius sneered at him. "You obviously can't hold your drink, Aiden. Half a glass and you're already talking nonsense."

"I tell what I see, and just that, nothing more, no nothing."

Aiden tapped his forefinger on the table as if waiting for a response. Truman watched a subtle smile cross his lips.

"What are you talking about, Aiden?"

"That's all there is, all and no more."

Julius ran a finger across his throat, silently mouthing the words, 'don't encourage him'.

Truman shrugged. "Well alright, Aiden, I guess you were just talking nonsense after all."

Julius sighed with exaggerated satisfaction. "Thank you, Truman, for ending a pointless discussion, as well as my misery."

Hollis chuckled. "After all that and you boys still don't get it?"

"What do you mean?" Julius sat up.

"I mean our man Aiden here is the sharpest tack in the box. He sees and you don't. Now that's saying something when you happen to be blind."

Truman looked from Hollis to Aiden and back. "What he said is true?"

"It's been staring you fellers right in the face."

Truman glanced around the porch, the meaning slowly coming to him. "Of course, it has. We have Sam, Langhorn and Clem, right here with us."

"Has everyone gone mad?" Julius groaned.

"There's a method to my madness, Julius. I named my animals as a way of honoring Samuel Langhorne Clemens. I've read just about everything Mark Twain ever wrote." Hollis nodded toward the door. "I even have a collection of first editions."

"You collect rare books?" Truman glanced at the house, trying to reconcile the two images. "But you're a rancher."

"Just because a man lives way out in the country doesn't mean he has to be ignorant."

Julius moaned, putting his forehead to the table. "Can't we talk about the Weeks brothers so I can go home?"

Hollis took a breath and sat, his ruddy face turning grim. He motioned Truman to an empty chair.

"You wanted to hear what those rich bastards are up to so I'll tell you what I know. They aren't the only wing-nuts around these parts, mind you, but they've got the cash to make things happen."

"What sort of things?"

"The sort that worries me, Truman. They're using their wealth to stockpile all types of weaponry, from assault rifles to grenade launchers to shoulder-fired missiles."

"That kind of thing can be bought legally?"

"The brothers have no regard for the law. They do whatever they please and thumb their nose at the authorities."

Julius leaned his elbows on the table, sensing he might be able to use what he'd heard to his advantage. "How do they get away with it?"

"If you have money enough most anything's possible, I suppose. Some say they have the local officials in their pocket. I'm not so sure. We still have a few law-abiding folks left out here.

"You see, when the economy went belly up a lot of good people had to go find work elsewhere. Things got unbalanced, you might say, and the types that believe the rules don't apply to them, the ones that look on anyone different as the enemy, began to hold sway."

"I think Julius and I might have met a couple," Truman nodded. "How do the Weeks fit in with all this?"

Hollis shrugged. "I wish I knew, Truman. For now, I'm keeping an eye out and I advise you to do the same. And don't go poking around where you're not welcome."

Chapter Eleven

Nicolai crouched beside the whitewashed cabin, casting occasional glances up the hill to make sure he was alone. Nothing moved. Only the old oak rustled before a light breeze. Perched on a rock ledge, the small home seemed dwarfed by the towering house. He stood and peeked through a side window, curious about the serious-looking man Parfit had called Truman Birdsong.

Hurrying around the corner, he hopped up the wooden steps and onto the porch. The screen door stood ajar, its broken spring dangling from a hook. The freshly painted door behind it shone red in the afternoon light. He glanced up the hill again and twisted the knob, surprised to find it open.

The spare living room held a single upholstered chair and floor lamp, its shade yellowed with age. A table scattered with drawing paper, pens and pencils sat nearby, a stool next to it. On one corner, a half-empty beer bottle perched atop a stack of well-used texts.

Wondering what sort of books a caretaker collected, he bent to read the titles, tracing his finger along the faded words *Greco-Roman Architecture, Gothic Cathedrals of Europe* and *The Mathematical Expression of Curves*. He sounded out the words with difficulty. In the center of the table a page of scribbled notes sat next to several unfinished renderings of stained glass windows. In spite of their incomplete state, he found the drawings beautiful and mysterious. A snapshot of a church was taped to the tabletop.

He turned to survey the rest of the house, noticing how the bare walls gave the place a familiar feel, temporary and uncommitted. Before him a narrow hallway split the opposite wall, ending in an open doorway. He glanced toward the front door then started for the room. Halfway down the hall he froze as footsteps sounded on the porch steps. A wave of panic swept over him.

Swallowing his fear, he hurried through the doorway and into a cramped bedroom, silently praying for a place to hide. The tiny room had not even a closet. He held his breath, trying to hear above the sound of his pounding heart. Then he spotted a window standing half-open across the room. Seconds later he had slipped through and into the dry heat of afternoon.

Careful to stay below the windows, he crept along the back of the house. He had little idea what to do next. If he ran, could he make it across the thirty yards to the boarding house before being seen? He knelt, took a breath and started for the house just as a hand grabbed him from behind, stopping him.

"Find something you liked in there?" Truman said as he turned him around. "I didn't think I had anything worth taking."

Nicolai pulled free, angered by the accusation. "I don't steal."

"Then you broke in just for the fun of it?"

"I didn't break in."

He looked at Nicolai askance. "What do you call it then?"

"The door was unlocked."

"You think that makes it alright?"

"No, I don't think that." He turned his eyes, ashamed of his excuse-making.

"What *do* you think?"

"I didn't mean… what are those drawings for?"

Truman shook a finger at him. "You're changing the subject."

"You won't tell me?"

He sighed. "I'm designing some stained glass windows. They're for a church. I used to be an architect."

"Why aren't you still?"

"I lost my license."

"How'd you do that?"

"It's a long story."

"Did you get in trouble or something?"

"You sure ask a lot of questions." Truman scowled again, feeling the sting of his past. "Don't you need to get back home?"

"Carlisle is letting me stay here."

"Is that right?" He squinted at the boy. "Are you a liar as well as a thief?"

"I told you, I don't steal." Nicolai spit into the dirt, annoyed by the accusation. "And I'm telling the dang truth."

"I heard what Parfit said." Truman pointed a finger in his face. "But you can't just show up and expect to live here."

"You don't know everything. My probation officer came by and Carlisle didn't tell her I was here. That's as good as saying I can stay."

Truman stared at him, surprised by the news. "Kennis McDuff came here?"

"Carlisle said she wanted to talk to you, but don't bother now."

"Why's that?"

"It won't do any good. I'm not going back to that dang foster home, not now, not ever." Angered by the thought of the place, he spit again. "You can't make me. I'll go where no one can find me if I have to."

"Relax. I'm not taking you to any foster home, at least not right now." He nodded up the hill. "We're going to see Carlisle. I want to hear what he has to say."

Nicolai hesitated at the doorway to Carlisle's room. The old man sat with his back to them, thumbing through a book and making notes on a yellow legal pad. After a moment, he spun his chair around, a questioning look on his face. Truman nudged Nicolai into the room.

"Go ahead and tell him."

He cringed, knowing how he had bent the truth. "Carlisle, I, uh... I told him you sort of said I could stay here."

Carlisle studied him in silence. Impatient for a response, Truman pointed a finger at Nicolai.

"You didn't tell him that did you, Carlisle?"

He ran a hand across his chin, considering the question. "This is an important and delicate matter, Truman, one not easily decided."

"You can't mean to let him stay."

"A boy's future is at stake."

"But his future is up to the authorities, not us."

Nicolai glowered at them. "Don't talk about me like I'm not here!"

Carlisle turned to him. "It's true that we must inform your probation officer sooner or later, but..."

"You promised you wouldn't," he pleaded. "Please don't tell her, Carlisle."

"But the way we tell her is worth some thought," he continued. "Miss McDuff had considered this a potential foster home but she said the judge became uncomfortable with placing a chronic runaway in such a remote location."

"She said that? Why didn't you tell me?" Nicolai's voice broke. "I'm not going back to that dang place, not even if some judge says I have to!"

Carlisle raised a hand to silence him. "Perhaps if we offer the judge an assurance that there will be no more running away, he'll reconsider."

"You can count me out." Truman shook his head, wanting no responsibility for the boy's welfare. "The house is my concern, not who lives in it."

Carlisle faced him, disappointment in his eyes. "Truman, you can't mean that."

"I've got enough on my plate. I can't take responsibility for a thirteen year old boy."

"We can all share responsibility, Truman. It's just a matter of... "

"What's the urchin still doing here?" Julius' voice called from the doorway. "Why haven't the authorities hauled him away?"

He shuffled across the threshold. Nicolai started toward him, his fists balled.

"Don't call me that! The only dang urchin here is you!"

Julius pressed himself against the wall, shocked by the boy's anger. Truman stepped between them.

"You've got yourself some kind of temper, Nicolai Tate." He took him by the shoulders. "I know a thing or two about that. Now take a moment and get a handle on yourself. You can do that, can't you?"

Nicolai took a ragged breath and locked eyes with Truman. "You don't want me to go back there, do you?"

He peered into the boy's face unable to answer, reminded of his own fractured childhood. Seeing his ambivalence, Julius decided to press the issue.

"Think carefully, Truman. This house is no place for a boy, is it? Besides, we're crowded enough already."

Truman ignored him, lost in a maze of childhood memories, his father still working, his mother before she became ill. What would life have been like if she had never gotten sick? Where would he have lived? Her image crowded his thoughts.

Carlisle grabbed his cane, pulling himself up. "I was just thinking how Simon's old room would be a perfect hideout for a young boy. A room at the top of the stairs is ideal. That is, until we get all this straightened out."

"But he'll just be bored in a house full of adults." Julius whined. "Besides, this is no place for a child. Those attic stairs are dangerously steep. What if he trips?"

Carlisle waved off his feigned concern. "If Simon could manage those stairs, Nicolai will have no problem."

"But what will he do with himself?"

"Why, he'll go to school, of course." Carlisle clasped his shoulder. "You're ready to return to class, aren't you?"

Nicolai turned his eyes to the floor, too embarrassed to answer. Carlisle leaned toward him.

"Is there something you haven't told us?"

"I got kicked out." His voice was just above a whisper.

"You got kicked out of school? What on earth for?"

"The teacher made me read aloud in class. I sounded like a complete dork, of course. I got so mad I keyed her new car down both sides." He shook his head, still amazed by his own stupidity. "The car was right below a video camera. That's why I'm on probation, or one reason anyway."

"Well then, if school is out we must find something else productive to occupy your time." Carlisle faced Truman. "Isn't that right, Truman?"

He looked up at the sound of his name. Carlisle tapped his cane on the floor.

"Nicolai will be out of school for a time, so…

Truman motioned him to stop. "Wait. Did you say he's not going to school?"

"I'll explain later. So, in view of that fact I was asking you if we might find something for him to do around the house, something that involves math or geometry or read…"

Julius interrupted, guessing Truman would never agree. "We have yet to decide anything. Truman, what do you say? Does the kid stay or go?"

They stood waiting for an answer. Though reluctant, Truman realized at once what he must do. A wry smile crossed his lips as he recalled Parfit's prediction.

"As much as I hate to admit it, that old witch doctor, Parfit, called it right. There are times around here when I could use an extra pair of hands." He faced Nicolai. "But we're going to have to tell your probation officer. And you can't go snooping around where you're not invited. If you're agreeable and willing to work then you can stay."

83

Speechless, Julius glared at him. Carlisle tapped the floor with his cane.

"I believe we have a decision."

Nicolai pointed at Julius. "What about him?"

"What *about* me?" He sneered.

"What do *you* say?"

Annoyed at the outcome but seeing further argument pointless, he shrugged. "I won't say no to it, but the less we have to do with each other the better."

"Then don't call names."

Truman turned to Julius. "Have anything else to say, Mister Rose?"

At once realizing the boy's presence might prove useful he chose his words carefully. "Perhaps I spoke incautiously. By that, I mean without thinking. Shall we declare a truce?"

Nicolai nodded grudgingly. Truman peered at them both, wondering how soon he would regret his decision.

Chapter Twelve

Nicolai pressed his forehead against the passenger window, tracing the ragged horizon on the glass with his finger. He knew without looking that the scattered buildings of the state hospital topped the opposite ridge. Images of his mother's distraught face flashed in and out of his thoughts despite his efforts to stop them.

To distract himself he counted the passing fence posts, seeing in them the days slipping by. He had little idea what his future held. Though he had been granted permission to remain at the boarding house, the judge had yet to make a final decision, leaving him little to count on. Maybe the spirit of Carlisle's sacred oak would come to his aid.

Truman pointed through the windshield at a white steeple rising above the treetops like a beacon. The cross atop it glimmered beneath the cloudless sky. They rounded a curve and a white clapboard church came into view, the scattered buildings of an abandoned town a quarter mile beyond, their dark windows blank, vacuous. He angled the van next to the church entrance.

"You wait here." He motioned Nicolai to stay put and grabbed a small leather portfolio. "And don't touch anything."

Though Truman had allowed him along at Carlisle's urging, he was in no mood to babysit. He stepped onto the gravel walkway and paused to study the chapel. A surrounding grove of pecan trees cast the small church deep in shade. Near the entrance a sign read "Lawson Free Evangelical Church".

He pushed through the oak doors into a shallow foyer and paused to let his eyes adjust to the dim interior. Crimson carpet stretched away from him, bisecting a double row of pews and ending at a short set of steps, the apse just beyond. Part of his project, a circular window now missing, would fill the rear wall. He moved closer to better view its progress.

Once Truman was out of sight Nicolai slipped out of the van, hurrying beneath the windows to the rear of the church. He rounded the corner and came upon a narrow entrance. Turning the knob with care, he stepped inside and down a short hall ending in an open doorway. He peeked around the threshold. Truman stood in the middle of the room bent over a makeshift worktable, his back to him.

Sunlight momentarily filled the church as the front door opened and closed with a creaking thud. Nicolai watched a silhouetted figure hurry down the aisle. Seconds later a heavyset man in a white shirt and tie emerged from the shadows. Sweat beaded on his cheeks. He glanced behind him before pointing a finger at Truman.

"What in God's name are you doing here in broad daylight, Birdsong?" He spoke between breaths. "If my congregation finds out a parolee is replacing our windows, I'll be out on the streets before you can say Jesus H. Christ."

"I'm on probation not parole, Reverend Butts," he said trying to hide his irritation. "I may have broken the law but I didn't go to prison."

"All I know is some San Antonio judge said you can work off your time by fixing our storm-damaged windows, and at no cost thanks to my lawyer brother-in-law." He pulled a handkerchief from his pocket and mopped his forehead, a look of disgust on his face. "I don't want or need to know anymore than that."

Truman held out the portfolio. "I'm here because I need you to approve the final design."

He cast a nervous glance at the foyer, ignoring the request. "Long as the windows have plenty of prophets and angels, they'll be fine."

"Just take a quick look."

Truman opened the binder and held it to the light, flipping through the pages. The reverend raised a hand for him to stop. He squinted at the page through bifocals.

"What the devil is that supposed to be?"

"It's an image of Moses and the burning bush, Reverend Butts."

"Lord God Almighty, it looks like a dang oil well fire. My congregants are oil people. They're bound to have a fit."

Truman pointed at the image. "The quotes at the bottom should clear up any misunderstandings."

"May God have mercy on me for allowing a criminal into his house." He took a breath and glanced toward the doorway again. "I'll just tell them the work was cost-free and maybe they won't fire me. Now you slip on out of here real quiet, quick as you can."

Truman slapped the portfolio closed and started toward the doorway without another word. Nicolai pivoted, rushing out the door and into the blinding sunlight. Dashing beneath the church windows, he reached the van just as Truman stepped out the door. He leaned against the fender, trying to look relaxed.

Truman passed him in silence. The reverend paced the church steps, glancing up and down the street until they climbed into the van. Then he hurried to his car, disappearing down the road in a cloud of dust.

Biting back his anger, Truman gripped the steering wheel. At times his life seemed nothing more than a long series of humiliations, one after the other, all of which he could only endure. Nicolai stirred in the seat next to him. Releasing his grip, Truman faced him.

"I thought I told you to stay put."

For an instant he feared Truman had spotted him. "What do you mean?"

He pointed toward the seat. "Staying put means sitting right there, not slouching against the van like some juvenile delinquent."

"I was leaning, not slouching."

"Call it what you want, you were supposed to be inside."

"I wanted some fresh air. It gets hot in here."

87

"Don't be a whiner," he snapped

"I didn't ask to come here."

"I didn't ask to bring you," he growled. "You can thank Carlisle for that, not me."

"Why are you so angry?"

Truman turned his eyes at once, ashamed of venting his frustration on the boy.

"It's not you, Nicolai." He took a breath, unable to face him. "You didn't do anything."

Nicolai suddenly wanted to say something, anything helpful.

"Have you ever heard of Jean Valjean? He made a mistake and then decided to make up for it by helping people."

Truman squinted at him, puzzled by the comment. "Where did you hear that?"

"I didn't hear it. I read it in a book."

"I know the novel. *Les Miserables* is a great story. But I'm wondering why you would bring it up now, just at this moment."

"I don't know what you mean." Nicolai cringed, realizing his mistake.

"Why did you decide to tell me about the book just now?"

"Carlisle gave it to me." He searched his mind for a way to change the subject. "He's helping me with reading so I must've been thinking about it."

Truman looked at him askance. "And the urge to tell me just came over you?"

"I guess so."

He gestured toward the dashboard. "You were here while I was inside?"

He nodded. Truman pointed a finger in his face.

"Damn it boy, tell the truth!"

Nicolai pressed himself against the window.

"You saw me, didn't you?" he answered, managing both to lie and tell the truth.

Nicolai watched him, hoping he believed the story. Truman sat back, deciding to let the matter go. He put the key in the ignition and spoke without facing him.

"I was wrong to raise my voice at you."

"It's okay."

"Are you hungry? I know a place not far from here."

Nicolai pointed to the church. "Can I see inside first?"

Truman sighed and nodded. Moments later they stepped into the foyer. Nicolai walked halfway down the aisle and turned a full circle, captured by the beauty. Truman followed his gaze.

"Beautiful, isn't it? This was a Catholic church before they moved to a larger building in town and the evangelicals took it over."

"What are evangelicals?"

"I suppose you could say they're people who are very serious about religion."

Nicolai pointed down the aisle. "What's that big circle for?"

"That's going to be a stained glass window, sometimes called a rose window because it resembles a flower."

Truman led him to the makeshift table where slabs of colored glass were arranged around a central hub like spokes on a wheel. Strips of lead solder sat alongside the glass. He lifted a section, holding it to the light.

"The glass crew cut and fit the pieces together with the solder based on my design. Once they're finished, they'll set the window into the frame." He pointed to the arched windows above the pews. "I also designed the stained glass along both sides of the sanctuary."

"Why do they call it a sanctuary?"

"It's meant to be a place of peace and safety."

Nicolai studied the soaring windows and tried to imagine the feeling. "My mom used to take me to church when I was little. I don't remember it much."

Truman studied him, again reminded of his own fractured childhood. "How old were you when she got sick?"

Nicolai faced him. "You know about that?"

"Carlisle told me. He has a doctor friend."

"I was in grade school, second grade I think."

"You've been thinking about her?"

"I couldn't help it when we passed the hospital."

"I can go a different way next time."

Nicolai cast him a skeptical glance, wondering why he had suddenly become so friendly. "No, that's alright."

"Would you like to go see her sometime?"

He stared at Truman for a moment. "You would take me?"

Truman nodded his agreement. Nicolai's last trip to the hospital flashed through his thoughts.

"I don't know, maybe."

Truman shrugged. "Alright then, let's go eat."

Half an hour later they pulled up to a low-roofed building painted a deep red. Flatbed trucks and pickups lined the parking area. Off to one side a huge outdoor pit, the lid controlled by counterweight and cable, poured smoke into the air.

A man in jeans and apron stood before the brick pit, a long-handled fork in his hand. He lifted the lid at their approach. Beneath a haze of smoke, charred slabs of brisket sat alongside turkey, sausage and ribs. The man pointed to the meat with his long fork.

"What are you men having today?"

Truman turned to Nicolai and raised his eyebrows in question. He pointed to the ribs. Truman held up his thumb and forefinger indicating the amount.

"We'll have ribs."

With practiced speed, the man sliced the meat onto a sheet of waxed paper before dousing it with sauce and wrapping it in a tight bundle. Taking the package, Truman pointed Nicolai toward the entrance. Minutes later they stood before a long picnic table.

He motioned Nicolai to sit and spread the barbeque before him. Then he disappeared, returning with ice tea and pinto beans. A grizzled man at the end of the table nodded to Nicolai and held up a half-eaten rib, flashing a gap-toothed grin. Startled, he turned his eyes. At the next table two hunters in camouflage shirts and caps hunched over their plates, eating in silence.

Nicolai lifted a rib and glanced at the old man before taking a bite. Sauce dribbled down his chin. He let the flavor fill his mouth, trying to recall anything that tasted as good.

Watching Truman eat, he wondered about his mysterious past. The reverend had called him a criminal yet he seemed decent enough, maybe more so than most. All at once he felt ashamed for eavesdropping. He searched his mind for something to say, blurting out his first thought.

"I shouldn't have gone into your house without asking."

Truman looked up, surprised by the confession. "Asking isn't so hard. You might be surprised how often people say yes."

Nicolai recalled the home's bare walls and spare furnishings. Other than the drawings, the place seemed practically empty.

"How come you have so little stuff?"

"I've moved around a lot. It's easier to travel light."

Having gone through home after home, Nicolai was mystified why anyone would prefer it.

"Do you like moving?"

"Not exactly." Uncomfortable with the questions, Truman shifted in his seat. "That's just the way things turned out."

"Have you ever had your own house?"

"I did once."

"What happened?"

"I lost it in a divorce."

"Were you homeless then?"

Truman stared at him, struck dumb by the question. He had never before thought of himself that way.

"I suppose in a way I was."

"But what about your mom and dad? Couldn't you go live with them?"

An image of his parents flashed through his mind and he was again reminded how seldom he thought of them. "My mother died when I was twelve."

"What about your dad?"

"I haven't seen my father in years."

"Why not?"

"We lost touch."

"But why did you?"

"I don't much like talking about it," he said, hesitating, pained by the memory but compelled to continue. "He was a drunk."

Nicolai stared at him, surprised by the news. "Did he beat you?"

"Sometimes he did, after my mother died and it was just the two of us. We were sad and angry, both of us, and we took it out on each other. Some families do that."

"At least he was still around. My dad is in prison."

He nodded. "I heard. How often do you visit him?"

"Never." Nicolai's eyes darkened at the thought. "I don't ever want to see him again."

"Why's that?"

"He was a bully."

"And he beat you?"

"That didn't matter. But I couldn't stand it when he hit my mother."

"There's no excuse for hitting, ever."

"He beat her so bad she ended up in the hospital."

"And you thought your job was to protect her?"

"Wouldn't you?"

"I suppose so. But you were just a kid and…"

A rising cackle of voices stopped him in mid-sentence. Nicolai peered past him, straining to find the cause. Near the back wall a bearded man in overalls stood and pointed toward a group of women and children, their dark hair and clay-hued skin shining beneath the fluorescent lights. They kept their eyes to the table as his voice echoed across the room.

"I say them bean-eaters have no business being here in this country. Set them on their donkeys and point south is what I say. Don't I have that right, Cecil?"

Truman turned, recognizing the voice from the gas station. The little man grinned, bobbing his head in agreement.

"You got it right for certain, Horace, right as rain."

"Maybe we ought to help them along."

Horace moved next to the family. Truman wondered if he still had the black pistol tucked into his overall bib. Cecil hurried behind him.

"Maybe we should, Horace. Maybe we should just point them south and say adios."

His anger rising, Truman stood. Shifting his gaze, Horace glared at him. Nicolai looked from one to the other, suddenly afraid something might happen, something bad, something involving Truman. An instant later a man in an apron emerged from behind the counter. He faced the men and gestured toward the door.

"We don't need any trouble in here, Horace. It's bad for business. Why don't you just move on? Times are hard enough around here without you adding to it."

Horace nodded toward the family, a disgusted look on his face. "You must be desperate if you allow their type in here."

Nicolai watched as the man from the pit rounded the counter, fork still in hand. Horace glanced at the family and then started for the door. Relieved, Nicolai turned back to his meal. Truman eased back onto the bench, his appetite gone.

Halfway to the exit Horace changed direction, moving between the tables to where he and Nicolai sat. Cecil hesitated in the aisle. The old man at the end of the table grabbed his barbeque and hurried out the door.

Horace stopped midway down the row and stood staring at the back of Truman's head. Nicolai lowered his eyes for a moment, fear filling his throat. Then he made himself look up. Suddenly an overwhelming anger moved through him and he stood, locking eyes with Horace.

"What are you looking at?" he sneered.

"Shut up, boy."

Truman flinched but kept his head down, hoping Horace would lose interest. He motioned with his eyes for Nicolai to sit. Ignoring him, Nicolai swallowed his fear and squinted at the big man.

"Why do you treat people the way you do? You're just a dang bully. What happened to you to make you so mean?"

"I told you to shut your damn trap."

"Didn't your momma teach you any dang manners?"

Truman reached across the table, grabbing him by the arm and pulling him to his seat.

"You mind your own manners so the man can be on his way."

"That's right," he said, glaring at Nicolai. "Put the boy in his place."

"So you can be on your way," Truman said without emotion.

"I hear you're taking care of the retards for that money-grubbing bastard, Mercer," Horace spoke to the back of his head. "He doesn't mind pilfering the taxpayer's money, does he?"

"What he does is not my concern." Truman continued facing the table, struggling to stay calm. "We're in the middle of our lunch here."

94

"In my view that means you're living off the dole too."

"You heard the owner. Best take your view and yourself on out the door."

"Are you telling me what to do?"

"I'm telling you we aim to finish our lunch in peace," he growled.

"We'll just have to see about…"

He went silent as a figure appeared at the edge of Truman's vision. Looking up, he found Hollis standing at Nicolai's shoulder, his eyes locked on Horace.

"This one giving you trouble, Truman?"

He gave his head a slight shake. "We're just having our lunch, Hollis."

Hollis lifted a pistol from his pants pocket just enough to show the handle. Horace took a step back, his eyes wide.

"You like shooting dogs?"

"Why, I… I…" he stammered. "I don't know what you're talking about.

"Oh, I believe you have an idea. Whoever shot my dog is a poor aim and only winged him. But that dog never forgets a face so you best stay well away or he'll have his revenge. He's so big there won't be a thing I can do about it."

"Why would I shoot a damn dog?"

"Because you're the sort that would," he said, turning to Truman. "I've seen this one hanging around the Week's place more than once. There's no telling what he's up to over there but I guarantee you it's not good. I would ask him to educate us about it but I believe he's on his way out just now. Isn't that right, Horace?"

His eyes never leaving Hollis, the big man hurried down the aisle and out the door, pushing Cecil ahead of him. Truman took a breath, relieved to see them gone.

"Thanks for getting rid of him, Hollis."

"You had the look of a man about to reach his limit."

"I might've done something stupid," he added, reminded of his first encounter with the two men.

"Well, old Horace usually carries a revolver in his overalls so I decided to even the odds."

"Did he really shoot Sam?"

"Someone did, but Sam's a tough old son," he chuckled. "He'll be alright."

He sat next to Nicolai, his expression turning grim. "The fact is those antigovernment types are feeling bold just now. Yesterday some modern day Bonnie and Clyde gunned down two sheriff's deputies for the fun of it. Then they did us all a favor by killing themselves. The couple was part of a radical militia group."

"What do you think Horace and his friend are doing at the Weeks' place?"

"I wish I knew. I did hear some of them are meeting on the sly somewhere in town." He stood. "But I won't ruin your meal with such serious talk. Besides, I need to get back to my goats."

Truman watched him leave before turning his gaze to where Nicolai sat picking at his meal. Truman could imagine the world through the boy's eyes with little effort, his mother ill, his father in prison, a world not unlike his as a child. That he could be slow to trust was no surprise.

Truman thought of his own father, not in prison yet often absent and little more available even when around. He had disappointed so often that Truman learned to count on nothing but himself and even in that proved unreliable. He wondered for a moment if a similar fate awaited Nicolai. Then he caught himself. Such matters were not his concern. He had his own problems to sort through.

Chapter Thirteen

Bored with verbs and an adverbs, commas and conjunctions, Nicolai slammed shut the grammar text. Try as he might, he could find no point in diagramming sentences. He glanced at the new book Carlisle had loaned him, something to do with a boy and a runaway slave. Though reading remained slow and laborious, he felt irresistibly drawn to the books, as if hidden within the pages was his own story.

He stood and stepped away from the desk, surveying the small room, the two-pane dormer window with the ancient oak visible just beyond, the narrow bed, the scratched and chipped dresser holding his meager belongings. His gaze came to rest on the attic door tucked beneath the sloped ceiling.

Many nights, unable to sleep, he had worried what spirits might lurk beyond the threshold. Bumps and groans sometimes echoed behind the wall. Now, in the bright light of afternoon his worry turned to curiosity then to preoccupation. He glanced down the stairs, listening for sign of anyone. The house sat quiet.

Easing the bedroom door closed, he crossed the room and knelt alongside the short wall. The door appeared to be painted shut. He wondered how long since anyone had passed through. His gaze moved to the glass doorknob, the bent world captured in its facets, shrunken and disorienting. He again puzzled over Parfit's spirits, good or evil.

Turning the knob, he heard the metal click but felt no give. He leaned against the door. Nothing. Returning to his desk, he retrieved a flashlight and a wood-handled pocket knife Truman had given him. He steadied his arm with his free hand and ran the blade along the top and side. Then he pressed his shoulder to the door. The paint crackled as it gave way.

Cool air smelling of mildew and pine resin spilled across the threshold. He peered inside, hesitated and then crawled through, brushing the cobwebs from his face as he went. Standing, he surveyed the dim space. A maze of pine rafters stretched into the blackness. The door drifted closed, the dark engulfing him, and suddenly he sensed he was not alone.

Biting back his fear, he fumbled for the flashlight, switching it on just as it slipped from his grip. The metal case clattered along the floor sending flashes of light skittering across the rafters. A ghoulish face rose above him for an instant then vanished beneath the dying light. He stumbled back.

Darkness again enveloped him. Never taking his eyes from where he last saw the image, he searched the floor with one hand, finally locating the flashlight. He pressed the switch. The beam slit the blackness, falling on a carved wooden mask painted garish hues of green and orange. The drooping nose stretched toward him nearly a foot. Relieved to find nothing alive, he stared at the strange figure and puzzled over how it had come to be there.

Then he took a breath and swept the light in a semicircle. Spare roofing tiles sat stacked between dust-covered piles of trim and molding. A rolled oriental rug leaned against a support beam. Otherwise, the space appeared empty.

Disappointed, he turned then paused as a flash caught his eye. He moved the beam across the area again, shielding his eyes from the glare for a better view. A glint of metal winked from beneath the rug. He scrambled to the spot, pushing the rug out of the way and pulling a small storage box onto the floorboards.

Holding the flashlight in his mouth, he flipped the brass clasp and opened the lid. A cardboard folder holding a sheaf of yellowed papers sat wedged beside a tattered black and white photo of two men standing before an oil rig. There was nothing more. He pulled out the photo and squinted at it, unable to decipher the handwritten caption across the bottom.

Ready to abandon the effort, he started to replace the photo when all at once it came to him. The faded scrawl read 'Birdsong'. He checked inside the folder and found the name again, this time in a clear typescript. Realizing he could not leave the box as he found it, he lifted it, grabbing the mask as he moved back through the cramped doorway. He set them on his desk and stared at the box, trying to figure what he should do, who he could tell. The safest choice was Carlisle.

Minutes later he stood before Carlisle's room, the mask in one hand, the folder in the other. He pounded his toe against the doorframe. Carlisle's cane rapped the floor in a halting rhythm before the latch clicked and the door swung open. He pushed his reading glasses over his forehead, blinked, noticed the mask and blinked again. Then he raised his gaze to Nicolai.

"Where in heaven's name did you find that?"

He held the mask to the light. "It was in the attic."

Carlisle coughed hard and doubled over, red-faced and gasping for air. Alarmed, Nicolai dropped the folder and grabbed his arm to keep him from falling. After a moment he regained his breath and slowly stood upright.

"I can't imagine where I picked up this little bug."

"Don't you need to see a doctor?"

He waved off the question, raising his cane and pointing to the carving.

"I had forgotten all about it, you know."

"The mask belongs to you?"

"It was a gift to my wife from a Nigerian shaman." He ran a finger along the tapered nose. "The design is ceremonial, meant to ward off evil spirits. They wear them and dance for hours to banish demons."

"Then don't you want to keep it in here? Maybe it will get rid of your cough."

His eyes dark with memory, Carlisle shook his head.

"Did I say something wrong?" Nicolai said, lowering the mask.

"The mask brings back many memories, some difficult to face in my current state. I want you to hold on to it until I'm feeling better. Will you do that for me?"

He gave a nod of agreement and retrieved the folder, pulling out the photo and papers.

"I found these too. I think they may have something to do with Truman, maybe something important."

"I'll take a look," he said as he took the folder. "Now, I must get back to my project. I'm afraid this cough has slowed me down and I've fallen behind schedule."

Nicolai watched him shuffle back to his desk. Then he started up the stairs, mask in hand. He paused on the first landing and peered down the hallway. Julius' door stood slightly ajar. He held his breath, again listening for footsteps. The house remained quiet.

Setting aside the mask, he started toward the room, casting nervous glances down the stairway. The wood floor groaned beneath his step. He told himself to turn around and climb back to his room but he kept on, curiosity overruling his better judgment.

Reaching the threshold, he leaned away from the wall and peeked inside. The room appeared empty. He nudged the door with his toe and watched it swing open, revealing the space in increments. Books covered virtually every surface, spilling onto the floor amid stacks of magazines and newspapers, some shoulder-high. A narrow path wound between them. A table in the far corner held an open laptop computer surrounded by empty bottles of beer.

Slipping inside, he followed the pathway past science magazines and star charts, physics texts and comic books. A makeshift shelf held a battered manual calculator alongside plastic statues of fantastical creatures, some grotesque, others strange yet beautiful. A yellowed periodic table filled the far wall.

He paused to study a legal pad covered with notes and diagrams but could make little sense of them. His eyes wandered to the table, landing on a thick folder topped with Carlisle's name. Next to it another file held Aiden's name, and another Truman's.

He cast a quick glance at the doorway and lifted the folder, sending the contents to the floor. Cursing beneath his breath, he knelt. At his knee lay a scattering of newspaper clippings, photos and scribbled notations. As quick as he could he stuffed them back into the folder, puzzling over their meaning.

Then the floor creaked behind him. He froze. Seconds later Julius appeared in the doorway. His eyes darted about as he surveyed the scene, finally settling on Nicolai.

"Did you find what you were looking for?"

Nicolai stood, his thoughts racing as he searched for an excuse. "I heard something, maybe a mouse."

Julius squinted at him, wondering how he might react if confronted. Would he bolt or fight? Then he realized Nicolai might prove a useful informant if he had something to hold over him. He proceeded cautiously.

"A mouse, you say? And what does a mouse have to do with the folder in your hand?"

Nicolai looked at his hands. "Why do you have folders on everyone? Are you spying on them?"

"Not that it's any of your business, but it's a hobby of mine, and a harmless one if you must know."

"Do you have a folder on me?"

"Excuse me but you're in my room without permission so I'll be the one asking questions."

"The door was open."

"It makes no difference."

"But do you have a folder on me?"

"The more important question is how judges deal with boys who are budding thieves."

"I'm not a dang thief."

"First, you break into Truman's house, and..."

101

"How do you know about that?" he shouted.

Julius pointed a finger at him. "And then I catch you in my room with private property, *my* property, in your possession. That sounds awfully like stealing."

"You'd tell the judge?"

"Perhaps not… that is, if we can come to an understanding."

"What do you mean? What kind of understanding?"

"I mean we can leave the judge out of this unfortunate situation." He gestured at the folders. "All you have to do is be my eyes and ears on a special assignment."

"How do I do that?"

"You know the abandoned hotel in town?"

"You mean the tall building across from the old train station?"

"That's right. During the oil boom it was called the Clayton Hotel, by all accounts the most exclusive establishment for hundreds of miles. All sorts of fat cat wheeling and dealing went on in that hotel, some legal, some not." Julius tried to sound mysterious. "Well, there's going to be a secret meeting there tonight."

Nicolai snorted. "It can't be all that secret if you know about it."

"Yes it can," Julius snapped. He moved next to Nicolai and leaned in as if conspiring. "If you must know, I have ways of knowing things, even what's supposed to be secret."

"You sound like Parfit." Nicolai peered at him, trying to guess his motives. "Why are you telling me?"

Julius stamped the floor. "If you weren't so impatient you might find out!"

"I can listen."

"That's better. Now, I want you to go down there, sneak in with the utmost care, and listen to what is said, listen very carefully." He patted the table. "Then you come here and tell me all about the meeting. Do you think you can handle that assignment?"

"I can do it." Nicolai nodded, his curiosity piqued. "I'm good at being quiet."

"Yes, but are you brave enough? This mission could prove dangerous."

"I'll do it as long as you don't turn me in to the judge."

"Then I believe we have a deal."

He held out a bony hand. Nicolai ignored the alarms sounding at the edge of his thoughts, dreams of adventure sweeping him along. He scarcely noticed the damp cool of Julius' palm beneath his grip. An instant later Truman's voice sounded behind him.

"What sort of deal would that be, Julius?"

He flinched but quickly regained his composure, raising his eyes to the doorway.

"This is between me and Nicolai. You will kindly mind your own business."

"As I see it, this *is* my business."

"And how, may I ask, do you arrive at such a ludicrous conclusion?"

"Whenever I see you getting all chummy with one of us, I know you're up to no good."

"You make me sound like a scheming Machiavelli."

"I doubt you're up to his standards, but the scheming part fits." He turned his gaze to Nicolai, making no effort to hide his anger. "You're supposed to be working on your English homework."

"Grammar is boring."

"That boring grammar can help you sound as smart as you really are, but only if you take the time to learn it." He pointed down the hall. "Now get to work and I'll come up to check on you as soon as I'm finished here."

Slump-shouldered, Nicolai slipped out the door. Truman pointed a finger at Julius.

"I don't know what you're up to but whatever it is, leave him out. He doesn't need any more trouble."

"You truly believe I'd put him in harm's way?" Julius feigned offense. "You judge me too harshly, Truman Birdsong."

Truman squinted at him. "Save the act for someone else, Julius. Just leave the boy alone."

Chapter Fourteen

Truman found the last open stool and sat, ordering green enchiladas and ice tea from the counter menu. The only sit-down restaurant in town, La Nunca often had a line of customers waiting for a table. A glass of tea appeared before him. He squeezed a lemon wedge over it, stirring the ice with his finger. Beads of sweat trailed down the tinted glass.

Taking a sip, he surveyed the crowded room. Strings of papel picados, colorful tissue cut-outs depicting flowers, birds and Aztec symbols, stretched from corner to corner. Painted clay pots and woven blankets from Mexico littered the walls. At the heavy wooden tables, oilfield roughnecks in mud-caked boots hunched over their plates.

A group of men in stained work shirts were gathered around a booth opposite him, their voices rising above the crowd noise. He watched them, recalling the scene he and Nicolai had witnessed over barbeque. Horace's treatment of the family still irked him. He was in no mood for more of such bullying.

The men parted and he spotted Kennis McDuff at the table, her expression strained but polite. She glanced his way, seeming to nod him over before disappearing behind the group again. He hesitated, wondering if he had imagined only what he wished to see. Then he started across the room.

The moment he rounded the group she reached for him, taking his hand and pulling him to the table. He tried to hide his surprise. A grumble moved through the men as they crowded in. She locked eyes with him before turning her gaze to the closest man.

"You'll have to excuse me now that my friend is finally here." She turned to Truman. "What took you so long?"

He peered into her dark, downturned eyes and hesitated, his mind searching for an answer, and then gave his head a slight shake.

"We ran into an unexpected problem. Sorry to make you wait."

"That's alright, Truman." She waved off his apology. "These gentlemen were keeping me company."

The man in front frowned and gestured at his companions. "We were having fun until you showed up."

Truman returned his stare. "And now I'm here."

"You just a friend or what?" The man squinted at him. "What do you think?"

He leaned in, his face inches from Truman's. "I think you're not too friendly."

Truman swallowed, struggling to control a growing anger. "You think wrong. I'm hungry is all."

"Is that right?" He shifted his gaze to Kennis. "A pretty lady like you can do better than his type."

"No doubt she can." Truman pointed toward the door. "But now she wants to have her lunch in peace, so you best take your leave."

The man glared at him. "Are you trying to…?"

Kennis stood and pulled a small leather wallet from her purse, flipping it open and thrusting it at the man. The gold badge flashed beneath the restaurant lights.

"You don't really want to cause trouble, now do you?"

Wide-eyed, he took a step back. "You didn't say you were the law."

"Didn't I? Well, I'd tell you all about it but I'm sure you men have someplace to be."

The others started for the door, leaving him standing alone, a look of confusion on his face. She nodded toward the exit.

"You'd better hurry or your friends will leave without you."

He pivoted, hurrying after them. She turned to Truman.

"They're called roughnecks but they aren't so rough after all, are they?"

He took a breath. "That's the second time in a week I've almost done something stupid. I must have a guardian angel."

"Truman, are you calling me an angel? That's so sweet." She stuffed the wallet back into her purse. "I rarely show my badge. It scares the kids, not to mention their parents."

"I'm glad you made an exception for me."

"You had a certain look, like you might…"

"Do something stupid."

"I was going to say act without thinking."

"Is there a difference?"

"You were very gallant to step in like you did, Truman. I am grateful."

"You could've handled them without my help."

"Maybe. Spending time around teenagers does encourage a sort of boldness."

"How'd you get into that line of work?"

"I wanted to make a difference. Working with kids does that for me. As a probation officer I have contact with them at a critical time, a time when the choices they make can follow them for the rest of their lives. Not every kid rises to the challenge but it's gratifying when I get to see their efforts pay off."

Recalling the pride he once felt as an architect he looked away, unable to imagine how he might explain to a beautiful woman like her the humiliation of being on probation. She leaned across the table, peering at him with her black, depthless eyes.

"You're troubled by something I said?"

He gave his head a shake. "Just remembering another time."

"I'd like to hear about it."

107

"Well, I…" He searched for a way to change the subject. "It would bore you, no doubt."

"Why don't you let me decide for myself?"

She frowned as a voice near the entrance drew her attention.

He glanced over his shoulder. "Is something wrong?"

"This is not my day," she mumbled, a disgusted look on her face.

Truman followed her gaze. Two men stood near the door, one in a red leather coat in spite of the warm day, his blonde-white hair stuck to his pale forehead, the bulge of a pistol clear beneath his chest pocket. The other wore a purple shirt and yellow pants. A black goatee sprouted from his chin. Kennis watched with interest as they moved to a corner table. Truman hailed her attention.

"You know those two upstanding citizens?"

She turned to face him. "The blonde one in the red coat is the father of a boy I worked with a long time ago. He's a hard case. That boy of his never stood a chance."

"What happened to him?"

"After years of beatings at the hands of our friend over there, he took up the hobby himself and ended up killing his girlfriend. If he behaves, he'll get out of prison when he's sixty."

"No one did anything about the beatings?"

"By the time the truth came out the boy was nearly an adult. Neither he nor his mother would testify against the bastard. Unfortunately, it plays out that way more often than not."

"Your pale friend has a pistol beneath his jacket."

"That's not a surprise. No doubt, he has a permit. All you need to get one is a pulse, brains not included."

"Does everyone around here carry a gun?"

"Most places it's legal as long as it's concealed, which basically means they're not waving it around in public. What bothers me most is people that carry a weapon but have no regard for the law. They think they're above it and can do whatever they want."

"What's it about, Kennis, this lawlessness I keep hearing about? You know law enforcement. What do the local authorities think about…?"

He stopped in mid-sentence as a man in a starched white shirt and jeans appeared at the table. A gold star hung from his belt.

"Speaking of the law…" Kennis winked at Truman and patted the seat next to her. "Don't stand there looking all sad. Take a seat, sheriff."

"Not sad, Kennis, hungry. I've had my lunch interrupted three times today before I could take a single bite." He pointed a thumb toward the back wall. "Isabel has been keeping it warm for me. Once she sees I'm back, she'll bring it out. If I get paged again, you can take the call."

She nodded across the table. "This is Truman Birdsong."

"The name's Tico Bauert." The sheriff thrust his meaty hand across the table. "You got yourself the best view in the house, you know."

"Don't pay Tico any attention, Truman," Kennis blushed. "He likes to pick on us probation officers."

"Maybe so but I'm not complaining."

"We once had a family around here by the name Birdsong, if memory serves." The sheriff ran a thumb across his jaw. "I believe they owned the big place north of town. Any relation?"

"We left when I was twelve. My father never talked about his past so I'm a bit fuzzy on family history."

"If it was their place, the bank got it through some shady dealings and then sold it off to a couple of rich brothers by the name of Weeks."

Truman wondered if a family connection might explain the familiar sense he'd felt at the brother's place. "You're sure it was the Weeks that bought it?"

"I'm sure about them. What I'm not sure of is who owned the land before they got their claws into it."

Kennis chuckled. "Why, sheriff, you don't sound like you care much for those brothers."

"They're trouble, Kennis, long on money and short on sense. I hear all sorts of rumors about what goes on out there."

Truman searched for a way to tell him what he'd seen without admitting to trespass. Then a waitress appeared, setting three steaming plates on the table.

"I've been looking for an excuse to go pay them a visit." Tico spoke between bites. "They have weapons and such but nothing outright illegal that I know of. I'd need more to go on before showing up unannounced. Besides, it won't do any good without a warrant. I'll need to look where I want instead of where they let me."

Kennis nudged Tico. "Speaking of brothers, your friend Jerome Bell is sitting over there with a pistol under his coat."

Tico gave a disapproving grunt as he stuffed the last of a tortilla into his mouth. Then he sat back, pulling a toothpick from his shirt pocket. Kennis pointed to the empty plate.

"Tico, you weren't about to let another call keep you from your meal this time, were you?"

"I haven't had a string of calls during mealtime like that in I don't know when. I figured it was past time to put a halt to it." He craned his neck, surveying the restaurant. "Jerome and his brother look like a couple of pimps. Yesterday I spotted them in town driving a brand new purple Caddy. They must've come into some money."

Kennis nodded. "Outside of the legal avenues, I'd bet."

"Maybe I'll go have a talk with them and see what they're..."

The beep of a cell phone sounded from beneath the table. Mumbling a silent curse, he pulled the phone from his belt and held it up, the screen inches from his eyes.

"Dad blast it, I left my reading glasses in the car." He pointed the phone at Kennis. "I'd appreciate it if you could tell me what it says."

"Uh-oh, there's a problem at the high school." She squinted at the screen. "I wonder if it's one of mine. I had a girl return to class yesterday and…"

A muted buzzing cut her off. She glanced at Truman, disappointment clear in her eyes as she grabbed her purse and pulled out the phone. Giving it a quick look she stood and nudged Tico with her knee.

"Let's go, sheriff, duty calls." She leaned across the table. "I'm sorry I have to go, Truman. But we're not finished, you and me."

He watched her leave, a part of him already wanting to see her again, to hear her voice, to gaze into her dark eyes, a part of him resisting it. The past ate at him. He still felt the sting of his wife's betrayal and failed marriage. Just the thought seemed to tire him. He stood and started for the door, trying to clear his mind, to focus only on the moment, on his job, on what needed doing.

Chapter Fifteen

Truman unloaded the last of the lumber, stacking it next to the house according to size. A section of porch needed replacing. He stepped beneath the massive oak and wiped the sweat from his eyes, squinting into the brightness. With autumn less than a week away the afternoon sunlight still held the heat of summer.

His eyes followed the undulating line of hills below the bluff, their curves voluptuous, womanly. In spite of trying to rid his mind of Kennis, her image floated in and out of his thoughts like passing smoke. He took a breath, chiding himself for such foolishness. Then Aiden's voice sounded from the porch steps.

"Truman Birdsong, you must come inside the house, and you must."

"And why would that be, Aiden?"

"Why would it be, and why?" He tapped his cane three times. "Carlisle of the protected tower, of the walled city, wants a meeting, an important meeting for all, yes all."

"Carlisle called the meeting?" He started toward the stairs. "In that case, I accept."

He followed Aiden down the porch and around the corner to Carlisle's room. Nicolai held open the screen door as they stepped through. Inside the crowded space Carlisle sat next to his desk, his face pale, his gaze unfocused. A sheaf of papers rested on his lap. He coughed deeply into a handkerchief.

Julius loitered near the hallway door as if waiting for a chance to slip away. Nicolai pointed Aiden to a chair and they all turned to Truman. No one said a word. He studied the group, puzzling over what could warrant such drama, his gaze finally settling on Carlisle's drawn features.

"Carlisle, are you sick?" Truman studied his face. "You're not looking so good."

"It's just a lingering bit of flu." He dismissed the concern with a wave of his hand. "I'll be fine."

"Alright, then what's this about?"

"I asked everyone to join me because what I have in my hand is about this house, the house where we all live, about its history." He gestured to Nicolai. "Start us off, son."

"Don't be mad at me." Nicolai grimaced as he shifted his gaze from Carlisle to Truman. "I just wanted to know what was behind the door."

"I don't like the sound of that," Truman grumbled, disapproval clear in his voice. "Have you broken in somewhere again?"

His eyes grew wide. "No, this doesn't have to do with breaking in. Well, not in the way you mean anyway. I was in my own room."

"Then what door are you talking about?"

"Do you know the attic door, the small one below the ceiling?"

He nodded. "What about it?"

"I wanted to see what was behind it so I pried it open. The door wasn't locked, just hard to open because of the paint." He glanced at Carlisle, who motioned him to continue. "Inside I found some papers with your name on them."

Truman peered at him, unsure if he'd heard him. "Did you say you found something with *my* name on it in this house?"

"He means your family name, Truman." Carlisle held up the file. "These are the papers Nicolai found. When he realized they might be important, important to you, he came to me for advice. I've tried to put together the pieces and I think I've come up with an explanation. Take a look at this."

He handed Truman the photo. Nicolai stepped next to him, leaning over his shoulder.

113

"I found the picture first but I couldn't read what was written across the bottom."

"It looks like it says 'Birdsong'." Truman peered at the image. "The man on the left resembles my father."

"That's correct." Carlisle pointed to Truman's right. "Can you make out the other?"

They waited as he held the photo to the light. Then a flash of recognition crossed his face.

"Mercer."

"Yes, Truman, that's Mercer and your father as young men."

"I knew there was something familiar about him." He pointed to the photo. "He and my father worked together in the oil business?"

"There's more to the story." Carlisle held up the papers. "Not only did they work together, they went on to become partners in a wildcatting venture."

"Mercer and my father were partners?" He glanced about the room as if the walls somehow held an answer. "How could I forget that?"

"Your father lost everything, Truman. We sometimes put out of mind what is too painful to remember."

"He always claimed his partner betrayed him. I never believed him." He stared at the photo, stunned by the news, ashamed for doubting his father. "I figured it was just his excuse for being a drunk."

Carlisle tapped the folder with his forefinger. "This shows that Mercer extricated himself from the partnership just before the business went under, leaving your father holding the bag, bankrupt and out of work. Mercer lost next to nothing."

Julius watched Truman, studying his reaction. Then he stepped into the room.

"Best to get the bad news into the open all at once, don't you think, Carlisle?"

"You know more than what's in here, I believe." He raised the folder. "Please tell Truman what you've learned."

Julius faced him, trying to sound sympathetic. In truth, seeing someone other than himself humiliated for once was elating.

"I imagine this is a bit of an embarrassment for you, Truman."

Truman squinted at him, in no mood for his gibes. "Do you have something of value to add, Julius?"

"I'm getting to that." He wandered about the room, gesturing with flourish. "According to those who knew him, your grandfather thought land was the only real wealth. He bought acres as he could afford to, an acre here, two acres there, gradually accumulating a large parcel of land. You must have been quite young when your father used the land as collateral for a loan to go into partnership with Mercer.

"He, with typical underhandedness, convinced your father to put up the bulk of the startup money in exchange for his so-called expertise. I suppose it goes without saying that your father lost the land to the bank when the business folded. That land, land that by rights should be yours, is now in private hands. Shall I tell you whose?"

"As much as you would enjoy saying it, you can save your breath."

"But…"

"The Weeks brothers own that land."

Aiden slapped his leg, his eyes darting about. "Truman Birdsong is a man of truth, and he is, he is!"

"Which one of you gave it away?" Julius glared at the others, disappointment clear in his face. "What did you do, give him some sort of sign? How did…"

"They didn't tell me, Julius," Truman interrupted, a wry smile crossing his lips. "You told me, you and the sheriff."

"But I never…"

"All that nonsense from you and Aiden about a so-called deserved visit to the wine cellar was enough. But earlier today Tico Bauert gave me a little local history lesson on the Birdsong family. All I had to do is put it together."

Looking deflated, Julius moved back to the doorway. Carlisle handed the folder to Truman before waving Nicolai over. Using him for support, he stood and gestured toward the hall.

"I'm sorry but I must lie down." He spoke between breaths. "Please see yourselves out, all except Truman."

He watched Carlisle shuffle across the room. Reaching a narrow cot tucked behind a folding screen, he sat and pointed Nicolai toward the door. Then he motioned Truman to a bedside chair. Closing his eyes, he eased back onto the pillow. For a moment Truman thought he had fallen asleep. Just as he stood to leave, Carlisle's voice, a near-whisper, stopped him.

"I need your help, Truman."

He sat and leaned in. "How so?"

"As you know, I have a friend at the hospital."

"I remember."

"He tells me an experimental medication has become available that may offer hope to Nicolai's mother."

"That's good news."

"Yes, it is. She has responded well, but to maximize her chances the doctors say she now needs contact with her immediate family."

"You want me to locate the family?"

Carlisle opened his eyes. "Nicolai is all she has, Truman."

"What about his father? He's in prison but…"

"He relinquished custody long ago. Nicolai is her only family."

"So you want me to take him?"

"I would do it myself but you can see how I am."

"*You're* the one who should see a doctor, Carlisle."

"I'll be alright." He locked eyes with Truman. "Learning of our past can prove disconcerting, Truman. Give yourself time to understand it."

He closed his eyes. Truman turned to leave, hoping he could follow Carlisle's advice.

Julius stood waiting just beyond the doorway. He wanted to be sure nothing interfered with his plan for Nicolai. He looked up at Truman's approach.

"I realize now that I should have mentioned your family connection to the Week's ranch before our meeting today." He did his best to sound apologetic. "Does better late than never count for anything?"

"Don't worry about it, Julius," he answered, in no mood for his games.

"Let me make it up to you, Truman. I'm told there's a new bar only twenty minutes from here. They say it has the rustic ambience of rural Spain. If we leave now we can catch happy hour. What do you say?"

He sensed another of Julius' schemes behind his words but nodded in agreement anyway. After all he'd heard he needed a drink, not to mention a change of scene. He gestured down the hall.

"Lead the way, Julius Rose."

Chapter Sixteen

The silver glint of a passenger jet winked between streaks of cloud edging the horizon. Truman followed the plane with his gaze, the lure of escape, of a life elsewhere, of no ties, no attachments somehow captured in the image. A web of expectations had wrapped themselves about him unnoticed, one by one, bit by bit. He could feel them. Carlisle, Nicolai, Parfit, all pulled him into obligations he seemed unable to refuse, as if some hidden part of himself had overruled his own wishes.

He stopped the van before a sharp-roofed stone building surrounded by cars and pickups. Drooping willows lined a shallow creek just beyond. Glinting off the rippled surface, sunlight cast the overhanging branches in yellow as if the leaves themselves were lit from within. For a moment the peaceful scene provided a welcome distraction from his troubled thoughts.

Julius stirred next to him and climbed from the van, making for the entrance. Truman followed with reluctance, his thoughts again crowding in. A sudden desire to be alone swept over him. He pushed through the thick doors and stopped before a spiral of wrought iron steps leading to a broad cellar-like room, a massive walnut bar filling the far wall. A waitress in a low-cut blouse stood at one end.

Julius watched from a corner table as he descended the stairs, trying to guess at his thoughts. No doubt the news he had just received still troubled him. More concerning was Truman's distrust of anything he might say or do. Perhaps he could win back his support by enlisting his help. He was determined to find some gain out of Mercer's past wrongs. Truman eased into the opposite chair, his back to the wall.

"You must be in a shock after learning how your father was betrayed." Julius said, trying to sound understanding.

"I don't want to talk about it."

"I'm only trying to make amends, Truman."

"I came here to drink."

"And drink we will."

Julius motioned toward the bar. The waitress, a half-eaten sandwich in her hands, tried to ignore him. He stood and whistled, waving two fingers in the air, and pointing to a nearby beer sign. She slapped the sandwich on her plate. Seconds later she stood before him, forcing a smile as she tucked a strand of auburn hair behind her ear. Julius raised his hands in apology.

"Please forgive me for interrupting your meal but we've had some shocking news...."

"And you need a drink." she interrupted.

"That's very perceptive of you, Miss..."

She eyed Truman with interest before turning back to him. "The name is Jewel, honey."

"Yes, I can see why," he said, giving her his most genuine smile. "Your eyes are like two sapphires. The word comes from the Greek sappheiros, meaning blue stone, a gemstone of the mineral corundum."

"What are you, a professor or something?"

"I am a mere a commoner, Jewel, but I appreciate beauty when I see it."

She squinted at him. "What does a commoner like yourself want to drink?"

"My companion here is Truman and I'm Julius." He gestured across the table. "I believe I'll have a draft beer."

She moved around the table, winking as she bent toward Truman. "What does the strong silent type want... from the menu, or elsewhere?"

He considered her offer. A fling with a waitress, no strings attached, might take his mind off his troubles for awhile. Somehow, he couldn't work up an interest.

"Just a beer for me."

Julius waved a hand in her face. "Make it the largest stein you offer."

"Around here we call them mugs, honey," she called over her shoulder as she started toward the bar.

"Now, as I was saying, I merely want to make amends." Julius leaned his elbows on the table. "What Mercer did to your father must make your blood boil... perhaps enough to want revenge."

"I've already told you, I don't want to talk about it."

"But there is more to the story than what you just heard, Truman. Don't you want to know the rest?"

Jewel returned with the beers, smiling at Truman as she bent to set a mug in front of him. She lingered a moment, making sure he noticed her cleavage. She gave him another wink before turning to leave. Julius watched, feeling a tinge of jealousy.

"She's none too subtle, I'll give her that much. If you want me to find a ride home just say the word."

"It worries me when you start acting nice." Truman looked at him askance. "What do you want, Julius?"

He feigned offence. "Do you mean to say I'm less than nice most of the time?"

"Don't get cute." He took a long pull on his mug. "Tell me whatever it is you have to say."

"Ah, now we're getting somewhere." His eyes brightened at the thought. "Carlisle allowed me to peruse the folder Mercer inadvertently but fortuitously left in the attic. Most of the records are financial statements and appear deadly boring at first glance. But upon closer inspection they show that Mercer bilked the government out of thousands in taxes."

"You're talking tax fraud?"

"He could go to jail if he were to be found out." He rubbed his palms together, relishing the thought. "How do you like that for retribution?"

"You want me to turn him in?"

"Good gods, that is in no way what I meant. I could inform on him myself if I wished that, anonymously of course. But federal prison is too good for him. I'm suggesting you use the knowledge as leverage to make him do your bidding, preferably involving cash."

"That's extortion."

"A lovelier word was never spoken."

Truman sat back, considering the idea. Making Mercer pay for betraying his father was a tempting proposition. Though reluctant to admit it, he did harbor a burning anger toward the man. Mercer's greed had devastated his family and in the process derailed his childhood. But using what he'd learned for his own gain would make him no better. He locked eyes with Julius.

"I want you to keep all this to yourself."

"So how will you make him suffer? His wallet is his soft spot, obviously." Julius' mouth watered at the thought. "I recommend a financial agreement, perhaps in the form of monthly payments for, say, the next thirty years. I'll make my own similar arrangement with him, of course."

"Like I said, you will keep it to yourself and do nothing."

His eyes filled with anguish. "But you must, Truman, you must! Mercer is vermin, the worst pestilence."

"Why are you so interested in seeing him pay? And I'm not talking about money." Truman studied him. "There's something more isn't there, something personal?"

Julius took a breath, unsure whether to tell him. He seldom confided in anyone. Hoping Truman might soften if he knew the story, he searched for a starting point, wincing as his mind filled with the memory.

"This may prove difficult." He swallowed, trying to clear the lump from his throat. "Several years ago we had a housemate with a progressive form of epilepsy. His father, a classics scholar, had named him Cassius after the Roman senator who led the plot against Julius Caesar. Ever ready for a bit of dark humor, he often kidded about my safety with two such names under the same roof.

"Over time the seizures worsened to the point the doctors began talking about a nursing home, a move he

121

found horrifying. He believed he would quickly die in such a place. After much convincing, the doctors agreed he could stay in the house if he got a specially trained service dog. The dog would warn of an oncoming seizure and help with things he was increasingly unable to do for himself.

"After securing funds and locating a dog, he asked Mercer for permission. Of course, he refused the request. He claimed the house does not allow pets because of the damage they inevitably cause, money his obvious priority. I argued with him at length, explaining that a service animal is not a pet. He would have none of it.

"I had just contacted an advocacy group for legal help when Cassius had a seizure while standing at the top of the stairs. He was dead by the time he reached the bottom."

"The dog could've warned him?"

"I will never forgive Mercer for his coldhearted greed."

Truman stared at him, surprised by the story. "Julius, you have a heart after all."

"Heart doesn't enter into it," he lied. "Mercer's arrogance and greed are a personal affront. I want my pound of flesh."

"If we steal his money we're no better than he is, Julius." He paused, lost for a moment to his thoughts. "But give me some time to think it through and then we can…"

Truman looked up as Parfit appeared at the table. He peered at Truman and cut the air with a wave of his hand.

"You'd be needing to hear what I have to say, Truman Birdsong."

"You're here to see me?" Truman starred at him, perplexed by his presence. "How did you know where I'd be?"

Parfit ignored the question. "Darkness awaits the boy. You must find him."

"You mean Nicolai? He's back at the house working on his homework."

"A cold darkness it is, cold and wet," he continued, passing his hand across the floor in a broad arc. "The blackness is of the land, the rock, the soil."

"I don't understand."

Julius leaned across the table and whispered to Truman. "I believe senility is setting in. It's affecting his speech."

Truman glared at him and then he turned back to the old man.

"You're saying Nicolai is in danger?"

"A deep darkness," he said, starting for the stairway, "deep, it is, and cold."

Truman called after him. "Can't you tell me anything more?"

"You must find the boy."

A sense of unease moved over Truman as he watched him disappear up the stairway. Julius quickly raised his mug, again worried that his plan for Nicolai might be upset.

"Enjoy good drink and good company while you can, Truman. You never know when your mind will go the way of poor Parfit's."

"He does seem a bit more addled than usual." He drained his glass and then stood. "Still, I think I'd better check on Nicolai."

"What?" Julius jumped up. "Don't worry yourself over the boy. I'm sure he's at home studying just as you said."

"I'll feel better when I can lay eyes on him."

"But I was planning to have another round," he pleaded. "I'll even pay."

"I'll have to take a rain check." He tossed a wad of bills on the table. "Let's go."

A wall of gray clouds crowded the horizon, blocking the sun and splitting the sky with broken shafts of light. Truman studied the storm as he pulled onto the road, puzzling over Parfit's enigmatic words of warning. He

123

could make little sense of them. In any case, he would be foolish to take an old man's ravings as truth. Nicolai was probably studying in his room at that moment as Julius had said. Yet he knew he could not relax until he was certain.

Chapter Seventeen

Nicolai hesitated on the fire escape of the decrepit hotel. Situated atop a steep incline, the uphill side of the building had no first floor, making a second floor window easily reachable by way of the metal ladder. A murmur of voices drifted from inside. He took a breath, trying to harness his fear before he climbed through. Shards of glass lit by the glow of dusk littered the floor below him.

Lowering himself, he stepped between the shards, cringing as the smaller pieces crunched beneath his shoes. The rotting floorboards sagged under his weight. He paused to let his eyes adjust to the dim interior, afraid to take another step. Within moments a gaping hole emerged out of the darkness, the room below visible through the jagged opening.

Keeping close to the wall, he crept around the hole to the doorway. Beyond the threshold an ornate metal rail separated the walkway from the hotel lobby two floors below. Dust-covered chandeliers hung from the ceiling at odd angles. He inched toward the rail. The voices grew louder, reverberating off the tin ceiling and impossible to understand.

Realizing at once he must find another vantage point, he backed to the nearest corner and surveyed the walkway in both directions. Except for a small stretch along the nearest wall the floorboards had been removed, leaving only four inch thick joists between him and the lobby below. Just the thought of creeping along the narrow passage took his breath.

He retreated into the room behind him, dismayed by the seeming dead end but determined to find another way in. Just as he turned to leave a rustle of wings sounded overhead. He squinted toward the ceiling. An oval-shaped hole opened onto the room above.

He righted an overturned dresser and climbed atop, pulling himself through the opening. The floor stretched away from him, solid beneath his weight. Discarded glass light covers lined the walls in short stacks. As he crept to the doorway voices drifted from the lobby, distant but understandable.

Lying flat, he inched to the railing and peeked over the side. Three floors below a restless crowd faced a makeshift stage where two men, obviously brothers, stood together. A Gadsden flag hung from the wall behind them. Next to it a heavyset man with a beard stood surveying the crowd, his hand in the bib of his overalls. At the sight of him Nicolai gasped, recognizing him as Horace, the man at the barbeque restaurant.

Moving to one side for a better view, he gave himself one final push toward the edge, jostling a stack of light covers with his foot and sending them sliding to the floor in a clatter. He ducked behind the railing and froze, fearing someone had heard him. Only the unconcerned din of men's voices drifted from below. He again inched to the edge.

The two men had moved to the front of the stage. Both had reddish gold hair, short on the sides and thick on top, the ends pointing into the air like bound wheat. Their pale skin and ruddy cheeks seemed to glow beneath the yellow light. The taller of the two men sat while the other raised a hand signaling the crowd to quiet. His voice reverberated off the brick walls.

"Now that you men have met with your contact and know your assignment, it is time for action. The treasonous agents of the so-called law want to deprive us of our freedom, our property, our free enterprise and above all our right to bear arms. We will not allow it!"

A roar of approval rose from the crowd. Several of the men waved rifles through the air. The man on the stage again raised his hand.

"We will not tolerate our rights getting violated or our constitution trampled." He gestured toward the man seated behind him. "To fight these evil forces my brother and I are dedicating our time and resources, our land to train on, our money to buy the tools of war. Make no mistake, this *is* a war and it is already upon us.

"All patriots must open their eyes to the travesty that is our current government. We need you men to go spread the word in your communities so we can muster a militia to take back our country and rid it of the unwanted elements. The border-crossing aliens, the anti-family gays, the liberal media, the welfare leeches and the so-called authorities all threaten our freedom. We must return to a rule by the people and for the people. Help us take back what is ours!"

The crowd erupted in cheers, some whooping rebel yells, others standing on their chairs, still others waving handmade militia flags. Nicolai watched as the two brothers moved through the crowd, shaking hands and slapping backs like seasoned politicians. The low rumble of diesel engines drifted through the open doors as the crowd began to leave. Within minutes the group had thinned to a small cluster huddled around the two brothers.

Two men, one pale-featured and wearing a red leather coat, the other dark and with a goatee, approached them. The taller brother pulled a thick envelope from his pocket, handing it to the man in the leather coat. With the last of the truck engines fading into the night and the lobby nearly empty, Nicolai could just make out their words.

"It is imperative you get this right, Mr. Bell." The shorter brother pointed at the envelope. "The district attorney's home address is there along with addresses for the others. The plan is a bullet to the head as soon as he opens the door, Friday at six o'clock. He'll have had a drink or two by then and be off his guard.

"The assistant district attorney comes next, and then a Molotov cocktail through the judge's front window. As long as the first two are eliminated, it makes no difference if the judge survives. Either way the authorities will think twice about sending one of our freedom fighters to prison again."

The pale man in the leather coat thumbed through the contents and tossed the envelope to his companion. The taller brother pointed a finger into the man's face.

"If either of you gets caught you're on your own. We don't know you and you don't know us. Turn on us and you won't last long." His smile held little warmth. "On the other hand, if you do good work we'll hire you to put the screws to Mercer. We need those ten acres of his in spite of the boarding house full of freaks. That property is sitting on top of a massive pool of oil."

Nicolai shivered, alarmed by the man's words. A sudden urge to leave and report back on what he had heard overcame him. Though he had promised to tell Julius, his instinct told him the others should know as well. He must tell them soon, most of all Carlisle.

He backed away, stood and turned toward the door. An instant later, footsteps clattered in the third floor stairwell behind him. He threw himself across the threshold. Behind the cover of shadow, he peered back across the lobby, spotting Horace directly opposite him, his hands gripping the railing, his stare locked on the doorway. Nicolai was sure the big man had seen him.

Shouts erupted from all sides. Without thinking he scrambled though the window, ignoring the broken shards slicing his palms. Lightning flashed in the distance. Scurrying down the fire escape, he dropped to the ground just as a short, wiry man in a grimy cap rounded the corner, grabbing him by the collar. Nicolai wheeled around, planting the toe of his shoe squarely on the man's shin. He yelped in pain.

Nicolai kicked again, sending the man to the ground. Twisting free, he scrambled up the steep slope and plunged into the vacant lot, too afraid to look back. The thick grass grabbed at his feet.

A spotlight slit the darkness, illuminating a metal fence to his left, a tear in the chain link visible just above the ground. He dove for the narrow opening, clawing his way forward, trying to disappear behind the taller grass. The shouts grew closer.

Without warning the ground gave way beneath him, vaulting him down a near-vertical incline, featureless and slick with mud. The earth seemed to rise above him. Reaching for a handhold, he grabbed at the slope, tearing at it with his hands. Shreds of dirt crumbled between his fingers.

In a sudden moment the cold air swallowed him, pulling him into a void, damp and without light. The solid earth slipped away. For an instant he seemed to float, adrift and weightless, and then the air began to move again, rushing past him as he flailed about upended and helpless. Seconds later a flash shattered his vision, then nothing.

Lightning zigzagged across the horizon, silhouetting a wall of clouds. Their roiling shapes twisted like braided hair. Truman watched from the porch rail. Through the massive oak's tangle of branches a gibbous moon appeared and then vanished, leaving only a trace of silver in its wake. The tree groaned before the wind.

Parfit's words ran through his thoughts in a jumble of possible meanings, none helpful. Had Nicolai simply gone missing again? Surely cold and darkness await any runaway. And the approaching storm promised a wet night. But what had Parfit meant by a 'deep darkness'?

He tried to clear his mind of distraction. As much as the boy's absence annoyed him, it unsettled him even more. He sensed something more to it than a teenager's antics, something threatening. He called over his shoulder, hailing Julius as he sat inside.

Reluctantly crossing the living room floor, Julius hesitated at the doorway and said a silent prayer to the gods of deceit. Nicolai should have already returned from his spying mission. With the boy missing, Truman no doubt had suspicions. Julius searched his mind for a plausible explanation.

Finding none he peeked through the screen. Truman stood in the shadows midway down the porch, staring into the darkness. Julius eyed him and tried to gauge his mood. Then he stepped through the door.

"Unless I'm hearing things, I believe you called for me."

"Something doesn't add up." Truman turned but his face remained in shadow. "And I think you know the reason."

"Do I?" Julius squinted at him, trying to read his expression. "And why might you think that?"

"Nicolai has been settling in, doing his schoolwork and taking care of his other responsibilities." He moved into the light, his look less than friendly. "Then I see you making some deal with him. Now he's gone missing."

"As boys will do."

Aiden appeared behind him, his eyes turned to the ceiling, his gaze roving about as if watching their words pass through the air. Julius frowned and moved away before continuing.

"Do I need to remind you he has a habit of running away?"

"Kids run because they're unhappy, because they feel disliked and unwanted. You know how good Carlisle is with him." Truman gestured at the house. "He feels at home here, Julius. I can see it, you can see it."

"What does any of this have to do with me?"

"That's what I'd like to know."

"I'm not responsible for the whereabouts of a thirteen year old."

"Then explain the deal I heard you make with him."

"I can't seem to recall what that was about." He avoided Truman's gaze. "All I remember is discussing my research. Perhaps I agreed to show him my blog."

"What blog is that?"

"Haven't I mentioned it? I make my meager living writing a blog, a sort of modern version of the serialized novel. I do have a fair readership." He peered at Truman and shook his head. "But you'd have to be a fan of swords and shields, knights and kings, to care. You don't strike me as the fantasy type."

"You're telling me you have no idea where Nicolai is?"

"Other than what I've told you, I can't imagine what deal I might make with the boy."

"Why do I have trouble believing that?"

"Are you accusing me of…"

"Julius knows, and he does, he does!" Aiden pushed through the screen door. "I heard him from the stairs. He made a deal with Nicolai, a deal to listen and tell, tell and listen."

Julius took a step back, looking for a way of escape. Truman pointed a finger at his chest.

"You need to tell me what you know."

"You do know, Julius, and you do!"Aiden sliced the air above him with his cane. "Tell him what you know!"

Julius pressed himself against the wall. "He's only off on a small errand, nothing to worry about."

"What sort of errand?"

"Just down the hill to the edge of town."

Truman squinted at him, clearly waiting for more. Julius eyed Aiden's cane before continuing.

"It was a small favor, a bit of an adventure in fact, and completely voluntary of course. Boys love adventure, do they not?"

"Where did you send him, Julius?"

"He went to observe a meeting."

"A meeting held where?"

"At the old hotel."

"What were you thinking?" Truman moved toward him, his voice rising with every word. "That building should be condemned. When was this so-called meeting?"

"Yes, well, I uh…" he stammered, pressing himself to the wall. "I must admit I thought he would have returned before now."

"How long before now?"

He shrugged. "An hour or so?"

"We have to go." Truman grabbed his arm and started for the stairs. "He could be in trouble."

Julius stumbled along behind him. "What do you need *me* for?"

"Aiden," Truman called over his shoulder. "Call the sheriff and tell him to meet me at the old hotel."

Chapter Eighteen

Nicolai's mother stood above him, her hand outstretched, her face impossible to read beneath the dim light. He peered into her gray eyes, trying to gauge her intent. Did she want him with her? He could not say.

She rolled her fingers as if to compel him upwards and he moved to stand then hesitated, mistrusting his own eyes. Did he see only what he hoped for? Was he foolish enough to expect her to take him back after so long now that he was older? After all, she had called him almost grown. A shiver ran through him at the thought.

She motioned to him a second time. All at once he believed she was ready to leave the hospital, to again be his mother, to fix his breakfast, to help with his schoolwork. An image of her in the garden came to him, the smell of turned earth, of fallen leaves surrounding him, clinging to him, damp and pungent. He stretched a hand toward her.

Reaching back with his free hand, he tried to push himself up but a searing pain shot through his side. He collapsed to the ground. He lay back watching as she vanished behind a veil of white. Her voiced sounded somewhere in the distance, rising, pleading with him to come.

He awoke with a start. Voices ricocheted past him like gunshots. His head throbbing, he struggled to clear the fog from his mind, unsure whether the voices were friendly or threatening.

Lightning flickered above him, followed by the thump of distant thunder. He looked up and blinked, trying to see through his blurred vision. A circle of gray emerged overhead. Suddenly he realized he had fallen into a cave, the cave Parfit had warned him of. He seemed to be on a narrow ledge, his back to a stone wall. He managed to sit up, the pain in his arm returning but less so.

A beam of light split the space above him, only feet away. He scrambled to one side, sending a cascade of rocks tumbling into the darkness. An image of Horace standing at the walkway railing raced through his mind. Biting back the pain, he pressed himself against the wall and strained to listen. Thunder rumbled overhead, louder than before. The shouts grew nearer.

A spotlight appeared near the cave opening, dancing from side to side as it descended the wall. He flattened himself on the ledge, trying to meld with the damp stone without slipping over the side. Voices called out just beyond hearing.

He struggled with what he should do, one moment believing they meant to help, the other terrified they would find him. A string of words sounded from above, closer than before. The voice belonged to the man in the red coat. Nicolai shrank back against the ledge and strained to listen.

"We only want to help you, boy." The man sounded friendly enough. "You can't stay down there forever. It's too cold. Besides, don't you know witches live in caves?"

Nicolai spit, trying to rid his mouth of the metallic taste of blood and the anger he felt over his plight. His head throbbed with every move. He hunched up his shoulders and shivered, unable to deny the cold. Perhaps the man truly meant to help him. For an instant he almost called out but then caught himself. What he had heard in the hotel had been clear.

Seconds later a flash of lightning pierced the darkness, illuminating the entire cave as a blast of thunder shook the air. Tumbling bits of earth peppered his face. He pressed to the wall while hailstones clattered outside the cave mouth. Suddenly the spotlight dimmed behind a wall of rain and then vanished altogether.

He turned his face to the stone, trying to ignore the pain in his arm. For a moment he again imagined his mother's dark eyes, eyes still impossible to read. He wished for her even while seeing it pointless. Closing his eyes, he felt the cold air surround him like a fog, and then everything again went black.

Truman stood at the porch rail and stared into the wall of rain, cursing the weather beneath his breath. Julius stood next to him. The sky had opened the moment they had started for the hotel, forcing a retreat. As much as he disliked the idea of Nicolai roaming the derelict building, he liked the thought of him out in the storm even less. Lightning flashed overhead.

Aiden appeared beside him, his eyes darting about as if surveying the dark sky. Wind splattered the railing with droplets. He rapped his cane on the floor.

"The rain is about to stop, and it is, it is!"

"How do you figure that?" Truman peered into the deluge. "We've got lightning and thunder all around."

"I will go with you to find Nicolai," he yelled into the storm. "I will go now."

"But, Aiden..."

As quickly as it started the rain ended, leaving only the dripping roofline and the massive oak beyond. Aiden started down the steps. Truman glanced at Julius and shrugged before motioning him to follow.

Minutes later they stepped into the dim confines of the hotel lobby. Truman followed the wall with his hand, locating a light switch and flipping it. The tilting chandeliers flickered to a dull glow. Julius pointed to the rows of chairs.

"The meeting must have been just there."

"You sent a thirteen year old to spy on a meeting in an abandoned hotel?" Truman glared at him. "What are you not telling us? What sort of meeting are we talking about?"

"Well, it would be difficult to say with any certainty." Julius avoided his gaze. "I only heard about it indirectly from a friend of a friend and..."

"Forget I asked." Truman raised a hand to stop him. "What do you know that might help us find Nicolai?"

"Well, that too is problematic. I know so little, only hearsay, and even that..."

135

Truman took a step toward him. "Damn it, Julius, tell the truth for once!"

Aiden pointed his cane at the ceiling. "Nicolai is not here, no not at all."

"But how can you know that, Aiden?" Truman surveyed the three floors above them. "This building is huge."

"Nicolai Tate!" Aiden swept his arm through the air. "Nicolai Tate, you must come out now, and you must!"

They stood motionless, listening. The thump of distant thunder rattled the windows, nothing more. Truman called out, again with no response. Making no effort to hide his anger, he fixed his gaze on Julius.

"You'd better come up with a plan real quick."

Julius scoured his mind for ideas. "What of Parfit's enigmatic prediction?"

"What of it? I couldn't make heads or tails of his odd talk."

"But might it prove useful?"

Again recalling the old man's strange words, Truman searched for some clue. "He said something about darkness and cold. It makes no sense, Julius."

The meaning came to him all at once. "Ah, but perhaps it does."

"What are you thinking?"

"His exact words were 'a deep darkness'."

Truman considered the phrase. "I think you're right but how does that help?"

"Throckmorton Hole is nearby." Julius gestured through the doorway. "Parfit sees magic in such places."

"You think he was talking about a cave?"

"He claims to know things before they happen."

Aiden slapped his thigh. "Parfit knows things, and he does, he does!"

"I don't buy that psychic nonsense." Truman shook his head. "Just because a crazy old man believes in something doesn't make it true."

"I tend to agree but unless you have a better idea…"

"We should search here first. He may be hiding out somewhere up there, unsure of who we are. Or he could be hurt." Truman pointed to the gaps in the walkways above them. "This is a dangerous place for a boy."

He started for the stairwell. Aiden stood in place rapping the floorboards with the tip of his cane. Julius glared at him before settling into a chair.

"Stop that infernal tapping."

"Nicolai Tate must be found, and he must," Aiden murmured.

"Clearly our counsel is neither appreciated nor wanted," Julius sneered as he watched Truman vanish through the doorway. "So I for one will wait right here."

The crunch of gravel pulled Nicolai from sleep. Wincing, he shifted his arm and turned from the wall, peering at the mouth of the cave. Stars littered the sky beyond. Though he had no sense of the time, he felt grateful to see that night had yet to end. Someone would find him, soon perhaps.

Water trickled from the opening in a halting rhythm. The din of rain had given way to a silence so dense that sounds above him seemed amplified beyond believing. Tree frogs chirped beyond the entrance. An owl hooted once then went silent. Moments later a deep voice, Horace's voice, echoed through the cave, followed by approaching footsteps. Nicolai pressed his back to the damp wall.

The spotlight reappeared, dancing along the cave walls like a manic firefly. Nicolai looked one way then the other hoping for a means of escape. He could see no further than the narrow ledge. The cave seemed to swallow all light, the space below him depthless, infinite. All at once a white coil of rope flew across the opening, unwinding as it fell.

"There's no way out but right through here, boy," Horace again called out. "Get your ass to the rope and we'll pull you up."

Hoping his dark hair would blend with the wall and hide him, Nicolai turned his face the ledge, trying to be still despite his pounding heart. Suddenly a chorus of curses filled the cave. Dirt and rocks peppered him, followed by a commotion beyond the cave opening. A red glow flashed across his hands, disappeared and then flashed again.

He raised his eyes to the opening, straining to listen. Silence once more filled the air, broken only by the fading hum of a car engine and the distant thump of thunder. Moonlit clouds crossed the opening like silver frigates. He blinked back the pain in his arm.

Parfit appeared out of the dark, floating before him like an apparition, his features vague and ethereal. He raised a hand and motioned Nicolai to lie back. Then he vanished into the blackness. Cradling his aching arm in his lap, Nicolai closed his eyes and leaned back against the damp wall, hoping help would soon come.

Chapter Nineteen

Truman emerged from the stairwell and paused to catch his breath. Julius turned his eyes, disgusted by the sight of him. What gave Truman the right to drag him out into the night in search of an errant teenager? Did he not have better things to do than chase a boy who in all probability had seen his chance to run again and taken it?

Aiden stood nearby fidgeting with his cane and mumbling beneath his breath. A chill breeze rattled the broken windowpanes. Popping and groaning, the old building shifted before the stiff wind. Truman pointed toward the ceiling.

"This place is a disaster. The floorboards have been scavenged and most of what's left is rotten. It's no place for a kid." He nodded toward the exit. "We'd better go check on that cave."

Julius sat up, suddenly alert to his chance of escape. "But surely you don't need me for such an expedition. I'd be of no help whatsoever."

"You're not weaseling out of this." Truman glared at him. "We wouldn't be here if it wasn't for you. Now get off your…"

Aiden jerked to attention. "I hear voices, shouting voices, and I do!"

"Psychosis has finally claimed him," Julius sneered. "Why am I not surprised?"

"And a car is coming down the road." He pointed his cane to the door. "Julius does not know everything, no, not at all."

Truman stepped onto the hotel porch, Julius in tow. Behind him Aiden's cane tapped a steady rhythm. A gust of cold air buffeted the doorway, sending a gunshot clatter of acorns against the metal roof. Truman squinted into the headlights of the approaching car.

Moments later Tico Bauert climbed from his brown and white cruiser, turning his collar to the coursing wind. A cloud of yellow leaves swirled about his boots. He moved below the stairway and studied them a moment.

"Does one of you men go by the name Aiden Burns? The office got a call to come to the old hotel." His gaze lingered on Truman. "I believe we've met. You're Truman Birdsong if my memory still works. The jury's still out on that one."

"Your memory works, sheriff." He pointed a thumb behind him. "We're looking for a missing boy, a thirteen year old. His name is Nicolai Tate. We think he came here but there's no sign of him now."

"I know the boy. He's the foster kid we've chased over half the county." He frowned at the dilapidated building. "We found a homeless feller froze to death in there last winter. It's no place for a boy."

"I've checked everywhere I could." Truman said, nodding toward the door. "I don't believe he's here."

The sheriff glanced up the street. "On my way here I thought I caught sight of a flashlight but decided it was just the lightning. Maybe I saw right after all, just up the hill a ways."

"I understand there's a cave up there."

"They fenced off the area years ago. It's even more of a hazard than this old hotel."

"Boys have a way of getting into places they shouldn't."

"You're right about that." The sheriff glanced up the hill again. "We best go take a look."

Nicolai woke to the sound of distant voices. The ache in his head pounded out a dull rhythm. Blinking back the pain, he tried to clear the fog from his thoughts. Did he hear the voices or only imagine them? Had Horace and the man in the red coat returned or was it someone else? Wind whistled past the entrance, whipping the tall grass and taking all sound with it. Knots of cloud roiled beyond the gray oval of light.

All at once the voices sounded overhead, Aiden's high twang carrying above the rest like a bird's call. He struggled to sit up. A spotlight danced across the opening, vanished and then reappeared. Footsteps echoed off the walls.

Leaning back, he cupped a hand around his mouth and called out once, then again. A wave of nausea swept over him, the pain in his arm matching his throbbing head. The darkness seemed to spin around him.

Hearing him, Truman scrambled up the hill, reaching a torn-aside fence that opened onto a rectangle of overgrown grass now trampled flat. The black oval of the cave entrance sat just beyond. Secured to a fencepost, a length of rope stretched toward the opening.

Following the sheriff's spotlight, he skirted around the cave to the far side, grabbing the rope and pulling to test its strength. The loose earth shifted beneath his feet, sending a shower of rocks into the darkness. He corralled his fear and steadied himself, peering into the black air and listening as the stones splashed far below. Nicolai's voice again rose from the darkness, thin and reedy.

"Truman, are you there?"

"I'm here, Nicolai." Hearing the weakness in his voice, his skin prickled with fear at what he must ask. "Are you hurt?"

"My arm, I think it's broken."

"Can you see the rope?"

All at once the spotlight found him. He squinted at the glare, blinking back tears as he surveyed the cave. The sheer walls glistened with storm runoff and seepage. Daggers of limestone hung from an overhang opposite him. Shifting his gaze to the right, he found the ledge growing wider as it stretched away. The rope dangled just short of it.

He pressed his back to the wall and tried to stand. A fierce pain shot through his arm. He collapsed to the floor, the earth spinning beneath him, and for a moment he

141

seemed to float, unmoored and weightless. Then blackness again swallowed him.

Parfit reappeared, his white stubble of beard sparkling like fresh snow. Waving his hand through the air as if blessing the earth, he leaned toward Nicolai and traced the outline of his face with a crooked finger. His eyes held a strange wildness, disturbing yet mesmerizing.

"Things are not as they seem, Nicolai Tate." His face glittered, bluish and ice-like, his breath frigid. Nicolai shivered to hear it. "Change comes without warning. But light hides beneath the dark times like the moon behind a cloud. If you will let yourself, you can see it. Them that believe will find their way, and believe you must, Nicolai Tate. Hold tight to it and you will get through."

Nicolai blinked and he was gone. In his place an endless expanse of darkness stretched away like a starless cosmos, empty and featureless. He felt it pulling him in, surrounding him in a cold shroud. The bitter chill coursed through him, rushing in his ears. Then all went silent.

Tico stood by as Truman squinted into the cave's narrow opening. Despite the chill air, sweat trickled down the back of his neck. The thought of entering the tight confines took his breath. He glanced to his right. Aiden stood with his back pressed to the fence, his cane held before him, his eyes darting about as he followed their movements. Julius loitered just beyond the chain mesh.

Tico bent and untied the rope, looping it behind his back and wrapping his palms around the length. At Truman's direction Aiden hurried along the fence, quickly locating the loose end. Bracing himself, Tico nodded Truman toward the entrance.

He turned to the cave, his heart pounding, his breath quick and shallow. The wind-whipped grass swirled about his feet, sending the earth tilting beneath him. All at once he stumbled backwards, landing at Tico's feet. He squinted down at him.

"You're looking awful pale, Truman. I've seen that look before. You've got the claustrophobia, don't you?"

Gulping for air, Truman could only nod. Tico held out the rope.

"You take my place and I'll go down and get that boy."

"No, I can do it." Truman scrambled to his feet. "I have to."

"Take a look at yourself, son." Tico pointed to his shaking hands. "You're not much good with all that adrenaline running through you."

Truman glanced back at the cave. "But we've got to get Nicolai out of there."

"You and Aiden can get me in and out. At least I think you can. I admit I've had a few too many of Isabel's tacos over the last few years. Still, I believe I'll be..."

Aiden's high twang rose above the wind. "I will get Nicolai Tate, and I will!"

"Mr. Burns," Tico said, casting him a sideways glance, "I have to admit you got yourself some real cojones for a blind man. But how in the hell are you going to..."

"Bats are blind but they live in caves," he interrupted, "they do, no two ways about it, they do."

He tossed aside his cane and followed the rope around Tico before Truman put a hand to his chest.

"Aiden, I know you're worried about Nicolai," he said softly, his voice shaking but determined. "But I'm the one to go in. I can't explain why but I have to."

Aiden stood still, his gaze darting above Truman's head. Without a word he reached out and placed his slender fingers against his jaw, tracing up along his brow and nose, and back down his face, letting his hand linger a moment. Then he turned and hurried back along the rope, taking his place behind Tico. Truman grabbed the end and took a breath, steadying himself as he lowered through the narrow oval, the wet rope creaking as he slipped into the darkness.

Nurses in blue surgical gowns and pink hairnets passed white-coated lab technicians as they pushed through the swinging double doors of the operating theater. Julius stood by watching. Across the waiting room a clerk carrying a clipboard chatted with a grim-faced couple before disappearing down the hallway. Rising above the clamor, the ungreased wheel of a passing gurney squealed like a trapped rodent.

Julius sat and hunched down in his chair, trying to distract himself from the scene and, even more so, from the smell. Visions of his many surgeries flashed before him, the constant pain, the slow recoveries, the endless humiliation of dependency. The memories tended to come at random moments, pushing aside all thought. Entering a hospital was guaranteed to bring them on.

Sitting in the row opposite him, Truman shifted in his chair and cast a preoccupied glance his direction. Lines of worry pulled at the corners of his mouth. Otherwise, he gave little clue to his thoughts. He stood and started for the exit, passing Aiden as he paced along a line of windows, his cane tapping like a windup clock.

Julius silently cursed himself for sending Nicolai to the old hotel. He should have known the boy would find trouble. If only he could find out what he had seen. Even some tidbit could prove useful. He checked the time, surprised at the late hour. He had assumed the boy's injuries were minor.

All at once Aiden jerked to a stop, holding the cane before his chest and cocking his head. Julius recognized the look. He sat up and turned toward the double doors.

Moments later a young doctor in green scrubs pushed through. Sliding the cap from his hair, he scanned the room and then started toward him. Julius searched his face for some clue to the boy's condition. The doctor stopped in front of him and ran a hand across his chin as if searching for a place to start.

"The nurse said a hunch… uh, a midg… uh, a short man with a limp was with the group that brought in the boy." He glanced around the room. "Are you the one to talk to?"

Julius turned to Truman's chair, finding it still empty. Aiden stood just beyond with his back to the wall, unmoving but for his darting eyes. Julius was sure he heard every word. He again faced the doctor.

"I suppose I'll have to do," he said, his voice more question than statement.

"Alright, he's had a compound fracture of his left forearm. We had to insert screws but the break missed the growth plate so the arm should continue to grow normally as long as he can avoid secondary infection."

"I'm relieved to hear it…" he said and then stopped, surprised at himself. He absently touched his own arm, imagining his many corrective surgeries, some of the plates and screws still in place. The doctor eyed him a moment before continuing.

"He also had a concussion." He glanced at a wristwatch pinned to his waist. "I called in a specialist and she said you should keep a close eye on him for the first twenty-four hours. He'll be a bit addled for awhile, trouble remembering, concentrating, that sort of thing. Seek help right away if he gets worse."

Truman appeared beside him, his face flushed with anger. "Why didn't you tell me the doctor was here?"

"You might have bothered to say where you were off to," Julius snapped.

"I needed some air."

"Don't we all?"

"You're a fine one to cast blame."

"I merely state the obvious."

"Excuse me!" The doctor stepped between them. "That boy needs your attention, your *undivided* attention."

"You're absolutely right." Truman looked away, ashamed of his selfishness. "What I mean is… when can we see him?"

"First, you need to understand this boy has had a very close call, and he's not out of the woods yet." The doctor checked his watch again. "Someone should be with you shortly to go over his aftercare. Then you can see him."

Without another word he started for the operating theater. Truman watched him disappear through the swinging doors. Worried families huddled nearby, speaking in hushed tones. He studied their drawn faces, reminded of his own lost family and the strange life he now led. Glancing at Julius and beyond him to Aiden, he again felt the truth of the doctor's words. Nicolai needed them all.

Chapter Twenty

Truman leaned his elbows on his knees and stared out the porch window, watching as the salmon-hued glow of dawn edged above the horizon. Silhouetted birds streaked across the sky in small flocks. Emerging from the darkness, the scattered hills took on strange and fantastical shapes before returning to their natural forms.

A sense of wonder moved over him, as if all at once he could see through Carlisle's eyes the strange beauty of the rough land. A memory of his parents passed through his thoughts, his mother still healthy, his father confident. Then the image faded and was gone. Probably just exhaustion, he mused.

Nicolai's ragged breathing brought him back to the cot, set below the porch window. With his face turned toward the wall, hiding most of the scrapes and bruises, he looked nearly normal. For a brief moment Truman could almost believe he had never fallen into the cave.

He rubbed his eyes and looked about the room. The wall clock read just past six. Nicolai stirred but did not wake.

After leaving the hospital they had set up a temporary bed in the dining room, placing the cot by the window in hope of speeding his recovery. Since then he had drifted in and out of a restless sleep. Truman had not left his side.

Julius lurked in the kitchen doorway, alert for any sign the he might come out of his stupor. Though anxious to learn if Nicolai had overheard anything useful, he had been unable to shake an annoying but persistent concern for his welfare. That he had sent him to the hotel and into the danger did not help.

Something about the boy, homeless and outcast, rejected by school and pursued by the authorities, had touched him. Gritting his teeth, he tried to banish the thought, determined to let no one, especially Truman, know of it.

147

The crunch of car wheels on gravel drifted up from the street. Truman puzzled over who would be about at such an early hour. He stood as footsteps pounded up the steps, followed by a rap on the door. Before he could reach the threshold, the knock sounded again.

He swung open the door and a man stood peering at him through the rusted screen, his white beard matching his coat, his shoulders hunched up against the autumn chill. Behind him, the big oak groaned before a brisk wind. Truman motioned him into the house.

He hurried inside and set his satchel on the floor, his blue eyes glinting behind wireframe glasses. He surveyed the big room, his gaze finally pausing at Nicolai's cot. Then he turned and studied Truman a moment.

"You must be Truman Birdsong. I'm here to check on the boy, sent by children's services. They contract with me now and again for medical care." He shook Truman's hand. "The name is Silas Macallan."

"You're a doctor?"

"Was it the white coat that tipped you off?" he snorted. "Perhaps it was the bag? I suppose it could've been the stethoscope. Am I getting close?"

"Uh, I…," Truman stammered, confounded by the questions.

"Don't worry yourself, son." He gave Truman a quick wink. "A man has to keep his sense of humor around pain and suffering if he's going to last."

"Did you say your name is Macallan?"

"Just like the Scotch, of which I'll gladly partake if you have any."

"To be honest, we weren't expecting you."

"Does that mean you have no drink?"

"It's six in the morning."

"It's never too early for Scotch." He winked again and moved to the cot, easing into Truman's chair with a sigh. "The truth is I just delivered a baby girl near here, so I figured now was as good a time as any to make a visit. How is the boy?"

"It's hard to say." Truman tried to sound optimistic. "The pain medication has left him groggy. He's been sleeping mostly."

The doctor reached into his coat pocket, pulling out a handful of pecans. Truman watched as he squeezed them together in his fist. The shells popped beneath his fingers like distant fireworks. He tossed a nut into his mouth, dropping the broken remains to the floor, and leaned over the cot, his face only inches from Nicolai. After a moment he began to stir.

The doctor dropped another shell to the floor and crushed it beneath his heel. Nicolai's eyes fluttered at the sound. Pulling a link of dry sausage from his pocket, he took a bite and sat back, chewing thoughtfully. A frown crossed Nicolai's brow. Then he slowly opened his eyes and turned, squinting into the doctor's unfamiliar face.

"Who are you?"

"If you tell me your name, I'll tell you mine."

"What's that awful smell?"

"I can see you like to be the one asking questions." He held up the link, his jaws still working as he studied Nicolai. "I have a bit of German dry sausage here. I carry some when I'm out doing my rounds. You see, I never know how long I'll be and I do get hungry after a time. Would you like a bite?"

Nicolai winced. "Keep that away from me or I'll be sick."

"So, you can still smell then, uh…" He stuffed the sausage back into his pocket. "What did you say your name was?"

"I didn't, but it's Nicolai Tate."

"And how old are you, Nicolai Tate?"

"You forgot to tell me your name."

"You remembered that, did you?"

149

"You just said it." He cast him a skeptical glance. "How could I forget?"

"Then I'm Dr. Silas Macallan. Now you were about to tell me your age."

"I'm thirteen. What sort of doctor are you?"

"There's another of those questions." He leaned toward the cot. "I meant to ask you your exact date of birth, your birthday."

"I'll turn fourteen next April tenth. That means I was born in two thousand and one, or…" he paused, for a moment lost in thought. "That means I was born four thousand nine hundred and fifty-six days ago."

Dr. Macallan sat back, pulling a calculator from inside his coat and tapping in the numbers. He cast a glance at Truman before shoving it back into his coat.

"You did that all in your head just now?"

"Sure I did. I'm good at math."

"I want you to sit up follow this with your eyes," he said, holding a finger before Nicolai's face. "But don't move you head, only your eyes."

Nicolai pulled himself upright, wincing as a stab of pain gripped his arm. He took a breath and nodded, staring as the doctor waved his hand back and forth, up and down. Pulling the blanket from his arm, the doctor stood and prodded here and there beneath the bandages. Then he took hold of Nicolai's wrapped hand.

"Now, squeeze as hard as you can."

Nicolai grimaced as he pressed his meaty palm. The doctor sat again and peered into his face for a moment before speaking.

"What happened to your arm?"

"Can't you tell? I hurt it." Nicolai glanced at the bandages. "That's why I have a cast."

"How did you hurt it?"

"I, uh…" He stared at his arm, trying to summon the memory. "Well, I was… I must've done something…"

"But you can't remember what exactly?"

150

"No, I can." He struggled to concentrate. "Just give me a minute, I'll remember."

A cascade of images filled his mind. He recalled going to the hotel, climbing up the fire escape and through the window but everything after was a blur, like something out of a dream. Exhausted by the effort, he fell back against the pillows. The doctor put a hand on his shoulder.

"That's right, son, you will remember in time." He lifted his bag and stood. "But now you should rest."

Truman followed him out the door and onto the porch. The doctor paused at the top step.

"His memory will likely return in time, although it might be best if it didn't." He turned his collar to the biting wind. "Falling into a cave is not exactly a normal experience for a boy. As a result he may have some residual symptoms, nightmares, flashbacks, anxiety, that sort of thing."

"He'll be alright otherwise?"

"His arm is healing. But you should get him up and moving. Treat him as normal as possible."

"Do you know about his mother?" He whispered and glanced toward the house, concerned about the effect of a hospital visit. "She's in the state hospital."

"I know her. I've been consulting on her case."

"Before all this happened I had planned to take him to see her. Now I'm not so sure."

"As I said, don't baby the boy. He needs to see that you believe he can handle whatever needs doing."

"But *can* he handle it?"

"I don't know, but *you* must believe he can." He pointed to his eyes. "He'll know by what he sees here."

Julius listened to the low murmur of Truman's voice drifting in from the porch as he eased into the chair opposite Nicolai and leaned toward the cot.

"Nicolai, can you hear me?"

His face turned aside, he did not stir. Julius whispered again. The only sound was the boy's breathing, deep and regular. He sighed and sat back, for the moment abandoning his hope of jogging his memory. A report on the meeting would have to wait.

Nicolai rolled toward him. Lying there he seemed younger than his age, his purple and yellowing bruises garish beneath the dim light. Julius grimaced, overcome but unable to move his eyes. An image of his childhood self, bent and misshapen, mistreated by his peers, filled his mind and he reached out, almost touching his battered face. Then fearing he might be seen, he stood abruptly, turned and started for the stairs.

Chapter Twenty-one

"You're sure you don't remember anything, not even a little?" Truman made no attempt to hide his irritation. "How can you recall what happened before and after the meeting but not the meeting itself?"

Nicolai shrank beneath the questions. Try as he might, he could not escape feeling he was a disappointment. He stole glances as Truman paced the living room floor. Carlisle watched from a corner chair, saying nothing. Truman stopped and again faced Nicolai.

"What *do* you have to say about it then?"

He grimaced, wishing he had different answer. "I want to remember, I just can't."

"And what's with this sudden ability to figure large sums in your head? Where did that come from?"

"I don't know. I just…"

"You don't know?" Truman interrupted.

"I don't know the answer and then I do. It just happens. I've always liked math. Maybe that's the reason."

"You can do all that but you can't remember a meeting that happened only two weeks ago?"

"It's not like I haven't tried," he snapped, sulkily.

"Why should we believe you?" He nodded toward Carlisle. "Maybe you're up to no good again."

"I'm not!"

"Words are cheap."

"Why won't you trust me?"

"Because you…"

Carlisle rapped his cane on the floor, stopping him in mid-sentence. With much effort, he pushed himself up from the chair.

"Nicolai, I need a word with Truman… in private. Please wait for me in my room."

"But, Carlisle…"

"And close the door behind you."

Casting angry but furtive glances at Truman, he slunk out of the room. Carlisle moved to where Truman stood, taking care to keep his voice low.

"I trust him, Truman," he said, his tone impatient. "You should too."

"But he has a habit of avoiding the truth," he grumbled. "How do we know he's not doing it again?"

"Because he has changed since he first came here. You said it yourself, did you not?"

"I did."

"Nicolai says he doesn't remember and I believe him. Listen to his words, Truman. He needs you to trust him."

"You could be right," he mumbled, recognizing his mistake. "I know I push too hard."

"Have you asked yourself why?"

"I don't know why… no, that's wrong. I do know. I had no one to push me, to have expectations for me, and look where it got me."

"William Faulkner said something like 'the past is never dead. It's not even past'…"

"And I'm taking it out on the boy," he interrupted.

"Try to be patient, Truman. Given time his memory might return." He softened his tone. "In the meantime there is something you *can* do for him."

"What are you thinking?"

"The doctors still believe it would help his mother if she were to see him."

"Of course," he said, silently chiding himself for forgetting. "With all that's happened…"

Carlisle placed a hand on his shoulder. "Then take him to her, Truman, the sooner the better."

Nicolai watched the wrought iron gate with its blue and white sign appear over the road, the hospital buildings looming just beyond. The rough brick shone a dull red beneath the harsh light of midday. Down an adjacent walkway a man in a blue jumpsuit rushed across the courtyard, stealing glances at them before slipping through a side door. Two men in white uniforms hurried after him.

The chapel bell sounded twice, marking the two o'clock hour. Nicolai climbed from the van and cast Truman a worried glance, trying to gauge his mood. He had said little on the drive over. He motioned Nicolai to follow and started toward the nearest building.

Moments later they stood before a nurses' station. A large woman with orange hair and heavy makeup sat at the counter, a thick stack of files next to her. Nicolai kept his eyes averted and head down. He had no way of knowing who had seen him as he fled from his mother's room weeks before. The nurse tossed a file onto the desk and gave a heavy sigh.

"Visiting hours are over," she barked, making no attempt to hide her annoyance. "There's a sign right behind you that says so plain as day. You all can read, can't you?"

"I called and spoke with the doctor on duty," Truman said, ignoring her attitude. "She told me it would be alright if we came now."

"She... she did what?" she stammered, jumping to her feet. "I decide what happens on my ward, not her!"

She pivoted and vanished around the corner. Nicolai turned to Truman.

"She's not going to let us see her, is she?"

"It's starting to look that way." He scanned the hallway in both directions. "If only we knew which room..."

"I know," he interrupted. "Follow me."

They hurried down the corridor, ducking into doorways while keeping an eye out for the nurse. A darkened hallway appeared to the right and Nicolai hesitated, unsure whether to take it. The sound of approaching footsteps echoed behind them. Grabbing Truman's arm, he slipped into the shadow of an open entry.

The footsteps fading, they continued down the corridor, moving from doorway to doorway. Room after room appeared empty. All at once Nicolai stopped, backtracking to an open door. A soft thread of music drifted from inside. He waved Truman to follow.

Reminded of his last visit, Nicolai peeked around the corner. For a moment he feared he had picked the wrong room. Sunshine spilling through an open window reflected from the floor onto the far wall, filling the room with light. A nearby turntable popped and crackled with a tune familiar from his past.

In one corner he spotted his mother in an overstuffed chair, a book in her lap. She looked nothing like he remembered her. Thick hair held back by a chartreuse scarf spilled down her shoulders. Her cheeks glowed in hues of rose and pink. She raised her eyes and a look of recognition slowly transformed her face. She jumped from the chair.

"Nicolai, you've come to see me!" She started toward him. "I was just wishing for you and somehow you came, like magic."

He stood still, unsure what to expect. A memory of the last time he had seen her flashed through his mind, her wild eyes, her terrified screams. Then the image from the cave replaced it, her hand outstretched, her face beckoning him. He took a breath and stepped through the doorway.

Truman followed him in. Seeing him she hesitated, smoothing back her hair as she glanced about the room. A wave of anxiety crossed her face. Nicolai moved next to her, taking her hand.

"This is my friend, Truman," he said, nodding over his shoulder. "He brought me to see you. The doctor told him your new medicine is helping and it would be good for me to visit."

"Thank you," she whispered, giving him a brief glance.

Nicolai studied her. "You're looking better, mama."

"Could you really be here, Nicolai?" She cradled his hand in hers. "I've dreamt of it so often that now I don't know what to believe."

"I'm not a dream, mom. I'm really here."

"I believe you are." She sat and studied his face. "You've gotten so big, almost a man I would say."

"I'm only thirteen," he said, sitting opposite her.

"Are you really so grown already?" Noticing the bandage, she ran her fingers along his forearm. "But you've hurt yourself."

"No, I'm alright." He waved his arm before her. "See, it moves fine. The stitches come out in a few days."

"But why do you have stitches, Nicolai?"

"Let's not talk about that, mama." He gestured toward the doorway. "Let's talk about you leaving here. How soon can we start looking for a place to live?"

"But this is where I live."

"Don't you want a house, a house like we had once?"

"Why do I need a house when I have a home here?"

"I mean, a house for us both, a place to live in after you leave."

"Oh, no, Nicolai, I can't leave."

"But why can't you? Your medicine is working now, isn't it?"

"You don't understand." She glanced at the window. "I need to be where it's safe. It's safe in here."

"There's nothing to be afraid of out there, mama." He placed a hand on her arm. "I'll be with you."

"There are things out there, Nicolai, unsafe things." She pulled away from him, drawing her knees to her chest. "There are things you can't control."

"What are you talking about, mother?"

"No one can control them, no one," she mumbled, wrapping her arms around her knees, her gaze preoccupied and distant.

"But mother…" He felt Truman's hand on his shoulder.

"Maybe your mother needs time to get used to seeing you again before making any big plans."

157

"Is that what you want, mom, more time?" Nicolai leaned toward her. "Mom, are you listening?"

"I don't want to leave." She turned to face him. "Please don't make me."

"Try not to worry, mama." He pulled her hand free and cradled it in his palm. "You don't have to leave unless you want to."

Voices echoed down the corridor. Truman disappeared and returned, nodding toward the doorway.

"We're going to have trouble if we don't get moving."

Nicolai kissed his mother's cheek and stood above her, a mixture of hope and disappointment filling his throat. She dropped her gaze, her eyes again lost to an inner world. Without a word he turned and followed Truman out the door.

Chapter Twenty-two

Nicolai opened his eyes and squinted at the silhouetted figure standing over him. The sound of dripping water echoed far below. He glanced to either side, realizing at once he was back in the cave. The narrow ledge stretched away from him, vanishing into the darkness. The surrounding walls glistened with seepage.

He turned back to the figure. Parfit bent down to him, the white hair framing his face, halo-like, glowing. Then he pointed a gnarled finger into the air.

Nicolai leaned to one side, peering past him. Two silhouettes appeared at the cave entrance, blocking out the narrow oval of sky as they learned over the edge. Suddenly the sun moved from behind a cloud and the scowling faces of Horace and the pale man with blonde-white hair appeared above him.

He sat up with a start, his heart racing. The bedroom stood quiet around him. Sunlight streamed in through the dormer window, the big oak beyond flickering before a light breeze. At once he realized that his memory had returned, the hotel, the cave, and most of all the two brothers' plan to take over the boarding house property. He hurried to dress, impatient to tell Carlisle.

He was halfway down the stairs when the doorbell rang once, then twice. He paused on the landing. Down the hall Aiden stood erect, his eyes darting as he listened to Truman's voice drift up from below.

Julius appeared in the doorway to his room and stood watching. An unseen woman's voice droned downstairs just out of hearing. Nicolai turned and peered down the stairway, spotting Truman as he reached the front door. With his free hand he motioned behind his back, waving him away. Ducking behind the wall, he darted into the hallway and moved next to Aiden.

"Who is it?" he whispered. "What are they talking about?"

159

Aiden bent toward him. "You must leave, Nicolai Tate, and you must now, not later, no not."

"But why, Aiden?"

"A lady from children's services has come to take you away, and she has," he said, speaking under his breath. "She is saying you broke into the cave so you must go to another place, a place for troubled boys, a place not here, no not." He slapped his thigh. "So you must leave this house or be caught, and you must!"

"But how do I leave, Aiden? The stairs go right by front door. They'll see me." He glanced down the hall. "There's no other way out."

"Julius will take you, and he will."

"What the... have you gone stark-raving mad?" Julius hissed as he approached them. "I'm not responsible for...."

Aiden whipped his cane through the air, narrowly missing his head. Julius pressed himself to the wall.

"Julius knows a secret way out." He pointed down the hall. "He will take you now."

"But I... I just can't... it's simply not possible," he stammered. "I can't and I won't."

A memory passed through him in a sudden wave, taking his breath. Lying on the floor of the school bathroom, his arms around his head, his face pressed to the floor, he gasped at the knee pressed to his back. The rank breath of the other boys burned his nostrils, their whispered curses echoing about him, filling him with dread. Then all at once they were gone. A dense silence covered him and he drew his knees to his chest, trying not to cry.

Aiden's shrill voice brought him back into the moment. "You can take him and you will, Julius Rose!"

"But, Aiden," he pleaded, "I can't possibly..."

"And I will be a decoy, a distraction," he interrupted. "I will be a red herring, a smokescreen for Nicolai Tate."

At that he started down the steps, the metal tip of his cane rapping the floorboards, sending echoes down the narrow stairwell. Nicolai turned to face Julius, unsure what to expect. Julius eyed him for a moment, trying to conceal his fear. Then, seeing no alternative, he sighed and put a finger to his lips, motioning him to follow.

Moments later they were standing in his bedroom. Nicolai looked about the room, wondering if he should take his chances on the stairs. Julius was far from trustworthy. He stepped aside as Julius swung open the closet door.

"You've got to be kidding," he sneered. "You expect me to hide in your closet?"

Julius waved a finger at him. "It is a mistake to rush to judgment before you have all the facts."

Pushing aside a stack of boxes, he pointed inside. Nicolai peered into the cluttered space, trying to puzzle out his meaning.

"I thought Aiden said there was a secret way out," he said, half to himself.

"And he was right." Julius pointed inside. "I discovered the passage when I dropped a valuable coin and it rolled under the door."

"What are you talking about?" Nicolai surveyed the dusty confines. "I don't see anything."

"You're not using your eyes." He pushed him forward. "Try looking again."

He stepped inside and studied the walls and ceiling before his gaze settled on a discolored patch of flooring. He knelt for a closer look. A slim line marking a trap door emerged from beneath the dim light. Slipping his fingers between the boards he lifted the lid and peeked inside. A narrow set of stairs vanished into the darkness below.

He stared into the cave-like oval and the room began to spin about him. Fear gripped his throat. Grabbing the doorframe, he steadied himself as Julius moved next to him.

"Is something wrong?" he asked, searching his face and seeing the fear behind his gaze. "You've gone pale."

"I'll be alright."

He took a breath and let go of the door, not wanting to give himself away. Julius gestured toward the stairway, seeing a chance to sidestep his own fear. The thought of being alone with a teenager terrified him.

"The steps go to a tunnel that leads to a storm shelter on the far side of the hill." He nudged him forward. "Go ahead and look for yourself."

"But it's dark down there."

"I have a flashlight. You'd better hurry. I think I heard a deputy asking to see inside the house," he lied. "Finding you hidden in a closet would just be too easy."

Nicolai stared at the dark opening. "You're not coming with me?"

"There's no need." He tried to sound reassuring. "You'll be fine on your own. Just take the..."

"But I can't!" he blurted out. All at once he felt he was back in the cave, the damp chill again surrounding him. He pressed himself to the wall. "I can't go alone."

Julius eyed him. "Why in heaven's name can't you?"

"I just can't," he muttered, shivering.

"But you must go now or be found." He glanced toward the hallway. "I believe I hear them coming."

"I'll go but only if you go too."

"You're afraid, then?"

"No."

"Come now, I can see it on your face." Julius peered at him, sensing an advantage in the boy's pride. "Admit it. You know I'm right."

"You think you're so dang smart but you're not," he sneered, not wanting to give him the satisfaction. "I'm not scared."

"Well good, because there's nothing to be afraid of down there." He forced a smile. "It's just a quick trip down a tunnel to the storm shelter and you're all safe and sound."

Nicolai watched the corners of his mouth strain under the false grin.

"You've been before?"

Julius looked away. "I've had no need to."

He eyed him skeptically. "Then how did you get your coin back?"

"I simply used my brain," he said, his tone dismissive. "All I had to do was lower tape on a string to retrieve it. Now, be on your way."

Voices echoed up the stairwell. Nicolai glanced at the trap door, the fear again rising in his throat.

"Please come with me, Julius," he pleaded.

"Why must you be so obstinate?" Julius moaned, tired of arguing. "There's nothing to it. Just down the steps and off you go."

"That's easy for you to say. You weren't chased into a cave by a bearded maniac and his pale friend."

Julius stared at him, the meaning of his words slowly coming clear.

"You... you remember that night?" he asked, trying not to sound overly interested.

"I had a dream and when I woke up I could remember."

"You're sure it wasn't just the dream?"

"I didn't dream it. I remember what really happened, everything... or most of it anyway, from when I left here until I woke up in the hospital."

"Everything, you say? Well, perhaps I was a bit hasty." Julius stepped closer, his mind racing with questions. "I believe I will accompany you after all. Just let me find the flashlight."

Within minutes they were halfway down the narrow staircase, the house creaking and popping around them as if protesting the intrusion. Julius regretted his decision as soon as he lowered the trap door. The suffocating darkness closed in around him. His heart pounded in his ears. Concentrating on each step, he limped down the stairway, struggling to regain his composure.

"Now, tell me about that night."

"I can't."

163

"What do you mean you can't?"

"I just can't," Nicolai called over his shoulder as the spotlight jumped along the walls, "not until Carlisle can be there."

"Keep the blasted flashlight steady!" he yelled back. "And tell me exactly what you remember about the night in question. I want to know who you saw, what you heard. Or have you forgotten our little arrangement?"

"I haven't forgotten," he mumbled from the bottom of the stairs.

Moments later they were moving along the tunnel. Trying to distract himself from the wall of darkness following at his heels, Julius continued peppering him with questions.

"Now, as I was saying, I want to hear everything. Any seemingly insignificant detail could be important. Do you understand me?"

Nicolai said nothing.

"Do you intend to answer or shall I give the sheriff a call?" Julius said between breaths, struggling to keep up. "And slow down. You're practically running."

Nicolai slowed his pace, wishing he could run and never look back. Images of Horace's cold glare swept over him like ice water. His head throbbed in rhythm with his aching arm. All at once he was gripped by a dread the flashlight would go out, leaving them blind and lost. Panic filled his throat, stopping him.

"I said slow down, not cease moving altogether." Julius peered past him. "Why did you stop? Did you hear something?"

The house groaned, shaking the crossbeams overhead. A veil of dust drifted through the flashlight beam. Julius glanced at the darkness around them, blinking the grit from his eyes.

"It's only the wind," he announced, trying to sound convincing.

"You don't believe that." Nicolai pointed past him. "I want to go back."

"Why on earth would you want to go back now?"

"I'm afraid."

"But we must be halfway there."

Julius peered into the darkness, his own fear rising. Nicolai sighed and pressed his forehead to the wall.

"I'm tired of being afraid. I'm tired of running. I'm tired of failing at everything I ever..." he stopped, unable to finish.

"You heard what Aiden said. They're sure to send you away if you go back."

"I knew it would happen sooner or later," he whispered. "Living here with all of you was too good to last."

"You mustn't think that way, Nicolai," he said, taken aback by his sincerity. "Things will get better. You'll see."

"But I'm afraid things won't get better," he mumbled, despondent. "Soon I'll be back in another miserable foster home. There's no way to avoid it."

"There's always a way."

Nicolai turned to face him. "Aren't you ever afraid, Julius?"

"Well, of course I am," he said softly, seeing his chance for questions slipping away.

"But not so much you want to run away?"

"Of course I've had my dreams of escape." He pointed to his chest. "Don't you think I've dreamt of escaping this? How many girlfriends do you think I've had looking like I do? Go ahead and guess."

"I don't want to."

"We all have our fears, Nicolai. But don't believe everything you see in the movies. Lack of fear is just a form of stupidity." He spoke as much to himself as the boy. "Yet fear can be managed, even mastered, using your intellect."

"You mean thinking your way out of a problem?"

"That's one way to put it."

"Could you teach me?"

"Well, I suppose I might be able to…"

"Please, Julius, I'm a fast learner. I promise to listen."

Julius peered at him in the dim light, struggling with himself over whether he would help him, over whether he actually had something to offer the boy. Suddenly the questions he had wanted to ask seemed unimportant, even trivial. He lifted the flashlight from Nicolai's hand.

"Come now and we'll go see about this mysterious storm shelter." He pointed the beam down the tunnel. "I hear it's carved out of solid rock."

Chapter Twenty-three

Truman hurried through the courthouse doors and up the stairs, anxious to find Kennis. He guessed she would be talking with Tico Bauert as she often did on Friday mornings. The lilt of her voice drifted down the hall as he neared the sheriff's office. He quickened his step, convinced Nicolai's only real hope of remaining at home rested with her.

Stepping into the entryway, he spotted her across the room, hands on her hips, a glint in her eye. Tico sat facing her. He reached across his cluttered desk, absently shifting a stack of papers from one corner to the other before looking up at her.

"I'll bet you lunch at La Nunca that boy ends up in detention before the weekend is through."

He sat back in his chair, a self-satisfied smile on his meaty face. Shaking her head, she squinted back at him.

"I think I'll be having the green enchiladas." She tried without success to suppress a smirk. "You can go ahead and put in my order."

Noticing Truman, Tico sat up and nodded toward the hall. "I believe you have a visitor, Kennis."

She pivoted, a mixture of surprise and pleasure on her face. Struck by the sight of her, Truman stood in the doorway, speechless. A questioning smile crossed her lips. Tico shuffled the stack of papers on his desk again, finally tossing them in a drawer.

"I believe I have an important meeting to get to."

"You have a meeting?" Frowning, Kennis turned to face him. "Weren't you just complaining about all the paperwork you have to do?"

"Well, I guess I forgot," he mumbled as he stood.

"What is this important meeting about?"

"It's confidential sheriff business."

"Oh, is that so?" She gave Truman a quick wink, bringing him out of his trance. "Well, if it's secret then it must be important."

"I said confidential not secret."

"Is there a difference, Sheriff Bauert?"

"Well, I'd best be on my way then," he muttered, ignoring her.

Truman stepped into the room and raised his hands in apology.

"Don't leave on my account, Tico." He nodded toward Kennis. "I've come because I've got a problem and hoped I'd find her here."

Her smile vanished. "What is it, Truman?"

"A children's services supervisor showed up at the house looking for Nicolai. They want to send him to some sort of reform school."

"Without talking to me first?" Her eyes grew dark with indignation. "We're supposed to be working together."

"I thought there might be trouble." Tico sat again. "A supervisor from children's services was here the night we got the call on the boy."

"That explains it," she said, her tone angry. "She has no liking for teenage boys and must have overruled Nicolai's caseworker."

Truman nodded. "She seemed to be on some sort of vendetta."

"Where have they taken him?"

"Nowhere yet. He slipped out while I was talking to her."

Tico snorted. "That boy goes missing more than a stray cat."

"To tell the truth, I signaled him to make an escape while I stalled her."

"Now there's a surprise." Tico stared at him. "You don't seem like the type to go against the rules."

"He's where he needs to be, Tico. It's not right for them to send him away, not now."

"The judge has a hair trigger when it comes to problem teenagers. The fact is he doesn't want to be bothered anymore than that supervisor."

"He just needs someone to explain that Nicolai should stay where he is, that we're his best bet." Truman shifted his gaze to Kennis. "You can do something, can't you?"

"I don't see how, Truman," she answered, cringing. "The judge grumbles whenever I enter the courtroom."

Tico's phone rang. He answered it, said a few words and replaced the receiver.

"I need to leave, this time for real."

"Is this another of those confidential meetings?"

"Hell if I know, but it's important," he said, his expression turning grim. "Ever since that district attorney and his assistant got murdered over in Rains County, people have been on edge. The last straw came when the judge's office got fire-bombed."

"That was a bad business, alright," she said, nodding.

"It's not over yet."

Grabbing his hat, he disappeared through the doorway. Truman watched after him and then turned to Kennis.

"Isn't there anything you can do for Nicolai?"

"The way things are between me and the judge, I'd probably make it worse."

"But I was counting on you, Kennis. I have no one else to go to, no contacts, no connections, no inside line to the court. I know a handful of people is all, people with disabilities, with eccentricities, people who have little or no say so in their own lives much less the life of a boy."

He looked away, his concern for Nicolai twisting in his gut. Kennis studied him a moment.

"You really care for him, don't you?"

"What? I, uh... I... I'm not sure what you mean," he sputtered, surprised by the comment.

169

"I can see it in your eyes." She searched his face. "You've grown fond of him, haven't you?"

"No, I'm just… I'm only trying to…" he said as a flood of conflicting thoughts swirled about him. Confused and overwhelmed by it all, he retreated behind cliché. "Anyone would do the same."

"The sad truth is few would ever even consider befriending a teenage orphan, not to mention commit to it. But you have."

"A lot of good it's done. If only I could…" he mumbled, his voice trailing off.

Feeling ineffective and helpless he glanced at the doorway, wishing for escape. A rising anger filled his throat. Kennis stepped closer, reaching for him.

"Truman, I wish there was something more…"

"I didn't figure you'd help," he interrupted, jerking his hand away. "I don't know why I bothered."

She reared back as if he'd slapped her. Then she leaned in toward him.

"That's not fair," she said, her eyes flashing. "I've told you already, the situation is unworkable."

"Excuses are always there if you want to find them."

"You don't understand the situation… or you won't."

"I understand the boy is out of luck."

"How can you say…?" She stopped as a voice in song drifted through the door, the words in Spanish. Seconds later a short, caramel-colored boy stumbled into the room, followed by a thick-necked deputy. The boy leered at her, clearly drunk.

"Hey, it's my favorite chica, Kennis the Menace," he slurred. "What's up, woman?"

The deputy pushed him into a chair and turned to her, a wry smile on his face.

"Good thing you're here." The smiled disappeared. "Otherwise he might accidently hurt himself."

"He was drunk at school?"

"A group of them broke into some old lady's house and raided her liquor cabinet," he said, smirking. "Genius here is the only one that got caught."

The boy grinned at her and nodded toward the deputy.

"That there is the man, Officer Raymond the Ray-gun," he said, chuckling to himself. "Check out his boss pistol, miss. All black metal with antler grips. I could definitely handle one of those pieces. You know what I mean, miss?"

She cast a disappointed glance at Truman as he turned and started for the door, anger and disappointment sweeping him along.

Julius crouched on the storm cellar's narrow set of concrete stairs and eased open one side of the double door. A sliver of yellow sunlight split the steps beneath him. He breathed in the fresh air, relieved to be free of the suffocating darkness. Pushing the crack wider he peeked outside, alert for any sign of the caseworker.

The lawn leading to the rear of the house stood empty. He started to lift open the door when he caught a whiff of cigarette smoke, brief but unmistakable. He froze in place, his mind racing. Could the smoke be from the caseworker? Could the odor have traveled all the way from the front porch?

Easing the door back into place, he moved to its mate and lifted it slightly. An alleyway edging the back of the property came into view. He squinted through the narrow slit, spotting a green sedan parked halfway down the gravel path, facing away from him.

A bearded man with a broad, ruddy face sat in the driver's seat, his gaze fixed on the house. Next to him a figure slouched with his head on the seatback, the stub of a cigarette in his mouth. His skin and hair were the color of ivory.

Julius lowered the door and squinted down the stairs, letting his eyes adjust to the dim light. A bare bulb dangling from the ceiling cast pale shadows along the rough walls and shelves stacked with cans of soup, canvas bags of rice and jars filled with dried beans. Nicolai peered up at him from the bottom step.

"There's something wrong, isn't there?"

"Now is the time to tell me what you remember about that night, especially the part about the bearded maniac and his pale friend."

"Well, they were at the meeting. I saw them. Why are you asking me now? I want to get out of here."

"If you want to leave then finish telling me what you remember."

"First two red-headed brothers made a big speech about war and the constitution. There was lots of cheering. Then everyone left but the maniac and the pale one. The red-headed brothers told them they were going to make us leave here so they can have it for themselves."

"They want the house?" Julius paused to consider the news. "Now I have to wonder what use they could possibly have for a dilapidated Victorian."

"Then they gave the white-haired one an envelope and talked about bullets. They said they had a plan but I didn't understand it."

"This gets more intriguing by the moment. Tell me more."

"What's a Molotov cocktail?"

"Never mind that," he barked, "what else can you recall?"

"They said they were going to put the screws to Mercer. Is he the same one Truman knows? There was something about oil. I was going to tell Carlisle but forgot everything until I woke up this morning and..."

Julius raised a hand to stop him. "This will require a careful going through and now is not the time. What about your bearded friend? What more can you tell me about him?"

172

"I was trying to leave when he spotted me. I ran and would've gotten away too if I hadn't fallen into the cave. His name is Horace and he scares me."

"And the pale one?"

"He was at the cave with Horace. They tried to lure me out but a storm came. Then they came back but something scared them away. Why do you keep asking about them?"

"They're sitting in a car a short way down the alley."

"They're here?" he yelled, glancing back down the tunnel. "We have to go. We can make it back to the house."

"You don't understand, Nicolai. They're here looking for you."

"They can't be. They don't know where I live."

"Apparently they do." Julius shrugged. "Come and see for yourself if you don't believe me."

He lifted the cellar door and sunlight again sliced the stairway. Nicolai hesitated, unsure whether to trust him. But the lure of seeing for himself proved too strong to resist. He hurried up the stairs and peeked through the narrow opening just as Horace leaned out the window and spit. Nicolai slumped onto the steps.

"But how could...?" All at once an image of the big man standing before him at the barbeque restaurant came to him. "He saw me, the one with the beard. And he knew where Truman worked."

"That would explain their presence." Julius pondered the implication. "You're going to have to leave here, at least for awhile."

"But what will I do, Julius, where will I go?" He glanced toward the tunnel. "Now that I've come this far I can't just go and turn myself in."

"I have a plan. You'll need to sit tight until I return. You can manage that, now can't you?"

Nicolai lifted the door again and squinted into the bright sunlight, realizing with regret that his fate rested in

Julius' hands. He glanced at the bent form crouched next to him, reluctant to trust him but seeing no alternative. Then he nodded his agreement.

Chapter Twenty-four

Truman pushed through the scarred wooden door fronting Pinkie's Lounge and took a seat at the bar, hoping to free his mind from thoughts of Kennis. He surveyed the dim interior, recalling how his father had frequented the bar after his mother's death. The place had changed little from what he could remember.

The bartender looked up from behind the counter, his broad face the color of ham, his eyes like punched holes. A grease-stained apron stretched across his belly. He squinted at Truman, studying him as if reaching for a lost memory. Giving up, he motioned toward the rows of bottles behind him.

"What'll you have?"

"A double shot of peppermint schnapps and a beer."

Moments later the man slid the beer next to a brimming shot glass and stood lingering. Truman tried to ignore him, in no mood to talk. The man spread his thick fingers on the countertop and leaned toward him.

"Do I know you?"

Truman downed the shot and half the beer before answering. Memories of his father flitted through his thoughts like fireflies. He raised his gaze and stared into the meaty face.

"I don't think so."

"You sure about that?" He peered at him. "You have a familiar look about you. I reckon it's the eyes."

He leaned on the counter as if awaiting an answer. Truman glanced to either side, wishing he would go bother someone else but the early crowd was thin for a Friday afternoon. He shrugged, hoping to end the conversation.

"I just remind you of someone."

"Sure, sure, you might be right. I've owned this place for thirty years and seen a lot of folks come through."

He pushed himself upright and began washing a row of dirty glasses, stacking them below the countertop. The rich aroma of fried potatoes drifted in from the kitchen. All at once the man flinched and turned to Truman, a dripping glass in one hand, a towel in the other.

"You that actor from down near San Saba, you know the one I'm talking about?"

"I know the one," Truman mumbled, hoping to end the conversation. "But I'm not him."

The man huffed and returned to his dishes as a waitress passed though the kitchen door and moved along the bar. Truman relaxed and motioned to her for another round.

He was beginning to feel the effects of the schnapps when the owner appeared before him again. He pointed a sausage-size finger at Truman's chest.

"You any relation to Royce Birdsong?"

Truman stared into the coal-like eyes and sighed, giving him a slow nod. The man slapped the countertop and a grin spread across his ruddy face.

"I knew it would come to me sooner or later." He held out his hand. "I'm Pinky Stiles."

"Royce is my father."

"Sure, sure, I can see the resemblance now. You came in here with him from time to time."

"He made me wait in the car mostly," he said, his voice flat, his memory of the time bitter.

"Sure, sure, I remember now. He was in some kind of bad shape back then." He grimaced, wagging his head from side to side like a huge hairless dog. "Your mama passing like that hit him hard. He needed time to himself, time to unwind, take the pressure off, recharge the batteries, you know what I mean. This is where he came."

"He did plenty of unwinding," he snorted. "I'll give him that much."

"You don't sound too happy about it."

"Well, that's what drunks do, isn't it?"

"Sure, sure but you got to understand how it was for him having to care for her and you both at once like that, it

176

all falling on him, no other family around to lend a hand."
His face clouded with the memory. "I helped him out
where I could but I had my own concerns, my sick daddy
and a new business to tend to, this place here. I had only so
much time to give. Still, I wish I could've done more. I
could see he was headed for trouble."

"And he made it in grand fashion."

"Sure, sure he did, but Royce was a good man, one of
the best before your mother passed on. I believe he
would've come through it alright if his business hadn't
folded like it did."

"There's always an excuse."

"Sure there is, sure, but you've got to understand it
wasn't that simple. Royce was a reliable, determined man
back then. His whole life was about caring for your mother
and you. That's why he put his heart and soul into his
wildcatting business. He thought if he tried hard enough,
saved up enough, it would all work out and he could care
for your mother and you proper until she got better. He
always believed she would you know, right up until the
end."

"How do you know so much?"

"Like I said, this is where he came when he was
feeling down and out. I was his confessor, sort of like his
priest, always here to talk to, to listen as he poured out his
troubles like bailing out a boat. I heard more than I ever
wanted but I know what I'm telling you. He treated people
right. I heard it from the roughnecks, the land men, all of
them. He treated people fair and with respect, like he was
no better than any one of them even though he had struck it
big. Well, for awhile anyway.

"Then it all went bust, and look at the town now, all
sad and falling down, like an abandoned homestead, like I
get to feeling some days living here. He was right to get
out and take you with him. He had to hit bottom but then
he came out of it and got on with his life. Did alright too."

"What do you mean?"

"Well, he'll never get rich teaching school but he's doing the world good, that's a fact. We need more kids learning science and all, becoming doctors and engineers and such, making a better life for the rest of us."

"Are we talking about the same Royce Birdsong?"

"Why sure, sure we are." He peered at Truman, the meaning of his question slowly sinking in. "You're telling me you don't know? When did you last see him?"

"I left for college and never looked back."

He slapped a heavy palm on the countertop. "Good Lord God Almighty, how could you do such a thing?"

"I'd had enough of him, his lies and excuses. I was done with him."

"Sure, sure, but even if you might've been done, he wasn't. He won some award for his teaching, went to the Capital to get it from some hotshot politicos. But he didn't let it go to his head, no sir."

"You keep in touch with him?"

"Not so much, but he lives down the street from my daughter over in Abilene so I see him now and again. He even taught my grandson." He chuckled to himself. "Although I have to say that boy is not cut out for a science career or anything close to it. He hates math more than I hate exercise."

"I have a hard time seeing him teaching school. From what I remember he didn't have much use for kids."

"Listen to me, son. That was a long time ago. You have got to go see him. He's a changed man."

"He said the same to me more than once, but it never lasted. You'll understand if I leave well enough alone."

"Sure, sure but you've got him all wrong so I'm going to tell you a little story to set you straight." He glanced around the room, speaking under his breath. "Now I have to enforce the rules around here so I got a reputation to maintain or I'll have men making trouble. You've got to keep this to yourself."

The big man leaned in.

"After my wife of twenty years walked in here one night to tell me that she'd had enough of small towns and bar life, and that she was running off with some city feller, I took it hard. You know what I mean?"

Truman nodded, his mind again filling with thoughts of Kennis. Pinkie leaned closer, speaking under his breath.

"I was in bad shape for a good long while. Your father took me into his house, gave me a bed to sleep in, and kept me from doing something stupid until I got over her leaving. He didn't have to do that but he did. That's the kind of man he is.

"Now you don't have to believe me but I know what I know," he grumbled. "And I know you should go see him."

He turned and disappeared through the kitchen door. Truman looked up as a couple sat across the bar from him, talking in low tones, their shoulders touching. He thought of Kennis again and chided himself for his impatience. She had been right. She could do little to help Nicolai, at least for the time being. He would tell her as much now if he could.

A sudden wish to see her overcame him and he stood, tossing a wad of bills on the counter. All at once the floor corkscrewed beneath his feet. He gripped the counter. The room tilted as if it floated adrift on a restless sea. Cursing himself for having that second schnapps, he stepped away from the counter anyway, determined to leave.

Minutes later he angled the van onto a narrow side street and blinked through the windshield. The scene spread before him, still blurred and unsteady. He took a breath and tried to concentrate. Frame houses lined both sides of the street, most with wide porches and gabled roofs. Bright sunlight scattered the tree-shaded lawns with shadow.

He pulled to the curb and rifled through the van's glove box, searching for the torn scrap of napkin he had used to jot down her address and phone number. The paper eluded him. After sifting through the contents for the third time he gave up and slammed the box shut, instead pulling from the curb and cruising along the street with the hope something might jog his memory.

After three passes he stopped beneath a sprawling live oak, dismayed by the scene before him. The houses all looked alike. He slapped the steering wheel in frustration and cut the engine. If only he had her phone number. She had told him she kept herself unlisted due to the peculiarities of her job. The last thing a single woman needed was an irate parent calling or showing up in the middle of the night. He leaned back in his seat and closed his eyes, wishing the world would stop spinning around him.

From a distance, a voice called his name. He opened his eyes to find a thick fog surrounding the van. He climbed from behind the steering wheel and stepped onto the concrete, squinting into the haze. The metal keys of a typewriter clicked somewhere beyond his sight, stopping and starting over and over. The voice called again, still distant but recognizable. Kennis was somewhere ahead. Without hesitating he ran toward her, the wall of fog blinding him as he stumbled forward. The metallic typing grew louder with every step, pounding in his head.

All at once the ground slipped from beneath him and he began to tumble down and down. The white world slipped uncontrollably past. A yawning hole suddenly opened under him and he became airborne, sailing into it, his stomach turning, his head throbbing. Nicolai's face flashed before him. Then all went black.

He jerked upright. The metallic tapping echoed through the van, scrambling his thoughts. He blinked, trying to clear his aching head. An instant later Kennis appeared in the passenger window. For a moment he imagined he was still dreaming. Then she raised her hand and rapped the glass with her keys, motioning him to unlock the door.

Instead he jumped from the seat and rounded the van. She turned at his approach, looking at him with a mixture of disapproval and affection. He stopped feet from her, unsure what to expect. More than anything he wanted to take her in his arms. She took a long look at him.

"You're looking a little rough around the edges, Truman."

"I should know better than to drink hard liquor," he said, massaging his temples. "It always leads to trouble."

"Is that what this is, trouble?"

"What?" He locked eyes with her. "No, I didn't mean it like that."

"You just decided to take a nap on my street?"

"Not exactly." He glanced up the road. "How did you know I was here?"

"You can't hang around law enforcement types for long without picking up a few of their little quirks, like noticing strange vehicles lurking about the neighborhood." A hint of a smile crossed her lips. "So, tell me, how *did* you end up sleeping on my street?"

"I didn't intend to fall asleep."

"What did you intend then? Something to do with me, I hope."

"Kennis, I wanted to… I didn't mean to…" he stammered.

"You sound so serious, Truman. It's just me and you here."

He took a breath. "I was wrong to say what I did. I know you would help Nicolai if you could."

"You're right, I would." She moved to him, taking his hand. "You're a good man, Truman Birdsong, and I'd invite you into my home right now if I could."

He studied her face, imagining her reaction if she discovered he was on probation.

"I doubt you'd say that if you knew the real Truman Birdsong." He felt the burn of shame move across his forehead. "There are things about me you don't know."

"I'm a big girl. Why not try me?"

He realized at once he had to tell her now or risk never having another chance. He peered into her eyes.

"This is going to sound like a joke but, trust me, it is not," he said, sighing. "A year ago I got arrested for assaulting someone. Now I'm on probation."

"Is that what has you so worked up?" She gave her head a slight shake. "Don't be. I've known for weeks."

"You know?" He stared at her, nearly speechless. "But how?"

"I have friends in law enforcement, remember?" she said, chuckling. "They look out for me."

"I figured you'd walk as soon as you heard."

"It sounds to me like you had your reasons. Finding your wife in bed with another man, not to mention a convicted felon, is enough to cause most men to do things they'll regret."

"I only regretted it later," he said, cringing. "At the time I wasn't thinking about anything but revenge."

"I heard it involved a baseball bat."

"My favorite from when I was a kid, an old Louisville Slugger. I had to go home unexpectedly around lunchtime because I'd forgotten some blueprints. I heard noises and at first thought someone had broken in, so I grabbed the bat.

"Then when I found out what the noises were really about I sort of stopped thinking altogether. The guy was big and covered in tattoos. He started mouthing off, saying how he was going to cut my throat and watch me suffocate on my own blood, that sort of trash. I didn't know if he was armed but I knew my wife kept a gun in her bed stand. He started moving and the next thing I knew he was on the ground and she was screaming like she'd been the one hit."

"That sounds awfully close to self-defense."

"I'm not going to make excuses, Kennis," he said, unable to face her. "I was out of control. I hate to think what would've happened if my wife hadn't stepped between us. I could've killed the man."

"But you didn't, Truman. You stopped yourself."

"To tell the truth, I don't remember much." He sighed and shook his head. "What happened later I recall all too well."

"Well, I'm glad you told me," she said, her tone reassuring. "I'd like to hear the rest of the story if you're willing to tell it."

"Didn't you say something about inviting me in?"

"I did," she groaned, "but now is not the time. Carlisle is looking for you."

"You talked to Carlisle?"

"Tico gave him my number. Apparently they know each other, something to do with the state hospital."

"Is there a problem with Nicolai's mom?"

"I don't know. He asked for you and said they needed a hand, a hand and that was all. I'm almost certain I could hear someone else in the background," she said, frowning. "He was polite but very serious and it all struck me as a little odd.

"The strangest part was he didn't say that they needed you or they needed Truman, but that they needed 'a hand'. He repeated it enough that it stuck with me though I'm not sure what it means, if anything. The one thing I am sure of is he sounded worried."

Parfit's words of warning came back to him: '...we best steel ourselves for the darkness. But some need the help of a willing hand...' He glanced at Kennis. More than anything he wanted to be with her. As if reading his mind, she pulled him to her, pressing her hips to him, finding his mouth. Her warmth, her smell, her aliveness seemed to engulf him, to fill him. Then she squeezed his hand lightly and stepped back, locking eyes with him.

"You'd better get moving. Carlisle doesn't strike me as one to worry needlessly."

"I'd rather stay here."

"Your friends need you, Truman."

Chapter Twenty-five

Aiden crept along the side of the one car garage, his cane clutched to his chest. The small building sat downhill from the boarding house, facing the alley. He ran his fingers along the weathered siding and smiled as bits of paint sprinkled onto his palm. Then he blew the dust into the air and stepped back, grinning. The cloud drifted to the ground in a glittering rain.

Julius frowned and pushed him toward the corner as a coursing wind rattled the tin roof above them. Helpful to cover the sound of their footsteps, he thought. Without warning Aiden jerked upright, throwing his free hand into the air and cocking his head to one side. Julius knew at once they were within range. He laid his hand on Aiden's arm and whispered to him.

"Before we begin our little plan I want to know what they're saying." He gripped Aiden's wrist. "But be sure to stay out of sight."

Aiden felt along the corner, took a step back and raised a hand to silence him. Then he tilted his head toward the alleyway and stood listening, statue-like. Horace's green sedan sat parked forty yards beyond. Julius searched Aiden's face for any reaction, straining to listen but hearing the wind and little more. Moments later Aiden relaxed his pose and bent toward him.

"One of the men is named Horace and he calls the other one Jerome Bell," he whispered. They do not like sitting and doing nothing but spy on a house of freaks, no, not at all. They say if the Weeks want the oil, why don't they just run them off or get rid of them, like they did the others?"

Julius listened intently, his mind filling with questions.

"Yes, but, but... what else?" he sputtered impatiently. "There must be more."

"They wonder what the boy heard and how long before he shows himself so they can find out."

"Is that all?"

"And they worry about being so near the big house. Why live way up here, they ask. Are the freaks sick? They worry they could they catch whatever is wrong with them."

"But the oil," he hissed, "what about the oil?"

"They say there must be an ocean of oil beneath the old house."

"An ocean of oil," he murmured. "I need a moment to think."

"You need a moment to think," Aiden repeated, "a moment and no more, no, not a bit."

Julius considered his options, realizing at once he would need to revise his plan. Nicolai was supposed to make a break for Truman's cabin once they had distracted the two men. Perhaps they could do even better. He faced Aiden.

"You may start now but proceed slowly." He tapped Aiden's forearm with a pair of oversized dark glasses. "Put these on. I'll follow shortly."

Aiden snickered. "And short you are, yes, and you are."

Julius shoved him into the alley. He strode along the narrow path, his cane tapping the gravel with rhythmic purpose, his eyes darting about behind the sunglasses. Julius turned to the storm shelter where Nicolai watched from the steps and motioned with elaborate gesture for the boy to stay put.

Seconds later he stepped out from behind the garage. Dragging one leg, he moved slowly along the alley, coughing and hacking as if he might collapse at any moment. Twenty yards ahead, Aiden paused to listen before continuing on his way.

Aiden slowed as he approached the green sedan. Startled by the sight of him, Horace sat up and pressed his face to the half-open window, trying to follow his reflection in the side mirror. Jerome jumped to attention, pivoting in his seat and pulling out his pistol as he followed Horace's wide-eyed stare.

Aiden whacked the bumper with his cane, slapping his free hand along the fender as if unsure what he felt. He stopped midway along the rear door to again gauge Julius' progress. Then he turned back to the window. Horace addressed his image in the mirror.

"What do, uh… could I, uh…," he stammered, "is there something I can do for you, sir?"

Aiden made no effort to answer. Stopping feet from the rear bumper, Julius doubled over with an exaggerated fit of coughing. Horace leaned out the window, craning his neck for a clear view.

"What's wrong with him?"

Hailing his attention, Julius spoke between breaths. "Help, I need help… very sick."

"Did he say he's sick?" Horace said, jerking his head back inside the car.

"He said it and he did, he did." Aiden bent toward the window, his high twang filling the car. "He's got a disease, yes, a disease, a terrible disease, no two ways about it, terrible."

"Jerome, did you hear that?" Horace called over his shoulder.

"Hell yes, I heard it!" Jerome answered in a hoarse tenor.

"I knew they stuck these people out here for a reason," he said, his voice rising. "What do we do now?"

"What do you think?" Jerome yelled, pointing his revolver at the windshield. "We get the hell out of here."

"But we're supposed to be watching the place."

"I don't give a damn about what we're supposed to be doing." He waved his gun through the air. "I don't want that freak getting anywhere near me."

"What do we tell the Weeks?"

186

Aiden bolted upright at the click of a trigger. Horace's quavering voice drifted through the window.

"Is that your pistol I feel on my jaw?"

"Good guess, Sherlock," he said, his voice low and calm. "And you won't be telling the Weeks brothers anything if you don't get moving right now."

Aiden jumped aside as the engine turned and sputtered, sending a cloud of blue smoke into Julius' face. He coughed again, this time in earnest, watching as the car sped down the alley and disappeared below the sloping hillside. Aiden slapped his thigh, cutting the air with his cane.

"And they ran like cowards, and they did, they did!"

Hung-over and exhausted from searching his mind for a way to keep Nicolai out of reform school, Truman blinked at the pain behind his eyes and tried to focus on the road. The van crested a rise and the land opened onto a sea of limestone hills bluish beneath the afternoon sun. In the distance, a line of red brick buildings briefly rose above the trees before disappearing.

Julius stirred in the passenger seat, lost to his own thoughts. Since his rush to leave he had said next to nothing. Glancing at him, a whirl of questions filled Truman's head. His thoughts quickly turned to their destination. Julius had said only that they were going to see one of his so-called friends, a geologist. The stop had to do with a conversation Aiden overheard about the Weeks brothers. Other than that he knew practically nothing. The secretive nature of his short companion continued to irk him.

He sat up as the town came into view, a ramshackle line of resale shops, abandoned storefronts and crumbling churches. At a flashing red stoplight, the intersection of two farm roads, the painted windows of an empty building held a likeness of Willy Reiner, the rattlesnake-taming preacher who promised to cure any ailment by 'taming the serpent and banishing Satan'. A pair of writhing diamondbacks dangled from his teeth.

The van shuddered along the pockmarked, brick-paved main avenue. Pickups and flatbed trucks crowded the curb. Truman slowed as Julius pointed to an arched doorway set into a three-story stone building. The ornate façade rose above the town like a matron fallen on hard times, tattered yet still stately. Carved into the top lentil, an elegant script read 'Ganske Bank and Trust'.

He angled to the curb and cut the engine. A half-block down an early crowd stood outside the painted windows of Starlight Café, the only restaurant in town. Julius sat with his hands on his knees, silent and sphinx-like, staring at nothing, saying nothing. Then he climbed out and started toward the arched doorway.

Moments later they stood before a frosted glass and wood door, seemingly the only occupied office on the second level. The name 'B. D. Hobson, Petroleum Geologist' crossed the door in ornate letters. , Worn smooth by decades of use, a pink marble floor stretched away from them like a river of cherry ice cream.

Julius glanced at Truman, his earlier stupor replaced by a mischievous glint, and then without a word he pushed through. The office spread before them, a cluttered tangle of tables, cabinets and map drawers. Paper seemed to cover every surface. County maps, town plats and colored graphs littered the walls. Opposite them a row of windows faced a jumble of dilapidated buildings and the sundrenched, denuded hills beyond, their sides dotted with oil rigs and pump jacks.

Julius wandered the room, disappointment in his eyes. He clearly had expected his friend to be in. He turned as a door slammed somewhere down the hallway followed by the echo of approaching footsteps. Pointing a finger at the door, he nodded toward Truman.

"That will be the answer to our questions. Now, let me do the talking. Hob can be a bit testy around strangers."

Seconds later a short, round man appeared in the doorway, his face scrunched into an unhappy squint. Hair sprouted from the top of his head in thin tufts of gray. Seeing Truman, his ruddy face turned deep red.

Then he spotted Julius. Truman noticed a slight but perceptible change in him, an easing around the eyes and mouth. Otherwise, he stood still and statue-like, waiting.

"I have arrived," Julius announced, unfazed by his stern demeanor. "You're probably wondering what brings the two of us here, Truman and me. Well, I'd venture an explanation but this dusty air is choking me. Might you have something cold and wet stashed away for special occasions, Hob? It *is* a special occasion when I make an appearance, isn't it?"

His eyes narrowed but he made no answer. Julius had no choice but to continue.

"Well then, the truth is we have come here to learn from B. D. Hobson, Petroleum Geologist, the great sage of geologic knowledge," he said, bowing deeply, "the gnome of esoteric petro-chemistry, the guru of tectonic collisions, the scion of eons etched in stone, the..."

"Enough!" he barked. "It's a bad sign when you start sucking up, Julius. What are you after?"

"I'm wounded by that summary judgment of my intentions," he complained, feigning offense. "But I'll disregard the tone and instead get on with why we're here. You see it has to do with..."

Hob raised a hand to stop him and then faced Truman.

"Julius and I go back a long way so I know what a pain in the hind end he can be, but I'll not extend that sentiment to you. It is Friday afternoon, after all."

He moved to a small refrigerator tucked behind the door and pulled out two cans of beer, handing Truman one. Then he popped the top, taking a long pull. Truman did the same. Pained guttural sounds escaped Julius' mouth as he stood by watching. After another loud gulp Hob turned to him, flinching as if he'd just noticed his presence.

"Where'd you come from?"

Julius smirked and acted as if he was not the least bit perturbed.

"Do you want me to tell you why we're here or not?"

"Sure old friend but first you need some refreshment."

"Well, only if you insist."

He waited for Hob to return with the beer before continuing.

"We have reason to believe a certain piece of land has oil beneath it, a good deal of oil," he said between gulps. "I was hoping you could give us your expert opinion."

"And you know this how?"

"There was a secret meeting," he said, trying to spark Hob's interest. "A friend overheard someone discussing the prospect of oil. Now we…"

"Hold on a minute," Truman interrupted. "What do you mean he overheard?"

"When he was at the hotel, he heard them talking."

"Nicolai doesn't remember that night," he squinted skeptically, "does he?"

"His memory returned magically while he was sleeping." Julius shrugged. "No one can say why such happenings occur but they do."

"When was this?"

"He was on his way to tell Carlisle when the caseworker appeared," he said, suppressing a yawn. "He said he heard talk not just of oil but about bullets and Molotov cocktails. It was all rather confusing so I decided to postpone the rest until…"

"Stop!" Truman said, eying Julius. "When were you planning to tell me?"

"If you must know I needed time to think, to hatch a plan," he said, his tone dismissive.

"Now is as good a time as ever."

"But we can't go into that now, Truman. We have important questions to answer and we don't want to waste Hob's time. Will you allow us to address those first?"

Truman glanced at Hob, frustrated by the circumstances but admitting he had no right to subject Hob to their argument. He squinted at Julius.

"As long as I get the truth," he growled, "and I mean all of it."

"Of course you'll get it all," he answered. "Now, what do you say, Hob? Will you help us?"

Hob eyed him knowingly. "This is a business, Julius, not a charity."

"I have no money, Hob," he admitted. "But you already knew that. On the other hand, this could be an opportunity to get in on something lucrative."

"It sounds iffy."

"You oil people enjoy taking such risks, do you not?"

"Alright, Julius, I'll play along." He leaned on the edge of a table. "Tell me what you know."

"You're familiar with the Weeks brothers I take it?"

"Who isn't?" he said, frowning. "Those boys have way too much money. But they're not stupid. What do they have to do with this?"

Julius moved to a map of the town and pointed at a blue rectangle just off the western edge.

"The property in question is here, ten acres just outside the city limits."

"That land is not far from the Weeks' place. Is there a connection?"

"Perhaps there is. The brothers were overheard making plans to get hold of the property and the oil beneath it."

"But there've been no discoveries anywhere near there."

"Could they know something you don't?"

"With their kind of collateral anything's possible." He stood and paced the room. "They're supposed to be born again evangelicals but I've had dealings with them and I can promise you they have no scruples when it comes to making money. They've been stirring up unrest around here for years so they can grab up cheap property when landowners get intimidated and want to get out. I've even talked to the district attorney about them. But they're sly enough to keep a distance. If anything goes wrong their lackeys take the fall and they come out smelling like a rose."

"Yes, yes, but let's get back to the oil question. It's possible someone is trying to scam them. Can you tell us if the oil is actually there?"

"I'd love to get a hand up on those Weeks boys," he said, pacing the floor. "You really think you're onto something?"

"That's why we're here."

Hob's eyes lit up at the thought and he hurried to a table draped with long ribbons of graph paper, digging through the pile and tossing one after the other to the floor. After a moment he lifted one free and stretched the roll along the table end to end. Jagged lines of black ink ran the paper's length as if tracing a series of mountain ranges.

Hob studied the lines, following the peaks and valleys with his thick fingers. Then he checked the town map and returned to the paper, tracing the lines again until his finger settled on a single grid. He bent to read the tiny array of numbers and then stood to face them.

"Most oilmen would skim past this data. It's too close to the town. Drilling could be contentious and you might end up spending all your profits in court. But if you have money to burn you don't worry about details like that, especially if you have a boatload of politicos in your pocket."

"Are you saying the oil is there?"

"You're never sure until you drill but I'd bet my hat on it. Now, what's your connection to this property? I might be interested in getting in on the action."

"What's my connection? Oh, it's nothing other than I happen to live there."

Truman slammed his beer on the table and rushed to the map, running his hand along the town perimeter until his fingers came to a rest on the blue rectangle. Then he slowly turned around.

"The Weeks brothers want to buy the boarding house so they can get at the oil beneath those ten acres? Is that what I'm hearing?"

"After learning what Nicolai overheard, I had my suspicions. But I needed confirmation the oil was actually there. Now I have it," Julius said, beaming.

"What are you so happy about? We'll be out on the street soon."

"There are many hands yet to be played, Truman Birdsong," he said, waving off his concern. "You must have faith."

Hob peered at the map again. "If I remember right, that money-grubbing crook, Mercer, owns this property."

"Right you are, Hob. Speaking of hands to be played," Julius said, grinning, "that will be a most gratifying round."

"Glad to be of service if it means Mercer and the Weeks get their comeuppance."

Truman stood lost in thought, a thread of conversation nagging at the back of his mind. Julius turned and started for the door.

"We are in your debt, Hob, and with luck will repay you handsomely. I'll be in touch," he called over his shoulder.

Julius waited beside the van as Truman stepped through the exit, pausing on the broad staircase fronting the old building. The street stood empty in both directions. Julius rapped his fingers on the passenger window impatiently.

"There's no time to waste now that we know the oil is a near-certainty. We must return to the house without delay and devise a strategy."

"I'm not leaving until you tell me what you know."
He moved toward him. "What did Nicolai hear? What did
he tell you?"

"There wasn't time to ask him any details, as I told
you."

"Then tell me what you did learn."

"If I must," he sighed. "My sources said the meeting
was intended to galvanize disaffected locals into an
antigovernment militia of sorts. Nicolai heard talk along
those lines, including bullets and bombs, nothing all that
surprising I can assure you. Although one thing he said,
something about an envelope that I had intended to follow
up on, but when the Weeks brothers' goons appeared the
boy was quite upset. Besides, at that moment I had other
concerns."

"What goons do you mean?"

"Didn't I tell you? Oh, it all happened so fast and then
this pressing question of oil…"

"Tell me about the goons, Julius."

"When we were fleeing the caseworker, I discovered
them lurking behind the house, a big bearded baboon and
his pale companion. They were after the boy, of course.
One of them, Horace I think his name is, spotted him at the
hotel and…"

"He was at the house?"

"They were in the alley to be precise."

"And we just left Nicolai back there? What were you
thinking?"

"Not to worry, Truman. With Aiden's help I managed
to banish them," he boasted, a self-satisfied smirk on his
lips. "To be honest, I considered relocating the boy but
then I realized how easily we could fool those brainless
morons. After my little ruse, the house is the one place
they'll not go again."

"How can you be so sure?" Truman squinted at him.

"Oh, trust me, I'm sure."

"Those types don't give up easily."

"You weren't there and I was," he snapped, his tone dismissive. "They were scared out of what little in the way of wits they have between them. Now, we must make haste if I am to hatch a plan."

"We need to hurry alright but Nicolai's the reason, not you. And you'd better hope he's okay when we get there."

Chapter Twenty-six

Carlisle stirred in his chair, his eyes closed, his breath a slow wheeze. Nicolai glanced at him and continued reading aloud from *The Adventures of Huckleberry Finn*. He squinted at the pages, concentrating on each word, each syllable, sounding them out, stumbling along but making it through one sentence after another, paragraph by paragraph, the images springing to life in his mind, the boy, the slave, the broad river. He could scarcely believe he now read with an enjoyment he once thought impossible.

He paused in mid-sentence and cocked his head toward the porch window, alert for any sign of a car, prepared to run if necessary. The caseworker had not returned but the order for his removal remained in effect. Twice before he had rushed up the stairs, making for the tunnel, only to find it was a false alarm.

Carlisle suddenly jerked upright and looked about the room, his eyes red-rimmed and glassy. He leaned forward and peered at Nicolai. For a moment Nicolai thought he must be dreaming. Then he stood abruptly, pointing to the open book.

"Haven't you completed your exam yet? Time is almost up."

"What exam?" he said, confused.

Grabbing his cane, Carlisle pushed himself up and stumbled to the window, pulling aside the curtain. Then he pivoted. Nicolai stood, alarmed by the change in him.

"Carlisle, what's happened, what's wrong?" he said.

"Why have they switched classrooms on me?" he barked, a scowl twisting his face. "I always have the same room for exams!"

"I don't understand."

Carlisle whipped the cane toward him.

"You must stay seated until the exam is finished!"

"Why are you yelling?"

For a moment Carlisle stood in place staring at nothing, his eyes glazed. Then he swayed slightly before the cane dropped from his hand and he collapsed to the floor. Nicolai rushed to him and knelt, listening for his breath but hearing nothing. He put his head to his chest, again finding no sound. Grabbing his arms, he shook him once then again, the fear rising in his throat.

"Carlisle, please, please wake up," he pleaded. "Please don't..."

Unable to finish, he bent to listen again and then rose up, tears blinding him.

"Please, God, do something, help him."

Carlisle lay still. Nicolai drew back, fearing he was dead. Carlisle was the constant in his unsettled world, the calm center, the always reliable touchstone. Life without him was beyond imagining. A wave of panic surged through him and he jumped up, making for the door, thinking only of escape, to run, to hide.

Truman angled the van beneath the massive oak and climbed out, turning at the sound of an approaching car. Moments later Silas Macallan pulled his car next to the van. He ambled to where Truman stood waiting. Julius limped along behind him, annoyed by yet another delay.

"Ah, Truman, just the man I'm looking for," he announced. "I've come to collect on that drink you promised me."

Truman frowned and pointed him up the stairs. "I don't remember promising any drink, Dr. Macallan."

"Please, call me Silas or I'll feel positively ancient."

Truman joined him on the landing. Julius followed and retreated down the porch, brooding in silence.

"I don't remember promising anything, Silas." Truman glanced at the front door, his thoughts still on Nicolai.

"Well, yes," he murmured, pulling on his beard, "maybe it was more like an implied promise. Scotch tends to have that effect on me."

"I don't mean to be rude, Silas," he glanced toward the house again, "but I'm pressed for time. Is there something I can do for you?"

"Yes, yes, well I can see you've a lot on your mind, Truman, so I'll get straight to the point. Nicolai's mother has made a breakthrough with the new medication. She'll be leaving the hospital posthaste. I don't particularly like the decision but there it is. Social service has already arranged an apartment for her and she'll be moving in next week. The important bit is she wants the boy to come along."

"She wants him to live with her?" he said in disbelief. "But the people at child services want to send him away."

"Yes, I heard. That could pose a problem. On the other hand, judges tend to side with the mother if she's able to provide proper care."

"Could she be that much better?"

"I know it's unexpected but these new medications can work wonders. Besides, it's policy now for patients to leave the hospital as soon as they're deemed ready, as a cost-saving measure, of course. The bean counters always prevail. I wanted you and the boy to know as soon as I…"

His words vanished beneath the rumble of a car engine. Seconds later Mercer's white Cadillac crested the ridge, sliding to a stop in a cloud of white dust. He threw open the door and grabbed the sides of the car, straining to pull himself up. Sweat glistened on his cheeks.

Pausing to fish a handkerchief from his pocket, he ran it across his face, and then with a final effort pushed himself out. Julius peered at him over the porch railing, suddenly alert. He stepped next to Truman.

"Now what do you suppose brings our rotund landlord for a visit?" he said, speaking under his breath.

"He doesn't look too happy, whatever it is."

"Look at him," he hissed, "you can see the greed oozing from his fat face. Could it be he has been contacted by the Weeks brothers? He looks a tad nervous, I'm glad to say. Nothing gives me greater pleasure than to see Mercer squirm."

"It's clear he's here to talk but I intend to keep it short." Truman started for the stairs. "I want to check on the boy straight away so let me take the lead."

Julius gave no response. Truman moved to the top step.

"What do you want, Mercer?" Truman called down to him, making no effort to sound friendly.

"That's a fine way to talk to your employer."

"I'm busy."

"Yes, yes, of course. Time is money," he said, puffing as he climbed the steps. "Speaking of money, I've come to tell you people there's going to be some changes around here."

"What sort of changes?"

"We're going to be parting ways soon. You see, I've decided to get out of the landlord business and..."

"You're selling the house to the Weeks brothers." Truman interjected.

Mercer stared at him in disbelief, his mouth half open.

"How the devil could you know?"

"But we'll be able to keep living here," Truman said, ignoring the question.

"Uh, well, uh, not exactly," he stammered. "To tell the truth, the brothers have other plans for the property."

"What sort of plans?"

"They wouldn't say and, well, they're a secretive lot. But since this is a deal of a lifetime, I didn't see any reason to push it. You can understand that, now can't you?"

"I understand that all you care about is the money."

"Listen to me, son, it's not as plain and simple as that. You don't say no to the Weeks if you value your safety. They made an offer, a generous offer, and I didn't argue. I can't for the life of me understand why they'd want this old money pit but they must have their reasons. Maybe they plan to bulldoze the place and start over."

"Either way, we're out of luck."

"Life is like that, son."

Having stood by patiently, Julius stepped forward and pointed a bony finger at Mercer's chest.

"Before you start counting your gold coins there is something you should hear."

"Look, Rose, I don't need to hear anything from you," he groused, "especially more of your complaints."

Julius squinted up at him. The slightest hint of a smile crossed his lips then vanished as he leaned in, his voice slow and deliberate.

"What I have to say this time you *will* want to hear," he continued, barely containing his pleasure. "We found something very interesting in the attic, a box of old records, *your* records…"

He paused as the heavy grip of Truman's hand fell on his shoulder. Truman bent to face him, giving his head a slight shake.

"Not now, Julius."

"But why not let me?" he pleaded. "If I could only…"

"Now is not the time."

"What's wrong, Rose?" Mercer snorted. "Cat got your tongue? Well, I don't have any use for whatever it is you're trying to sell. It can't be worth much. Besides, I don't remember any so-called records."

"You said what you have to say," Truman announced, pointing him to his car, "so leave us. I'm too busy to waste time on what might or might not happen."

"Yes, leave us and go count your money," Julius sneered, "or whatever it is you slum landlords do for fun."

"Rose, you bastard, you're one I won't mind putting out on the street," he growled. "I have half a mind to…"

Aiden burst through the door, his face pale, his eyes darting.

200

"Truman must come quick! Carlisle is hurt, and he is!"

Truman gave Julius a glance before rushing through the doorway. Seconds later he stood over Carlisle's crumpled form and knelt next to him, trying to find a pulse. Silas appeared opposite him and pressed a stethoscope to Carlisle's chest. He nodded to Truman as Carlisle began to stir, his eyelids fluttering for a moment before easing open. He looked around the room.

"Where am I?" he croaked, trying to rise up. "Whose classroom is this?"

"Don't you worry about that just now," Silas said, putting a hand to his chest. "You rest easy. You've had yourself a fall."

"But where is my student?"

"Carlisle, you ornery mule, listen to your old friend. Let me take a look at you." He studied Carlisle's face. "Did you hit your head?"

"No, I didn't hit my head!" he shouted. "I have an exam to complete. My student was still working."

"Do you have any pain?"

"Stop badgering me. I have an exam to…" He suddenly fell back, panting. "Just give me a moment."

Silas turned to Truman.

"The fall isn't the problem. I need to do some tests but I suspect this has to do with the encephalitis."

"Why does he think he's was back at the college."

"Post-infection complications can involve dementia, delusions, that sort of thing. That lingering flu may have weakened him. And there may be a secondary virus or infection. Either way, he's delusional and imagines he has a student with him."

Truman glanced around the room, spotting the open copy of *The Adventures of Huckleberry Finn* where it had fallen.

"Maybe he did have a student," he said, facing Aiden. "Where's Nicolai, Aiden? He was here, wasn't he?"

"I heard him, and I did, reading to Carlisle. But I had a talking book so I put on my earphones."

"You don't know which way he went?"

"I don't know, no, I don't," he murmured. Then all at once he snapped to attention. "No, I do remember, I do. I felt footsteps running, running to the back of the house."

Truman pivoted, spotting Julius pressed to the corner, his eyes on Carlisle. Truman called to him with no response. He tried again.

"Julius," he yelled, "snap out of it. I need your help."

He slowly shifted his gaze. Truman locked eyes with him, speaking deliberately.

"We need to find Nicolai. I'm guessing he got scared and went to hide, probably at my place. Go check."

"But Carlisle..." he whispered.

"Silas will take good care of him. Go find the boy."

The alleyway stood empty as Nicolai slipped out of the evening half-light, through the garage door and into the dim interior. Darkness surrounded him, stopping him. All at once the damp of the cave filled his senses, engulfing him, suffocating him, the dank smell of mud, the wet chill of glistening rock.

The heavy air closed in around him. He gasped for breath. Voices called from far above, loud and threatening. Images flashed before him, the open hole, the swirling earth, and a wave of nausea moved through him, rising in his throat.

Then in a flash it all vanished and he was back in the garage. He could breathe again. Another set of odors drifted past, the sour of mildew, the reek of stale cardboard, somehow comforting in their newness.

He squinted into the dim confines, spotting a silhouette of stacked boxes along the back wall, beyond a side door. Feeling his way along, he made for the corner, seeking escape from his thoughts, his fears. He wedged himself between the wall and the boxes and closed his eyes.

The space stood still around him. Nothing stirred beyond the door but the rattle of wind, the rustle of dry grass. He leaned his head against the rough siding. Carlisle will be alright, he told himself.

Suddenly, the untruth of the thought seized him. He should never have left the room. He had heard Aiden find Carlisle but they still might need help, an extra pair of hands, his eyes. He knew he must return in spite of his fear.

He started to pull himself upright and then froze as a shaft of light split the darkness. Someone had opened the door. Holding his breath, he strained to listen as he eased back into place. Footsteps moved near the doorway, starting and then stopping. His heart pounded in his throat. Had Horace and Jerome returned? Had others been sent in their place? Then a voice sounded across the room, Julius' voice.

"Are you here, boy?" he whispered.

Nicolai said nothing, unsure of himself, unwilling to trust anything.

"Carlisle was asking after you," he continued, his voice stronger. "He was awake, talking nonsense but talking nonetheless. The doctor is with him now."

Nicolai took a breath, relieved at the news. Julius edged along the wall, peering into the near-darkness, trying to guess where he might hide.

"You believed Carlisle had died, didn't you? I know how much he means to you. That's why you ran." A note of frustration crept into this voice. "Is that why you're refusing to talk now?"

Nicolai sat unmoving, unable to speak, his thoughts racing with all he had heard.

"Why won't you answer, boy?" Julius hissed, his patience gone. "Do you think I like stumbling around in the dark?"

Nicolai started to stand when sunlight again pierced the darkness, filling the garage. He ducked back behind the boxes, squinting between them as he surveyed the bright room. The door stood half open, Julius nowhere in sight.

Nicolai sat back, wondering why he had left so suddenly. It made no sense. He rose again, planning to leave as well when a shadow fell across the doorway, followed by the backlit bulk of Horace's hulking form. Stepping inside, he seemed to fill the entire room. Nicolai pressed himself into the corner, unable to breathe, unable to think, panic gripping his chest.

He looked about the room. The side door was open a crack. Horace turned toward the opposite wall. Without thinking Nicolai bolted for the door, sending cardboard boxes flying in all directions. Bottle-filled crates crashed to the floor in a din of shattered glass. A stack of wooden poles followed, clattering onto the concrete, nearly tripping him as he made for the exit.

The side door seemed almost within reach when a massive hand grabbed him by the hair, jerking him up and off the ground in one motion. He landed hard, for an instant losing his breath. Scrambling to his feet, he leapt toward the door but Horace snatched a handful of collar and yanked him backwards. He twisted around, freeing himself and in a flash planted his toe just under Horace's left kneecap. The big man staggered briefly then backhanded him, launching him against the wall. He slid to the floor in a heap.

Looming over him, Horace raised his club-like fist. Nicolai pressed himself to the wall, closing his eyes and waiting for the blow. Instead a high-pitched scream filled the room. He looked up as a wooden pole caught the big man in the jaw, sending him careening toward the opposite wall.

Nicolai jumped up and turned to see Julius standing on a crate, pole in hand. Wielding it with both hands like a long sword, he swung again but managed only a glancing blow. Horace lunged at him, knocking him from his perch and to the floor. On his back, Julius swung again, catching him on the shin. He groaned and fell to his knees. Jumping up, Julius raised the pole again, pointing Nicolai to the door.

"Run, you fool!"

"But what about…?" he yelled as Horace clambered to his feet.

"Run!" Julius called out, again turning to face the big man.

Chapter Twenty-seven

Truman stepped off the ladder and entered the tunnel. The top of his head nearly touched the stone ceiling. According to Julius' description, the storm shelter sat somewhere ahead. He took a breath, trying to reign in his dread of tight spaces. His pulse pounded in his ears. Reason can win over fear, he mumbled to himself, dismayed to hear doubt in his voice.

Aiming the flashlight on the path ahead, he forced each foot forward, thinking of the shelter itself, imagining it open, roomy, a place of air and light. The tunnel seemed to narrow with every step, grazing his arms, grabbing at him. He hunched his shoulders, pulling himself in tight, keeping his eyes to the floor.

His thoughts shifted to Nicolai. His dream was to live with his mother. What could possibly be wrong with that? That he would no longer live in the house was the inevitable result. Yet Truman was unable to imagine the place without him. He silenced the troublesome thought. For the time being, finding the boy was enough.

All at once the tunnel opened onto the low-roofed shelter with its single hanging light bulb and shelves of canned goods. He swung the flashlight into the corners and back up the tunnel. The space stood empty.

Mounting the short set of steps, he threw open the double doors and took a breath, relieved to be back in the open air. He surveyed the wide lawn. Nothing seemed out of place. Then the creak of a rusty hinge caught his attention and he shifted his gaze to the garage, spotting the open door. A sinking feeling settled in his gut.

The western sky, blood red and fading, hovered above the horizon as Nicolai crouched next to Truman's cabin. He glanced back at the garage. Seconds earlier a crash followed by a scream had trailed off to silence, leaving him shivering in spite of the warm evening. He would not let himself imagine a reason.

Abandoning his plan to reach the house, fearing he would be seen, he instead slipped through the cabin's back window, the same window he had climbed out when Truman caught him sneaking in. He crept down the hall, pausing to peek out the windows for any sign of Horace. An odd odor, one he could not place, drifted past. He guessed it must be Truman's paints or something to do with stained glass.

Reaching the kitchen door, he hesitated, something in the back of his mind sounding an unspoken alarm. All at once, it came to him. Horace was not the type to act alone. He stepped to the window, hoping for a view of the garage when a hand circled his neck. He froze. The earlier smell, the stale odor of cigarettes and beer, swept past him. He first imagined Horace but another voice spoke from behind his ear, followed by the cold steel of a knife blade pressed to his cheek.

"A pretty boy like you doesn't want to get all cut up," the voice rasped, "now does he?"

Nicolai recognized Jerome's hoarse tenor and silently cursed himself for his stupidity. He should have known he would return.

"Answer me, you little twerp."

"No," he mumbled, disgusted with himself.

"No, what?"

"What do you think?" he sneered, self-loathing blotting out his fear. "You know anyone who *wants* to get cut?"

"You best not get smart with me, boy. I don't care if the Weeks want you in one piece." He set the knife on the counter. "Besides, I don't need this pig-sticker. I know how to hurt so it doesn't show."

"Let me go!" Nicolai yelled, struggling to free himself.

Jerome clamped his forearm across Nicolai's throat.

"You're a nasty little kid and never should've heard our plans for the judge and district attorneys," he hissed. "The Weeks brothers don't want you talking to anyone. Maybe they'll let me cut your tongue out."

Nicolai glanced at the switchblade and all thought, all intention vanished, leaving him primal, instinctive, an animal meaning to survive. All at once he wrenched free, kicking blindly but with luck, hitting Jerome in the groin and sending him to the floor. Grabbing the knife, Nicolai jumped over him, making for hallway, the only way out. Jerome scrambled after him.

He reached the threshold an instant before Jerome tackled him, hurtling them both into the wall. Kicking his way free, Nicolai jabbed the knife at him, slicing his forearm. Jerome cried out before slapping him hard and sending the knife skittering to the corner.

The second blow was a closed fist. Nicolai collapsed to the floor. The room swirled around him, tilted and cloaked in a white veil. Jerome floated past, his shirtsleeve drenched in blood. Nicolai struggled to focus, using the wall to push himself upright. Jerome turned toward him, the switchblade in his hand. Nicolai pushed himself from the wall, stumbling toward the door, the white veil returning, blinding him. A muffled cry sounded behind him. Then all went black.

Stepping lightly, Truman slipped through the garage door and pressed himself to the wall. He forced himself to wait as his eyes slowly adjusted to the dim space. Horace's hulking shape emerged in the far corner, a blood-stained dowel in his hand. Julius' lay crumpled at his feet. Truman stood frozen in place, unable to move as Horace raised the pole over his head.

All at once he came to his senses. Leaping across the room, he grabbed the dowel and pulled with all his strength, wrenching it free. Horace pivoted. His bloodied face held a mix of surprise and rage. He lunged at Truman, knocking him to his back. Concrete tore at his elbows as he slid backwards. A tower of boxes tumbled to the floor.

Horace rushed at him but he managed to free the dowel, giving a tight, forceful swing. All at once time seemed to slow, the light becoming crystalline, the arcing of the pole, the whisper of it slicing the air, the crack of wood on bone. For an instant Horace stood suspended, hovering above him like a gargoyle, his nose shattered, his mouth spitting blood. Then he collapsed in a groaning heap.

Truman pulled himself free and scrambled to his feet, ready to strike again if necessary but Horace raised himself and then crumpled to the floor. Truman rushed to where Julius lay face down, relieved to find him still breathing. His eyes fluttered open and he peered at Truman as if to ensure he had his full attention. Then he pushed a hand toward the doorway.

"The boy... Nicolai... he ran there," he wheezed, speaking between breaths. "You must go find him."

"He was here?"

"He was hiding... wouldn't show himself." He nodded weakly. "I left... but then I spotted the oaf..."

"You came back for him."

"No choice..." he whispered, struggling for breath. "You must find him."

"I can't leave you like this."

"You must. The other one, Jerome, I saw him... near your house," he whispered, grabbing Truman's hand. "The boy would go there first. I'm sure of it. You must go now."

He squeezed Truman's hand and fell back, gasping. Truman glanced out the door, torn between the man lying before him and the boy's safety. Julius was hurt, how seriously he could not tell, but Nicolai's life was at risk. He knew then what he must do. Using his belt, he quickly bound Horace's hands to his feet. Then, patting Julius' shoulder to let him know, he rushed out the door.

209

Moments later he stepped onto the cabin porch and gave the partially open door a shove, letting it swing open on its own. He slipped through and jerked to a stop, baffled by the strange sight before him. A figure lay stretched across the living room carpet, arms folded on the chest, head tilted at an odd angle. A yellowed handkerchief had been draped across the face.

Truman lifted the rag, recognizing Jerome at once. He guessed his neck was broken. Glancing around the room, he could make little sense of the scene. He hurriedly checked the rest of the house and returned to the porch, scanning the hillside. Nicolai was nowhere in sight.

Moments later he burst through the front door of the house and checked the living room, dismayed to find no sign of the boy. He hurried to Carlisle's room. Against the far corner Aiden stood rocking back and forth in a manic rhythm, his face pinched with worry. To Truman's relief, Silas was still there. He yanked off his stethoscope as Truman pointed toward the back door.

"It's Julius," he gasped, trying to catch his breath. "He's in the garage... badly hurt. Come with me, quick."

Silas stared at him as if he was speaking a foreign language. Aiden jerked to attention.

"I will help Julius, and I will."

"No, Aiden, stay here with Carlisle," Truman said, trying to clear his jumbled thoughts. "Call the sheriff and tell him to get up here right away. We'll need an ambulance."

Silas stood, grabbing his bag. "I thought I'd misheard you. What's happened?"

"I'll tell you on the way."

"But what about the boy?"

"He's still missing."

Chapter Twenty-eight

Sirens wailed in the distance. Truman stood by the garage door as Silas knelt beside Julius and gently rolled him onto his back, running his fingers along his ribs. He winced weakly. His breath filled the small space with a panting gurgle.

Truman turned away, pained by the sight. In the near corner Horace stirred and groaned weakly. Truman glared at him, fighting the urge to kick him. When he turned back, Julius had opened his eyes. Truman crouched next to him. Julius waved him closer.

"The boy... Nicolai..." he wheezed, "you've found him?"

"Not yet," he answered, gripped by the sudden realization that Julius was lying there because of him. "Julius, if I'd had any idea what I was sending you into, I..."

"Not at your cabin?" he interrupted. "I was sure he would go there."

"I found Jerome instead," he said, shaking his head. "I think his neck was broken. He was stretched out on the floor in some sort of burial pose."

"A burial pose... as in a ritual?" His eyes flickered wide for an instant before narrowing. "Not relevant. You must stay focused on the boy. Need I explain the danger?"

"But we've got to get you to the hospital."

"No time for that," he murmured, shaking his head. "Leave the doctor to his work and go find Nicolai."

Truman looked up at Silas, spotting a momentary glint of resignation in his eyes before he turned away.

"You can't do anymore here," he said, busying himself with Julius. "Get yourself moving and find the boy. I'll flag down the ambulance."

Nicolai crouched in the hollowed trunk of the giant oak, blocked from the outside world by a thick wedge of iron-like heartwood that rose wall-like above him, eventually melding with the living outer layer. Biting back tears, he muttered a prayer for Julius. A vision of him facing Horace's hulking form rose in his thoughts, blotting out all else. He closed his eyes and tried to block the memory.

Instead, the old hotel where he had overheard Jerome talking with the two brothers filled his senses, the stale stench of mildew, the clattering glass. The red-headed brother's words echoed through his thoughts, now clear and understandable. Suddenly their meaning became clear. The brothers wanted Jerome and his brother to kill a judge and district attorney. The envelope held instructions and payment. Might they have a similar plan for him? He shivered at the notion, again trying to banish his dark thoughts.

On impulse, he reached out to touch the rough wood surrounding him, feeling for the great tree's spirit, praying that it might banish all evil, all danger. Even knowing his foolishness, he was unable to resist. He felt somehow responsible for all that had happened, as if all the harm, all the bad, had followed his arrival like thunder follows lightning. Tears welled beneath his closed eyes.

An image of his mother came to him, her face calm, her eyes clear. She stood alongside a tree-lined sidewalk, beckoning him to join her. A warm yellow light filled the street. A voice called his name. For an instant, he imagined the voice as hers but her lips were unmoving. She waved him closer, seemingly unaware of the sound. The voice called again and he strained to listen, the cadence familiar, almost recognizable.

Truman scanned the yard and alleyway as he hurried toward the house, scouring his memory for some clue to Nicolai's whereabouts. He could find nothing. Did the boy encounter Jerome in the cabin and, if so, what happened? Did he have a part in Jerome's death? And why would he or anyone else take the time to stretch the body out on the floor just so? He turned as an ambulance roared up the alley, sliding to a stop beside the garage.

Troubled by the image, he continued up the hill, rounding the corner and spotting Tico and a deputy at the top of the porch stairs. Aiden stood behind them slumped against the wall, his eyes tilted skyward as if listening to an unseen world. Something pulled at the edge of Truman's thoughts as he hurried up the steps.

"Aiden, shouldn't you be with Carlisle?" he said, panting.

"Carlisle of the protected tower, of the walled city, is sleeping, yes, sleeping. Silas said he is out of danger, out and not in, no not in."

"Alright, Aiden, I understand." Truman put a hand on his shoulder as he turned to face Tico. "Jerome Bell is laid out on the floor of my cabin. I'm guessing he has a broken neck."

"Now there's some news," Tico said, his eyebrows jumping. "Any idea who did us that favor?"

"No, but his friend is down at the garage."

"Does he have a broken neck too?"

"More like a bad headache. He was sleeping it off when I left."

"Better go take care of that one," Tico said, motioning to the deputy. Truman watched him leave, and then faced the sheriff.

"They were after the boy, Tico," he said, shaken by the thought. "And now he's gone missing."

"Well, it may not mean much. I'd run too if I was him and had Jerome Bell on my tail." He leaned over the rail and spit. "He's a nasty piece of work, that one... or he was anyway."

"I can't figure where Nicolai could've gone. I've looked everywhere."

"That boy likes to run. I'll bet he's halfway to Abilene by now."

Suddenly, Aiden jerked upright. Truman ignored him, his thoughts on Nicolai, but something again pulled at the edge of his mind. He turned and studied Aiden's face, the turn of his head, the glint of his darting eyes.

"What is it, Aiden?" he said, straining to listen. "What do you hear?"

Aiden stepped away from the wall, waving his cane like a divining rod as he started down the stairs. Truman followed close behind, the hair on the back of his neck rising with each step. Aiden stopped beneath the massive oak and leaned toward him, speaking under his breath.

"Carlisle's oak is a place of wonder and refuge, and it is," he whispered, nodding toward the tree. "You must see for yourself, Truman Birdsong."

"What do you mean?"

He made no reply.

Pulled from his dream, Nicolai jumped to attention. He looked about, confused for a moment by the dim, unfamiliar space. The muffled voice called his name again. He clambered up the wall-like wedge and then hesitated, untrusting of his own senses. He had heard a voice but how could he be sure whose? Fear gripped him that he would come face to face with Jerome or Horace or both.

He stood frozen, unsure what to do. Leaning against the trunk, he pressed himself to the heartwood, feeling its solidity, its strength, reminding him of his vow to no longer live in fear. Then he squeezed into the narrow opening, working his way out.

Pushing through the last of the passage, he paused and squinted into the dying light. For a moment, he could see nothing. Then a face emerged from the silhouetted mass of branches, Truman's face. Without hesitating, he scrambled out. Truman lifted him over the gnarled roots, clutching him to his chest and then pulling away, embarrassed by the display.

"You're safe now." Truman held him at arm's length, looking him over. He pointed to his swollen jaw. "What happened here?"

"I guess that was Horace…," he said, wincing as he fingered the spot, "or maybe Jerome Bell when he knocked me down."

"Jerome was at my place when you saw him?"

"He was waiting for me but I got away."

"Tell me exactly what happened, everything you remember."

"I kicked him but he grabbed me. That's when he hit me. I was woozy but I ran." He pointed to the tree. "Then next thing I remember, I was here."

"He was alive when you left him?"

Nicolai stared at him, confused by the question. "What do you mean?"

"I found him on the floor of the cabin, dead."

"But I… I took his knife… I cut his arm. Can you die from that?"

Truman gave his head a shake. "Not this time. Someone broke his neck."

"But who…?" He glanced up the hill. "What about Horace? Is he also… you know?"

"You don't need to be afraid."

"I'm not afraid!" he snapped. "I just want to know."

"He's alive. The sheriff has him now."

"The sheriff is here? I need to talk to him."

"What, you mean right away?"

"I mean now. It's important."

Nicolai looked past him, spotting Tico beside the porch stairs, listening.

"I'm all ears, son," he said as he approached, "but don't be wasting my time. I can't be bothered with a child's fairytales."

"I'm not a dang child!" he barked. "I'm thirteen and I'm not wasting your stupid time! You'd be sitting around drinking coffee if it wasn't for me."

"You sure do have an attitude, boy."

"Just because I'm a kid with no parents doesn't mean I lie about everything."

"Well then, get on with it," Tico grumbled.

"And keep hold of your temper," Truman added, laying a hand on his shoulder, "so you don't forget something important."

"I'll try," he said, his thoughts returning to the scene. "I remembered what happened that night in the old hotel, the night I fell into the cave. Will you believe me if I tell you?"

"We trust that you'll tell the truth, Nicolai." He cast a quick glance at Tico. "Isn't that right, sheriff?"

"Go ahead," he nodded, "and say your piece."

"I was up on the third floor but I could hear what was said. The meeting had ended and most everybody was gone when these two red-headed brothers, the Weeks I think they're called, met with Jerome Bell and his brother right below where I was hiding. I could see real good. The red-headed brothers told Jerome they wanted him to kill a district attorney and a judge."

Tico looked at him askance. "You're telling me you witnessed all that yourself?"

"And then they gave Jerome an envelope with addresses and money in it."

"This is important, son," he said, moving closer. "You've got to be sure what you're telling me is what you remember and not just something you dreamed up. I don't have time to go chasing after a bedtime story. Judges tend to frown on that sort of police work.

"Besides, I'll bet you a donut Jerome's brother will call you a liar. Too bad you don't have a way to prove what you say is true. Judges tend to like that."

"I do have a way."

Tico squinted at him. "Alright, I'll bite. What can you give me?"

"Horace was there when the brothers paid them."

Tico pulled at his ear, for a moment lost in thought. Then he refocused his gaze, locking eyes with Nicolai.

"Yes, I believe we can make that work if we play our cards right. You just sit tight."

Pulling out his phone, he started for his car.

Chapter Twenty-nine

Truman hurried through the sliding hospital doors and into the hallway, a sense of dread creeping over him with every step. Mercurial pools of fluorescent light shifted and jumped along the gleaming corridors in manic rhythm. Stripped of linens, floor-bound rows of plastic mattresses edged the walls like corpses.

He rounded the corner and the sharp odor of antiseptic and cleaning fluid wafted past him. Silas stood midway down the hall, waiting outside of the emergency room. He moved away from the doorway at Truman's approach.

"He's been asking for you," he said, his expression grim. "You'd best hurry. They'll be taking him in for surgery soon."

"Is it bad?"

"He's had a punctured a lung and lacerated liver, but the worst of it he's got no room in there, twisted up as he is. It puts a tremendous strain on his organs." He placed a hand on Truman's shoulder. "You should know that he's refused pain medication until he speaks with you."

"But doesn't he need it?"

"Of course he does. The pain must be intense."

"Why would he refuse?"

"He's a secretive bugger so I don't know for sure and won't guess," he said, pulling at his beard. "Whatever he has to say, it must be important. He wants only you to hear it. I won't be in there with you. You can handle that, now can't you?"

Truman nodded before stepping into the room. Surrounded by tubes and monitors, Julius lay curled on his side nearly swallowed by the bedcovers, his face like wax paper, yellowish-gray next to the white of the sheets. He seemed to be asleep. Truman hesitated, unsure whether to stay or leave. Then Julius stirred and slowly opened his eyes.

"I dreamt you were here," he whispered, "and here you are."

Truman stepped closer. "Silas said it was urgent."

"Sit and listen." He motioned him toward the bed. "I need your help if you'll give it."

"Of course I will."

"You remember when I told you of my books," he said, wincing as pushed himself up, "the ones I write when we lose a housemate?"

"I remember. The last was about Simon, if I recall."

"Yes, and now there is another."

"I don't understand. Silas says Carlisle will recover."

"The boy is going to live with his mother. I have been working on his book for some while, knowing his leaving for one reason or another was only a matter of time. The book is in the top drawer of my desk. You must finish it for me."

"You can finish it yourself when you get out of here."

"Don't patronize me, Truman," he wheezed, "I deal in truth only, remember? Now, will you do what I ask?"

"Tell me what you want," he said with a sigh.

"The boy... Nicolai... I was terrified of him in the beginning," he said between breaths. "I started writing his story to vent my anger and frustration, but over time I grew fond of him in spite of myself. I imagine he'd be horrified by the thought, so spare him that bit of confession.

"What's important for him to know is how brave, how strong he is despite his difficult life. I know something of that just as you do. You must help him come to believe, Truman, to believe in himself."

"I'm not much good at that sort of thing, Julius."

"But you'll try."

"I'll try."

"I know I've tested your patience and your trust. Please forgive my failings."

All at once he was gripped by a fit of coughing. Truman waited for it to pass before answering.

"You can make it up to me later."

"Truman, you must enjoy living in the land of denial."

"I call it hope."

"Then teach your trick to the boy. He of all people needs hope."

He fell back on the bed, exhausted by the effort. An operating room nurse appeared at the door. Truman bent toward his ear.

"You rest now," he whispered. "I'll see you soon."

A gusting wind coursed through the hospital courtyard, smelling of rain and live oaks. Unable to tolerate the sterile glare of the waiting room, Truman had moved outside. He paced the short stretch of sidewalk beyond the exit, keeping his eyes to the ground, trying to avoid the distraught faces lining the windows.

His mind went round and round ruminating on all that had happened, but his jumbled thoughts were beyond reclaiming. Shadows crisscrossed the concrete below him like prison bars. He looked up as a pair of competing sirens arose in the distance.

Silas appeared beside him, taking his arm and leading him to a nearby bench. He pulled a metal flask from his coat pocket and unscrewed the top, offering it to him. Truman peered into his face, knowing at once the meaning of the gesture. Julius was gone. He tried to speak and then lowered his head, unable to find the words. Silas pressed the flask to his arm.

"Go on now, it'll do you good. Death is no stranger to me, as you might guess. But some losses are harder than others. The surprise is that oftentimes the imperfect ones, those that test our patience and our trust the most, are the ones who hit us hardest."

An hour later, Truman stood alone in the darkness, his chest filled with a deep melancholy that slowly climbed into his throat. He could not return to the house. Lightning flashed over the horizon in yellow sheets, throwing the rooftops before him into silhouette. Moments later the headlights of a turning car swept along the street and then were gone.

Julius' voice came again, roaming his thoughts like a flock of birds, circling but never landing. He heard no accusation, no blame for what had happened to him. Yet try as he might he could not shake the feeling he was somehow responsible.

He stepped up onto the porch, wishing for escape, for something, anything to free his mind from all he had seen. Reaching the door, he hesitated, a part of him hoping he had other reasons for being there. Another part did not care.

He raised his hand to the door and held it there, unable to knock, asking himself what he wanted. He had no answer. All at once, the door swung open and Kennis stood before him in a bathrobe, her hair wet, her face gleaming beneath the porch light.

Without saying a word, she took his hand and pulled him inside, wrapping herself around him. He tried to speak but his throat choked with emotion. She pulled away from him, peering into his eyes.

"I know what happened and I'm sorry. But you're here now and you can leave it all out there for a little while," she said, nodding toward the door as if reading his mind. "Right now I want you to be here with me and nowhere else."

Seeing no question in his eyes she took his hand again, leading him to her bedroom. He did not resist. The past, the future seemed to fall away, leaving only the warmth of her skin against his, the lavender smell of her hair, the smooth curve of her back.

A narrow stream of water spilled over the fern-covered cliff, drifting into the small, circular grotto below. Truman watched it weaving back and forth in the shifting wind, sometimes disappearing quietly into an emerald green pool, other times ringing bell-like against a limestone ledge. Kennis lay stretched out next to him, her dark hair glistening, her face turned to the sun.

He looked up as a cloud appeared above the cliff, followed by another and then another, each one darker than the last. Mesmerized by the strange sight, he watched them swirling overhead, gathering, thickening. Within seconds a wall of blue-gray filled the sky, blocking out the sun and casting the pool deep in shadow. A chill wind rippled across the surface.

Disturbed by the change, he turned to Kennis. She had vanished. He jumped up, searching the grotto, finding no sign of her. The intermittent ringing of the stone grew louder, rising in tone. A growing anxiety gripped his chest.

A flash of light caught his eye and, instinctively, he turned toward the pool, its green depths lost in shadow. He squinted into the dark surface. For a moment he believed he saw movement. Then all at once, a shaft of sunlight pierced the water, throwing Kennis' face into relief, pale and unmoving.

He jerked upright and looked about, confused by the unfamiliar room, the creaking bed. The ring of a phone drifted through the doorway, followed by the hushed tone of Kennis' voice. Moments later she appeared at the threshold, disappointment in her eyes.

"That was Tico."

"He knows I'm here?" He jumped out of bed as if the sheriff might walk into the room at any moment.

She squinted at him. "Would it matter if he did?"

"No… I… it's just that…" he sighed, realizing his ridiculousness. "I was surprised, is all."

She moved to where he stood and pressed herself against him.

"He doesn't know. I can't say the same for the old lady across the street. Nothing gets past her." The hint of a smile crossed her lips. "Anyway, Tico said if I saw you to tell you he needs to see you right away."

"What about?"

"Something to do with Jerome Bell and the boy."

"That doesn't sound good," he said, reminded of his concern that Nicolai had something to do with the man's death. "I'd better get over there quick."

"Oh, I knew you'd say that," she moaned, again pressing herself to him.

"Well, I don't guess I have to leave right away."

"No," she said, pretending to pout, "you have to go where you're needed. But that also means you have to come back here as soon as possible."

Minutes later, he stepped into the sheriff's office. Tico stood bent over his desk, shuffling through a stack of tattered folders and muttering to himself. Nicolai sat slumped in a chair opposite him. Seeing Truman, he sat up, his glum expression brightening. Tico looked up.

"Truman, it's a good thing you showed up. Your boy here was pestering me with questions for no good reason and…"

"That's not true!" Nicolai jumped up, appealing to Truman. "He was telling lies about Parfit."

"Sit yourself down," Truman cast him a stern glance and pointed to the chair, "and let the sheriff finish."

"We'll get to Parfit in a minute. I was looking for you because the judge has ordered me to pick him up," he nodded at Nicolai. "Children's services are back on their high horse about sending him to reform school or some such place."

"They can't make me go," Nicolai sneered."I'll run away first."

"I have no doubt you will." He pointed a finger at his chest. "But before you make tracks, you'll hear what I have to say. Are we agreed?"

Nicolai squirmed as Truman squinted at him, waiting for an answer. He sighed and faced the sheriff.

"Yes sir, we are agreed."

"Alright, then. Now, I've always gotten along with the folks over at children's services. But I've never had much use for the supervisor. She's forgotten what it's like to be a youngster, if she ever knew, and she's too heavy-handed in her dealings with teenagers."

He leaned across the desk and peered at Nicolai.

"The reason I picked you up is so I could tell the judge I did what he asked of me. But then the question is where we go from here… other than reform school, of course. Well, it turns out your history of running away isn't so bad after all. It gives me an easy way of explaining to the judge why I wasn't able to hand you over to that witch of a supervisor. You just ran away again, no big surprise."

"But won't that get him in more trouble with the judge?" Truman asked.

"We're so far down that trail one more disappearance won't matter much. The important point is that it buys us time. I'm convinced the judge can be swayed with the right argument. But that's my department. You've got other concerns just now, like the conversation young Tate here nosed his way into."

"It had something to do with Parfit?" Truman said.

"Last night the old man checked himself back into the state hospital."

"He checked himself *back* in? You mean he's been there before?"

"The man has spent most of his adult life in and out the place. I believe they say he's got the schizophrenia but to my mind he's just a crazy old coot."

"He's not crazy!" Nicolai yelled, nearly coming out of his seat. "He was struck by lightning, is all."

Truman pointed him back to the chair. "You can have your say in a minute."

"I figure the lightning tale is just another of his crazy stories," Tico continued. "I've heard plenty. But that's neither here nor there. What's important is the evidence I found next to Jerome Bell's body."

"What sort of evidence?"

"The strange sort, the sort you don't see every day, a polished clam shell."

"What does that have to do with Parfit?"

"Boy," he said, turning to Nicolai, "can you guess?"

Nicolai stared at him, the meaning slowly coming clear.

"It can't be," he murmured.

"The shell was polished mother of pearl. There's only one explanation for finding it there."

"Maybe you made a mistake," he said, standing. "Lots of people collect shells."

"There was no mistake."

"Maybe it's some other kind of shell."

"You know better, don't you, son?"

Nicolai rose from the chair and began pacing before the windows.

"Parfit did it?" he said, his voice barely above a whisper. "Parfit killed him?"

Truman looked from one to the other, uncomprehending.

"Tico, what are you saying? What does a shell have to do with Parfit?"

"He always carries a clam shell for luck. He's known for it. In his mind it has some connection to the lightning story."

"It does have a connection," Nicolai said, stopping to face them. "He was carrying a bag of clams when the lightning hit. He said they saved his life."

"But Jerome had his neck broken," Truman said, still puzzled. "Parfit's an old man."

"I know the old boy seems harmless enough in a crazy sort of way," Tico said, wagging his finger through the air, "but he was a green beret in Viet Nam, trained to kill."

"So you're going to arrest him for murder?"

Nicolai leapt at Tico's desk, his face distraught.

"Please don't, please," he pleaded, leaning across the desktop, "he can't go to prison."

Truman placed a hand on his shoulder and gently pulled him back.

"Tico, if what you say is true, Parfit probably saved his life. That's got to count for something."

"Whoa, boys," he held up both hands, "no need to jump to conclusions. I believe our investigation will show self-defense. Jerome had a knife in his possession at the time. Besides, the judge has no stomach for tangling with the hospital over one of their oldest patients."

"So, as long as he stays locked up he won't go to prison."

"Truman, you have an interesting way of putting things." He shuffled through the folders again. "Now, I have to go see the district attorney. Our friend, Horace, is claiming the Weeks brothers hired Jerome and his brother to take out the D. A., assistant D. A. and judge just as the boy heard. But I doubt it will hold. Horace is not exactly your model citizen. Besides which, rich as they are, the Weeks will probably weasel their way out of it."

Truman watched him leave, ruminating over all he had heard. His thoughts turned to Nicolai. He stood facing the windows, staring at nothing. Truman studied him a moment, his mind refusing to accept the fact of his leaving. An image of Julius came to him, reminding him of his promise, and he moved to where Nicolai stood.

"With all that's happened I didn't get around to telling you something important. Your mother is going to be leaving the hospital and getting a place of her own. She wants you to come live with her."

"But how can she?" Nicolai stared at him in disbelief. "You saw how she was."

"Dr. Macallan said the new medications can work wonders. She's due to move into an apartment next week. That's good news, isn't it?"

"I guess it is."

"You don't sound so sure. Living with her is what you want, isn't it?"

"I thought I did but now I don't know. So much has happened."

"You've been through a lot, Nicolai, we all have."

"Everything seems different now. I seem different, like I'm not who I was."

"You need time. Life will return to normal, eventually."

"But it never will, Truman. Julius is gone. He won't be coming back."

"No, he won't."

"He died because of me, Truman."

"He died because he cared about you in spite of himself, because he wasn't going to stand by and let someone hurt you."

"He came back. He didn't have to. He knew Horace was there but he came back anyway."

"That he did."

"It's hard to understand."

"Give yourself time. You can do that, can't you?"

"I guess I have to," he said, turning back to the window. "I want to go home now, Truman."

Chapter Thirty

Nicolai watched Aiden rocking back and forth against the wall, his cane held to his chest, his fingers clasping one of Julius' strange figurines, what looked to be a dragon. Hearing of his death, he had become as silent as a breath of air, the muffled rhythm of his incessant rocking the only sound. Nicolai recognized the sadness in his face. In one way or another, they all had the look.

He turned as Carlisle lifted a tattered book from his desk and ran his hand across the red cover, turning it one way and the other. The edges had frayed at the corners but it was otherwise intact. He handed it to Nicolai. Cradling the book in his palms like an egg, he squinted at the faded title, now barely legible.

"*The Hobbit,*" he read aloud. He looked up at Carlisle. "Julius wanted me to have it?"

"See for yourself," he said, nodding at the book. "His note is just inside."

He lifted the cover, finding the tilted scrawl at the bottom of the page:

'To Nicolai, "There is more in you of good than you know, child of the kindly West. Some courage and some wisdom, blended in measure." J. R. R. Tolkein.'

"That quote is comes out of the story."

"No one ever gave me a book before."

"Julius liked doing things," Aiden's high tenor filled the room, "doing things when least expected."

Nicolai looked up at him. "You were thinking of him just now, weren't you?"

"I was thinking, yes, thinking now and then, thinking then and now."

"Then and now for me too, Aiden."

"As difficult as it sometimes is," Carlisle said, leaning back in his chair, "remembering Julius is a way to honor him. I think you'll find the same is true as you're reading the book. One memory or other will come to mind, or you'll find yourself imagining him the first time he read it."

Nicolai raised it into the air. "Should I start, Carlisle?"

He gave his head a quick shake. "You don't need my help anymore, Nicolai."

"I can read it on my own?"

"That book is best read while relaxing under a tree."

"I will go to the tree," Aiden said, slapping his thigh, "and I will listen to you read, Nicolai Tate."

A knock sounded behind him and Nicolai pivoted, finding Silas standing in the doorway. He pulled a handful of pecans from his coat pocket and crushed them in his palm, picking through the pieces with deliberate care. After a moment, he popped the nuts in his mouth and stepped into the room, eyeing each of them in turn until settling his gaze on Carlisle.

"Now, what is the status of my venerable, not to say ancient, patient on this fine morning?"

"I feel the same as you, old and decrepit," he quipped.

"That's because you don't eat the proper foods, Carlisle." He pulled a chunk of sausage from his pocket and bit off the end, offering him the rest. "A chew of this and a nip of Scotch are guaranteed to fix what ails you."

"No, I don't have any Scotch, so there's no need to ask."

"Then based on my observation of your orneriness, I pronounce you cured."

"What's the real reason you're here? It can't be to see me."

"I wish it was," he muttered, his expression turning serious as he faced Nicolai. "I'm afraid I have some bad news for you, son. Your mother has had a reaction to the new medication and they've had to take her off everything for awhile."

"But doesn't she need the medicine?"

229

"That she does. She relies on it."

"Will she go back to being like she was before?"

"That's more than likely to happen, I'm sorry to say."

"Then I won't be going to live with her."

"No, you won't, not for some time. But these things are hard to predict. Perhaps another medication will work. In any event, you can help her."

"I can?"

"You can go see her. She needs that just now. But you must remember that she is not at her best, that she must stay there and you can't expect her to be leaving for a good while."

"Will she know me?"

"You'll only find out by going. I've already arranged for a visit. What do you say, son?"

Aiden jerked to attention. "A car is coming, coming up the road just now, yes now."

Carlisle moved to the window, pushing aside the curtains and peering out. Resisting the urge to run, Nicolai stayed seated. A car door slammed and Carlisle disappeared down the hall. Rocking furiously, Aiden leaned toward him, speaking under his breath.

"Nicolai Tate, you must leave, and you must. I hear Carlisle talking to the children's services lady. She has come back for you. Leave now, now and not later."

Nicolai settled into the chair, knowing he had made his decision. He was through running. He would face whatever was to come.

Moments later, Carlisle returned, the supervisor walking behind him erect and without expression, her hard-soled shoes clacking on the floorboards. She stopped and stared down at Nicolai. He couldn't help imagining her as a witch.

"You are the boy, Nicolai Tate, I believe."

"Good guess, lady," he said, glancing at the others, "since I'm the only kid in here. You must be a real genius."

"I am with children's services," she continued. "The judge has decided you are to come with me."

"How can he decide that?" He stood abruptly. "He doesn't know a dang thing about me, and neither do you."

"You have repeated misbehaviors that require a more structured home environment."

"Where'd you get those shoes, from your grandmother?" he sneered, nodding at her feet. "Anyway, that stuff about my home is a load of bull. My home is fine like it is."

"Nevertheless, I have an order."

"Don't you have anything better to do than harass kids?" he said, his voice rising. "Why don't you go find someone else to bother?"

Carlisle placed a hand on his shoulder. Nicolai sat and looked around the room, letting his eyes drift across the shelves of books, the pipes in their rack, the jeweled dagger, all familiar, all part of him now. He wondered if he would ever see them again. Then he took a breath and pushed himself out of the chair, heading for the door without another word.

Truman watched the sunlight reflect off the lake in hues of crimson and gold, winking among the small waves, vanishing and reappearing in random patterns. The surface vibrated with blurred images of the trees and hills, the torn horizon beyond. To the southwest, an ominous wedge of clouds rose above the tree line.

He studied the ropes of cloud drifting overhead, their shadows turning the water gunmetal gray before moving onto shore. A rock-strewn beach stretched into the distance. The day seemed unusually warm for early fall as he squinted into the sun, gripped by a sudden urge to take off his shirt. Walking next to him, Kennis hummed an unrecognizable tune.

She reached for his hand. He glanced at her, the curve of her neck, the downward turn of her eyes, the flawed beauty that had captured him from their first meeting. An image of her without her shirt flashed through his mind, and he felt the power of her presence, the hold she had on him. He wanted her, to spend every spare moment with her, to feel her skin next to his.

All at once, a fear gripped him, a fear that sooner or later she would leave, that she would find someone else, that he would again find himself in the same spot, alone and bitter. An urge to protect himself swept over him in an avalanche of conflicted thoughts. Then he heard her call his name. He turned to find she had stopped twenty yards behind him while he continued on, unaware.

"What is it? What's come over you? Is it something to do with Nicolai, Julius, all that's happened?"

He had no answer.

"Wait, I know that look," she continued. "You're afraid we won't last, the two of us. You're pulling back, aren't you?"

She stood, hands on her hips, waiting for an answer. He stared at her, astonished by her guess.

"No, I...," he lied. "I'm just hot. It's hot out."

"You don't need to, you know," she said, moving next to him. "I'm not her. I'm not the type to run around behind your back. If I needed a change, I'd tell you to your face. But that's not likely to happen anytime soon."

"How can you be sure?"

"Truman, I don't know what's going to happen a minute from now, an hour from now or a year from now. All I know is I'm glad to be with you right now."

"But what if you want more than that, or I do?"

"Then we'll talk about it and figure out what comes next. But I don't want that now, do you?"

"I don't know what I want."

"So, you're hot, are you?" She ran her fingers across his cheek, ignoring his answer and instead tracing the outlines of his fading bruises. "Just thinking about that makes *me* hot."

"I was… uh… thinking," he stammered, unaccustomed to such frank talk from a woman, "to take off my shirt. That'll cool me off some."

"Maybe I like you hot." She lifted the edge of his shirt. "Or maybe I'd like you better if you took off all your clothes."

"It, it, it," he stuttered, "it's uncommonly hot for this time of year."

"Then we'd better do something about it," she said, whispering in his ear. "Let's go skinny-dipping."

Stripping off her clothes before he could answer, she ran splashing into the water. Truman looked up and down the beach, worried they might have company. The shoreline stood empty. He tossed his clothes with hers and in seconds was in the lake.

Kennis stood waiting in the deeper water as he waded out. Crystal-like droplets beaded along her shoulders and down her chest, following the curves of her body. Her dark hair lay heavy around her neck. She swam toward him, wrapping herself around him as he pulled her near.

The green water moved between them, warm and silk-like, transporting him to another world, a place of the moment and nothing else. He closed his eyes. Seconds later a bird called somewhere nearby, followed by a voice. His eyes flew open. Kennis gripped him, keeping him from turning.

"I heard something," he said, half-choking on her collarbone. "I think it was a voice."

"That wasn't just a voice," she whispered, "that was Tico. He's standing not fifty yards from here."

"What do we do?"

"You get to do the talking this time."

She turned him around to face the shore, keeping out of sight. Tico raised a hand to block the glare.

"I can't hardly see a thing with that sun reflecting like it is. I'm looking for Truman Birdsong. Is that him?"

"It is, Tico," he answered. "I'm having a swim. I didn't expect to see you out here on a Saturday."

"I wouldn't be here if it wasn't important. I saw Kennis' car up on the bluff."

"She's having a swim too."

Even from that distance Truman could see his eyebrows dancing.

"My hearing's not too good. Did you say Kennis is there with you now?"

Annoyed by his questions, she moved into the open, keeping low in the water.

"We're having a swim on a hot Saturday," she called. "Is there any law against that, sheriff?"

"None that I know of, but I'm going to have to cut short your fun. We have trouble that needs tending to the sooner the better."

"What sort of trouble?" Truman yelled.

"That dad blasted supervisor from children's services has taken the boy. She's determined to send him off. I need you to go down there with me right away and see what we can do."

Truman started for shore and Kennis yanked him back in front of her.

"You can't just walk out of here with him standing there."

Truman craned his neck, spotting their clothes down the beach. He pointed to the pile.

"Tico, we've got a little problem to solve before I can go with you."

"What sort of problem? We need to get a move on."

"Those are our clothes."

"You want me to bring them to you," he said as he approached the pile, "or what?"

He stood looking down at the clothes, his eyebrows working overtime.

"This looks like everything there is, including your skivvies."

"You just put your finger on the problem, sheriff."

He looked up. Even from that distance, Truman could see his face turn crimson.

"So, you two are...," he stuttered, "you're ... you're in the buff?"

"Okay, sheriff," Kennis yelled, pointing him toward the street, "enough questions. You just turn yourself around, move on up toward the road and stay there. I'm coming out."

Chapter Thirty-one

Nicolai slumped in his chair and fiddled with the loose veneer edging the supervisor's desk, pulling it free and letting it jump back into place. She flinched with every slap. Aiden stood off to one side. Hunched over a thick file, she flipped through the final pages and slammed it shut, turning her gaze on Nicolai.

"Apparently you have trouble controlling your anger, Mister Tate. I'm surprised you weren't sent to a more structured program without hesitation."

He glared at her. "Is that what they call jail now?"

"If I had been in charge of your case," she continued, "I would have recommended a change of placement long ago."

"Well, now you get your wish," he sneered.

"My wishes have nothing to do with it. You have brought this on yourself with your repeated inappropriate behaviors."

"You people always blame the kid when the dang grownups are the ones making trouble. I wouldn't have done the things I did if my foster so-called parents had treated me fair. Those people have no business taking in kids. All they know how to do is yell and hit."

"Well, you clearly refuse to take responsibility for your actions," she huffed. "You will learn to do so at your new home."

"You call a dang prison home?"

"The placement is a combined school and treatment center, not a prison."

"That's a load of bull crap. I've heard from kids who went there. I know what it is and I call it prison."

"Their stories are not trustworthy," she said, coolly.

"You don't trust anybody, do you, you old witch?" He stood, knocking the chair over. "Go ahead and send me. I don't give a damn."

"This is just the sort of inappropriate behavior that warrants the move."

"Are you one of those people that like tearing the wings off butterflies and feeding them to spiders?"

She winced. "I would never do such a thing."

"I bet you enjoy sending kids off to jail," he said, squinting at her. "You'd probably send your own dang kids if you had any. But who'd want to marry an old bat like you? They'd have to be crazy or blind or both."

She stood and stormed out of the room. Realizing what he'd said, Nicolai faced Aiden.

"I didn't mean to say that about being blind. It was my anger talking."

"No need to apologize, no, none at all," he whispered in his high twang. "She is a witch, yes, and she is."

"Well, at least we got rid of her."

He set the chair upright and moved to the windows. Below him, Carlisle stood on the sidewalk talking with Silas. In the distance, a line of clouds drifted over the hills, the hospital steeple winking between them. He thought of his mother again and the disappointment she must feel at the way things had turned out, that is, if she felt anything at all. He wondered if she understood the uncertain future awaiting them both, and quickly decided she'd be better off not knowing.

When he looked down again Carlisle and Silas had disappeared. He leaned against the windowpane, craning his neck to see where they had gone. Seconds later footsteps sounded behind him. He turned just as Tico strode into the room followed by Truman, his clothes still damp. Silas and Carlisle stopped in the doorway.

"Looks like you got the whole crew out for this party," Truman said as he eyed Nicolai. "You're not looking too happy about it."

"Talk to the dang stupid supervisor. This is her idea of fun."

"Sit down and be respectful," he growled. "That's no way to talk about an adult."

"She's not much of one," he muttered, slinking into the chair. "Besides, I wouldn't be here if it wasn't for her."

"Where the devil is she?"

Before he could answer, she appeared in the doorway, brushing past him as she moved to her desk. She frowned at Tico.

"Sheriff, I was forced to leave due to this boy's rude behavior and cursing. For that reason, I'll need a deputy to accompany us to the school."

"Now let's don't jump the gun here. I don't have unlimited resources to work with, you know."

"I refuse to be alone with a surly juvenile delinquent."

"That's some strong language for someone in your line of work. Aren't you supposed to be on the kid's side?"

"He's an ungrateful, foul-mouthed boy."

"You don't expect him to be glad he's going do you?"

Nicolai sat upright. "I wouldn't have cussed if she hadn't gotten me so dang mad."

Truman motioned him to stay quiet. Carlisle stepped into the room and stood before her.

"Might we review the judge's order?"

She sat, looking at him as if he'd slapped her. Then her gaze grew cold.

"You are his legal guardian?"

"I am his concerned friend," he answered, matching her cool tone.

"And what do you expect to find in these papers?"

"I would need to see them to know, wouldn't I?"

"Nothing in them will change the outcome. He will leave."

"Still, I'd like to see them."

"That is not possible," she barked. "Only legal guardians have access."

"You can't be serious, woman." Silas snorted skeptically. "There are ways around such requirements in exceptional situations like this."

"And who are you to be asking?"

"I'm his physician."

"Nevertheless…" she answered dismissively.

Truman leaned on the edge of her desk.

"You're telling us that the judge, the same judge who allowed him to stay at our house, would have a problem with us taking a look at his papers?"

"The judge is not saying it, I am."

"You imagine you have a lot of power in this little kingdom of yours," he said, struggling to stay calm, "don't you?"

"The decisions are mine to make whether you like it or not," she sneered back at him. "That's my job. I'm a professional."

"You sound more like a selfish child."

"I don't have to listen to this disrespectful blather," she said, jumping out of her chair and pointing to the door. "Get out of my office! All of you!"

Truman nodded to Nicolai.

"Fine! Come on, then."

Nicolai leapt from the chair, heading for the door. She scrambled to round her desk, about to cut him off, when Kennis appeared at the threshold. Everyone stopped at the sight of her. Her damp clothes were crisscrossed with wrinkles. She reached up and smoothed her windblown hair, and then she pulled a soggy paper from her jeans pocket and held it up.

"I just spoke to the judge. He says Nicolai can remain at home for the time being."

"You went to the judge looking like that?" Tico said, staring in disbelief. "Lordy, Kennis, what were you thinking?"

"Relax, sheriff, it's Saturday after all," she chuckled. "The man answered the door with a beer in his hand."

"You went to his *home*?"

"How else was I going to find him?"

She handed the paper to Truman. He glanced at it before turning to Carlisle.

"Will you and Silas take Nicolai downstairs? I'll be along soon."

Truman waited as Carlisle and the others disappeared through the door. Then he handed the paper to the woman. She snatched it from him without a word and retreated to her desk.

Truman grabbed Kennis by the arm and pulled her into the hallway, stopping near the stairwell. Taking her face in his hands, he kissed her hard and slid his hands to her shoulders, leaning back to study her face.

"You are a good woman, you know. Thank you for that gift. I should've never doubted you."

"We didn't have anything to lose so I thought why not try reasoning with the judge?" A sly smile spread crossed her lips. "Besides, I figured the wet t-shirt might help."

"Never underestimate a good-looking woman."

"Never underestimate a well-planned argument... and a wet t-shirt. He took some persuading but came around when I told him about you."

"You told him about me? But why?"

"He said Nicolai could remain at home as long as he was under the supervision of a responsible adult at all times. That means never alone, at least until the hearing. I assured him that would not be a problem. There was no way he would have agreed otherwise."

"I don't care what it takes as long as he doesn't get sent off to some reform school."

"He's not out of the woods yet. That bitter old woman could still be trouble."

"As long as we have you hanging around we'll be alright."

"Speaking of hanging around, would you like to come over later so we can take up where we left off? I can fix dinner and make you a special dessert, you know, the kind that's all warm on the inside. That is, unless you want to have dessert first."

"I always did have a weakness for dessert. But I may be late. I have to make a trip to Abilene."

"You don't exactly look happy about it."

"I'm going to see my father. I haven't spoken to him in twenty years."

"Can you tell me why?"

"Maybe someday I will. First I need to figure it out for myself."

An hour later, Truman angled the van onto a narrow lane lined with modest, well-kept houses. Toys and bicycles shared driveways with pickups and sedans. At the road's end an early autumn sun hovered above the horizon like an all-seeing eye, blood-red in the evening haze.

He squinted to the southwest where a towering cloud blotted out the sky, its flattened top, stark white against the indigo sky. Beneath the storm, a gray-green wall of rain slanted toward the ground. Thunder rolled in the distance, thumping in his chest like a failing heart.

He pulled to the curb opposite a white frame house crossed by a deep porch. Nicolai stirred in the passenger seat and peered out the windshield, wondering where they had come, and why. Truman had asked him along, but in a strange way that sounded more plea than request. Otherwise, he had made little effort to explain, instead brooding in silence on the hour-long drive.

Nicolai cast him a wary glance. With his wrinkled clothes and hair jutting in all directions, he resembled the drunks and transients he had seen prowling the rails outside of town. He sensed a tension in him, an unspoken edginess taut as a pulled bow and needing release.

He turned to the window as Truman cut the engine and sat studying the small house as if it held some great mystery. To Nicolai it seemed ordinary enough, almost

241

plain, except that unlike the other homes, it had no cars or toys in the drive. Taking a closer look, he realized all the blinds were drawn. A stack of yellowed newspapers sat beside the front door.

Truman climbed out and motioned him to follow, crossing the street and taking the sidewalk to the wide porch. Nicolai shadowed him up the concrete steps. Truman raised his fist to the door and then lowered it with a sigh. For a full minute he stood there facing the house, looking as if he expected the door would open on its own. He raised his fist again just as a voice hailed from the street.

Nicolai pivoted, spotting a thick-set man with sunburned cheeks and red hair, a can of beer in his hand. Nicolai decided he resembled a human fireplug. A spotted Chihuahua shivering next to him like a shrunken Dalmatian only added to the impression. The man tipped back the can, studying them with one eye.

"I don't guess you look like burglars, though I can't be sure. You look more like the derelicts that hitchhike the interstate preying on innocent, law-abiding people. If you're looking for a place to hide out, you best move on or I'll have to call the sheriff."

"You sure have a big imagination," Nicolai said, annoyed by his brusque manner. "Can't you see we came here in that van over there? We're not any derelict or burglar either."

"You must be trying to sell something, then," the man continued. "We don't tolerate solicitors nosing around here."

"Are you always this dang friendly?" Nicolai smirked.

Truman nudged him, motioning him to stop with a shake of his head. He tried to sound accommodating.

"We don't mean to make anyone uncomfortable. We're just looking for someone. Do you live nearby?"

The man pointed to a small frame house opposite them, the shiplap siding dirt-stained and peeling, the yard overgrown. The house looked like an out of place imposter among the well-tended homes.

"That there's my castle." He emptied the can and tossed it onto the lawn. "There's nothing worth stealing in there, if that's what you're thinking."

"So you know the people that live here?" he nodded toward the house.

"Did know is more like it," he said as he approached. "They all left, packed up and gone to stay with relations in Oklahoma or Kansas or someplace up north. I said I'd keep an eye on the place until they got their affairs sorted out. Now there's a sad story."

"What do you mean, a sad story?" he made himself ask, already regretting the trip.

"Feller that lived here had an accident about two weeks ago," he said, wincing. "He was on his way home after working late."

"He was drunk, no doubt," he guessed.

"No sir, he wouldn't touch liquor, said he had no toleration for it. You can see I have no such conviction. I offered more than once and he always refused."

"Alright then, but what about the accident?"

"We had ourselves a big storm that night, the rain coming hard, and they figure he lost control before he hit a big old live oak."

"And...?"

"Killed him outright."

"You mean he...," Truman muttered, "he... he's dead?"

"Like I said, it's a sad story if there ever was one. Did you know him? You didn't say if you're kin or not. Maybe your boy is a friend of his son. They look to be close in age."

Truman stared at him, unable to speak as a numb detachedness settled over him. The thought of his father dead, that he had a son Nicolai's age, swirled through his mind in a blur of images, all impossible to understand or accept. Nicolai looked up at him, puzzled why he would not answer. He turned to the man.

"Who was he? Who owns this house?"

"Why, this is Royce Birdsong's home."

Nicolai glanced at Truman, realizing at once why they had come.

"And he was once a drunk?"

"How's that any of your business?" he quipped. "You're just a kid."

"Well, was he?"

"What's wrong with your partner? He looks like he swallowed a goat."

"Are you going to answer the dang question or not?" Nicolai barked, worried over Truman's trancelike state.

"Don't get smart with me, boy," he snapped and then checked himself, casting Truman a concerned look. "Well, I don't reckon it'll matter now that the man is gone. The truth is, he said as much to me. But when he moved here he had left that life behind."

"Do you have a key to the place?"

"How else do you think I'm I going to keep an eye on things?" he said, the irritated tone returning.

"Then let us take a look around."

"Now why would I let two strangers into the house," he said, eyeing Nicolai skeptically, "when they won't answer a single question? Tell me that, boy."

"How'd you get so dang ornery?" he sneered. "First, you accuse us of being derelicts, and then call us burglars, and then…"

He went silent at the touch of Truman's hand on his shoulder.

"What did I tell you about being respectful?"

Nicolai faced him, relieved to hear his voice.

"Truman, if you heard the man," he said, searching his eyes, "go ahead and tell him who you are."

Thunder rolled across the sky, closer this time. The man flinched and scrambled up the steps.

"I don't like the look of those clouds. I believe there's a lightning bolt up there with my name on it. If you're going to tell me who you are, you best get on with it. Otherwise, I'll head on back home before the storm hits."

"Royce was my father," he said without hesitation. "I haven't spoken to him in twenty years."

"Then you didn't know about the accident," he said, running his fingers through his wiry hair. "And that's got to be a terrible shock, especially after so long a time."

"I would like to see inside the house." He motioned toward the door. "That is, if you'll allow it."

"Why sure, sure, now that I know who you are." He held out his hand. "The name's Harlan Cain, but everyone calls me Hurly. I did the shot put in high school."

He fished the key from his pocket and led them inside. The foyer opened onto a small, modestly furnished living room with a stone fireplace at one end. Family photos littered the mantel. Along the far wall, piles of papers, books and laboratory equipment crowded a row of plank shelves. A telescope stood next to a curtain-less window.

Truman wandered down the hallway and into the largest bedroom, looking for anything remotely familiar. He bent to study the bedside photos. Even his father seemed a stranger, a man clear-eyed and determined, living a life he could scarcely imagine.

He moved to the dresser. His father's glasses and wallet, coins and a house key, sat together in the center as if he had just come home. He cast Hurly a glance and flipped open the wallet. His father's driver's license and credit cards were still in place. Behind them, a row of plastic sleeves held more family pictures.

He was about to close the wallet when a wedge of paper poking from a side pocket caught his attention. He laid the wallet flat and gingerly pulled the tattered corner, lifting free a photo. He peered at the yellowed image. Facing the camera, he and his father stood together, a mountainside lake in the distance, a stringer of fish at their feet.

He remembered the day at once. They had risen before dawn, hiking into the mountains and to the bend of a narrow, boulder-strewn stream with a deep pool edging one side. Sitting together on a granite ledge, they baited lines with salmon eggs that faded beneath the black water like errant planets vanishing into space. Later that morning the aroma of coffee and bacon drifted through the still air as his mother stood behind the camera and snapped the picture.

The scene receded into memory as his mind filled with a host of conflicted thoughts and emotions. He had slipped the photo back into its pocket when a sound caught his attention. He turned his ear to the window. A low roar throbbed outside, rumbling inside his chest like a distant freight train. He nodded to Hurly and motioned Nicolai toward the door.

Moments later they stepped onto the porch. Thunder rolled overhead in a series of deep thuds, rattling the windowpanes. A blood-red streak edged the western horizon. Otherwise, the street stood in near darkness. Hurly fidgeted with the lock a moment, huffing with frustration before giving up. He hurried down the steps and turned his face to the sky.

"I don't like the look of that cloud, not one bit," he called up to them. "I'll come back later to lock the house. You boys best skedaddle while you can."

He scurried across his lawn and disappeared inside the house. Truman pointed Nicolai toward the van and followed down the stairs. A windless air surrounded them, thick and stifling, crackling with pent up energy. Stopping midway across the street, Truman turned and cast his gaze to the southwest. An approaching squall loomed over the house, green-gray and massive, beneath it an ominous wedge of cloud reaching toward the earth. Torn wisps scudded before it like giant swarms of bees.

246

All at once the wedge narrowed and began spiraling downward in a thin gray line. He watched, mesmerized, unable to move as it vanished behind the rooftops. The next instant the sky filled with dust and debris. For an instant, he thought a bomb had exploded the next street over. But instead of falling, the broken planks and twisted strips of metal began moving sideward in a swirling mass.

Nicolai appeared next to him, pulling him from his trance. Without a word, Truman grabbed him and made for the house, slamming through the door and past the living room to the kitchen. He hustled through the back door and onto the back stoop, scanning the yard for a storm shelter. There was none. The funnel had widened to a twisting wall a quarter mile across.

He rushed back inside, gripping Nicolai by the shoulders and locking eyes with him, telling him what to do. Scurrying from room to room, closet to closet, they searched the house for a safe room, the roar outside growing into a deafening howl. Seconds later they met in the living room having found nothing. Truman turned a circle, trying to squelch a growing panic, when his eyes fell on the fireplace.

Grabbing Nicolai, he ran to the adjacent room and dove into the closet, throwing aside boxes and clothes. A tiny door accessing the fireplace emerged from the corner. Kicking it open, he pushed the boy through and scrambled in behind him. The house shuddered beneath the howling wind. For a moment it seemed it would hold. Then the gunshot scatter of snapping beams exploded overhead. He threw himself on top of Nicolai. Then everything went black.

Chapter Thirty-two

Parfit emerged from the darkness, his hair wet, his face a pale blue. Moisture beaded on his jaw like gemstones, the droplets splashing to the ground in hues of amethyst and topaz, forming small pools at his feet. Nicolai watched as he waved his hand through the air, reaching upward and outward, motioning in a slow circle. Above him a vortex of clouds twisted in an ever-tightening circle.

He reached down and lifted Nicolai from the ground as if he weighed nothing. Astonished by his strength, Nicolai peered at him, wondering if in truth he had killed Jerome. Before he could ask, Parfit put a finger to his lips, silencing him.

He pointed into the darkness. In the distance the hospital chapel stood like an island in a featureless sea, pearl-like and glowing. Nicolai thought he could see his mother standing to one side. He squinted into the glare and blinked, but when he looked again she was gone.

All at once a yellow fog descended from the swirling cloud, surrounding him in seconds, dense and blinding. Parfit was no longer in sight. He struggled to breathe the putrid air, feeling as if a great hand had him in its grip. The fog burned in the back of his throat. For a panic-stricken moment he feared he would suffocate. Then the air exploded in a hail of flying debris.

He awoke with a start. Staring into the darkness, he labored to catch his breath, puzzling over the dream, if dream it was. What had Parfit tried to tell him? Had it something to do with his mother? Did the water and fog have some meaning?

A dim glow hovered just out of view and for a moment he wondered if Truman had installed a new lamp in the stairway. He often complained about the dim confines of the old home. In spite of its age, Nicolai loved the house, and in particular his bedroom. For the first time in his life he felt he had a place of his own.

Other than the glow, he could pick nothing out of the darkness. Yet the room seemed different, somehow small and confining, the bed harder, the covers heavier. He puzzled over why. Deciding to find out, he tried to move but a searing pain shot through his side, leaving him gasping for air. He thought he might pass out.

For a moment he stayed still, waiting for the fog in his mind to clear, hoping the pain was not his arm broken again. He tried moving his hand but found it stuck beneath something heavy. He could do little with it. Suddenly he realized he was not in his room and all at once he remembered the looming storm, the mad dash for the closet, Truman kicking in the door as the wood splintered overhead and then nothing. Just the thought left him breathless.

Managing to pull his other arm free, he moved his hand along his chest, finding a bruised area over his ribs. Nothing appeared broken. The pain he felt was not his arm, he decided with relief. He moved his hand further to the right, bumping against something solid. He ran his fingers along the length. A massive wooden beam crossed him from shoulder to waist, a beam that was slowly suffocating him.

He took a ragged breath, trying to stay calm and think through what he should do. If he was too hasty, the beam could shift in the wrong direction and crush him. If he went too slowly he could pass out and suffocate. He wedged his free hand beneath the board and gently pushed against the base, gradually increasing the pressure. A searing pain spread in a wave across his chest. Nothing moved.

He fell back panting. Taking another shallow breath, he pushed again, this time with more force, gritting his teeth against the burning ache in his ribs. The beam groaned and creaked in a dozen places above him. He turned away, waiting for it to come crashing down. Still, nothing moved.

Readjusting his arm, he pushed once again, his eyes watering at the pain. The beam shifted slightly. He stopped, holding still as he checked himself. The move was small but enough. He edged to the right and his arm and legs came free.

Pushing himself from beneath the timber, he spotted a rectangle of light to his left. He edged toward it, wincing with every push but determined to escape the confined space if he could. The concrete was cool and damp beneath his palms. Somewhere in the darkness, water dripped in a steady rhythm.

He reached the light and rolled onto his back. A gibbous moon appeared overhead, drifting amid a scattering of stars. Ropes of cloud scudded past like schooners before a gale. He had never been so glad to see the sky. At once his thoughts turned to Truman.

Sitting up with difficulty, he wrapped his arm around his chest to minimize the pain and surveyed the moonlit scene. The house had been leveled, reduced to wood and sheetrock. Behind him a mound of debris studded with pipe and lumber surrounded the chimney, the only part of the house still standing. Before him only the slab remained, and beyond it what had been the porch. The silhouettes of two mangled trees flanked the walkway.

Something stirred beyond the chimney, a scraping of wood on concrete. He pulled himself up with a broken table leg, overturning a chair and sending a flour tin clattering to the ground in a cloud of white. Rain-soaked books littered the floor. He staggered over the rubble, wading through a sea of bedclothes and curtains that grabbed at his legs like quicksand.

He rounded the chimney. Blocking his way, a wedge of rubble rose past the fireplace. Surprisingly, a row of photos still stood undisturbed on the mantle. He peered into the shadows, listening. A sudden clattering of wood and metal sounded beyond the pile, followed by a voice, Truman's voice, strained and hoarse.

"Nicolai… Nicolai… are you in there?" he called out.

More detritus went clanging to the floor. Nicolai scampered up the mound.

"I'm here, Truman!" he yelled as the trash slid beneath his feet, sending him to his knees. "I'm on the other side."

A hand appeared above him, followed by Truman's battered face. A deep cut oozed over his left eye. He took one look at Nicolai and vanished, reappearing seconds later at the edge of the pile. Scrambling over the wreckage, he knelt and lifted him from the rubble.

"Are you hurt?" He held Nicolai at arm's length, looking him over. "I was afraid you were…"

He stopped, unable to finish. Seeing the anguish in his face, Nicolai wrenched free and leaned into him, overcome with feeling despite the pain in his side. Truman draped his arms across his shoulders, listening to his soft sobs.

Hurly's voice called from the street and Nicolai quickly pulled away, embarrassed by the emotion. He wiped his eyes with the back of his hand and followed Truman through the mountain of rubble. A cloud of yellow smoke, acrid and choking, streamed past. He blinked into it, suddenly recalling his strange dream with a sense of awe and puzzlement. He half-expected to see Parfit appear as they threaded their way over the wreckage.

Moments later they staggered onto the sidewalk. Hurly stood at the curb, shaking his head and mumbling to himself. His was the only home left standing. Otherwise, the street looked like a warzone. Instead of houses, a forest of rubble stretched into the distance, the carnage a map of the tornado's path.

Halfway down the block a house smoldered beneath the moonlit spray of a fireman's hose. Next to it, another appeared untouched except for the missing roof. The flashing lights gave the scene an absurdly festive feel, as if a carnival had gone mad, melding the jovial and insane. Hurly turned to Truman.

251

"I don't know how in the hell my old house got skipped," he said, pointing to Truman's van, "but it's a good thing you parked in front of it instead of across the street. Otherwise, you'd be without wheels."

Dazed, Truman stared at him for a moment before understanding his meaning. He stepped next to the van and ran his hand across the door and fender, grateful to find it intact. A police car sped past him, the siren coming to life as it rounded the corner.

He wandered down the street to where Nicolai stood peering into the melee. Families sat along the curbside, the glare of emergency lights reflected in their unbelieving faces. A man wearing boxer shorts and an undershirt stumbled past, his face expressionless, his eyes glassy. Hurly hurried to him, taking his arm and leading him to a waiting ambulance.

Truman turned his gaze to the remains of his father's house, suddenly seeing the irony of the home collapsing around him. There was no going back. A bittersweet mixture of relief and exhaustion settled over him. Moments later, Hurly called out to him from the ambulance.

"These fellers say the phones are out all over the area, and a lot of the roads are closed too. You boys best stay here until first light."

Truman nodded his understanding. Opposite him a family wandered amid the wreckage of their home, picking through the rubble like a flock of birds. He laid a hand on Nicolai's shoulder and nodded toward the group, motioning for them to join in.

Hours later Nicolai stared through the windshield seeing nothing, his eyes heavy with fatigue. Images of the previous night roamed his thoughts like stray dogs, shadowlike and menacing, leaving in their wake a vague fear, as if some new disaster was destined to overtake them at any moment. His stomach knotted at the possibility.

Above the highway, pale fingers of light stretched over the horizon in bands of orange and teal. A distant thunderhead outlined in gold flickered like a Chinese lantern. He was suddenly aware of the strange marriage of death and beauty. For a brief, mesmerizing moment, the tornado bearing down on them had held both.

A thick forest appeared in a swale below them, only the treetops catching the sunrise. The road plunged into the thicket and suddenly night seemed to return. Stands of dense brush raced past the headlights. Nicolai glanced at his reflected image and, seeing the fear, turned away.

The van emerged from the thicket and they topped a rise. All at once the sun crested the hills, throwing the landscape into relief. A sunlit plateau scattered with stands of trees stretched below. He took a breath, hoping the light of day would lessen his fear.

A few miles further on the brush along the roadside began to change form, slowly at first and then dramatically, as if a giant hand had swept it aside in great swaths, leaving only matted grass scattered with leaves. Broken tree limbs littered the pavement, bone white beneath the brightening light. The acrid odor of chlorophyll filled the truck.

A hundred yards ahead a fallen tree blocked the roadway. Truman slowed the van and eased onto the shoulder. Nicolai stared through the window in disbelief. In both directions as far as he could see, a quarter mile wide path of twisted and mangled trees, most no more than limbless trunks, stretched away from them. In some places, even the grass had been stripped away.

Truman sighed and lowered his head, for a moment unable to continue. He refused to let himself imagine what might have happened to their home. He had just started moving forward again when Nicolai grabbed his arm, stopping him. In the middle of the tornado-torn swath a pale figure, what appeared to be an old man, wandered like a ghost among the broken stumps.

Truman pulled the van off the road and they climbed out. At the sound of the closing doors the man stumbled to a nearby tree and crouched behind it. Truman glanced at Nicolai, shrugged and then started toward him. At their approach the man rose with a sigh and stepped into the open, his arms outstretched, one high and one low as if feeling the air before him. One hand held a half-empty bottle of beer.

Truman blinked and looked again. The man stood before them stark naked. Short and wiry, his face and arms lined with scabbed-over cuts and scrapes, he peered at them with the dazed look of a drunk. Matted quills of white hair jutted from his scalp. He tipped back the bottle, tossing it aside and absently scratching the stubble along his jaw. Then, as if suddenly remembering he had no clothes on, he covered himself with his hands. He squinted in both directions.

"Any female types about?"

"Uh... no sir... no females here," Truman said, surprised by the question.

"You can call me Merton," he said, peering at Truman's face. "Looks like you got the bad end of a brawl."

"I'm Truman and this is Nicolai," he said, taking his hand. "We got caught by the twister, maybe the same one that came through here."

"The damn tornado was here alright. Took everything. I don't know why I bothered hiding like some scared critter," he said, letting his hands fall to his sides. "You can't rob a man who's got nothing left."

"We're not here to rob you, Merton. We just spotted you and thought you might need some help. Are you hurt?"

"Hell, I got a few bumps but nothing that a pint of Wild Turkey wouldn't cure," he said, squinting at Truman. "I don't guess you got any? That was my last beer."

"It's a bit early for me."

"I had just opened a brand new bottle when the dad-burned twister came along and snatched it right out of my hand along with my show pig, a half-smoked cigar, even the glasses off my face, sucked them up into the sky along with my house and johnboat. To top it off, the damn thing stripped the clothes right off me.

"If I hadn't taken the pig out for a stroll I'd be a goner. You got to keep those show pigs in shape if you want to win, you know. I had just put her back in the pen and was about ready for a drink. It was hot out despite the stormy weather. I tipped back the bottle but before I'd tasted a single drop the wind blew up all of a sudden-like. The next thing I knew I was sailing like a bird, clear over the barn. When I came to, the barn and everything else was gone."

"You're lucky to be alive, Merton," Truman said as he tried to check him over without seeming to.

"The only luck I see around here is the sorry sort," he grumbled, his eyes blinking, owl-like. "I expect it'll start raining rattlesnakes next."

"Rattlesnakes?" Nicolai yelled, jumping next to Truman.

"You won't believe me but just before I took flight I saw a big bull snake lift into the air like it had wings."

"Are you sure you weren't finishing off that bottle," Truman said with a chuckle, "instead of starting it?"

"Hell yes, I'm sure. I never drink while I'm walking the pig." His eyes grew wistful. "I sure am going to miss old Mona."

"You named your pig Mona?" Nicolai asked, stifling a laugh.

"Hell yes, I did. I name all my pigs. They're better company than most people, if you want to know the truth. Mona was a beauty. The feller two farms over offered to breed her with his boar, a big red, and split the litter. Those shoats would've been something to see.

"But those days are over, I reckon," he mumbled, shaking his head. "The worst of it is I'm blind as a stump without those glasses. That there is a problem when you're barefoot and there are snakes about."

"We'll take you out of here and then you can get yourself a new pair." Truman held out his hand. "Just give me your arm so you don't fall on your face."

Truman led him through the splintered trunks and fallen branches, settling him into the van. Then he pulled a blanket from the back and draped it over the old man's shoulders. Nicolai had just climbed into the passenger seat when a nearby wall of brush rattled to life and a huge pig burst through and onto the shoulder. Shocked by the sight, he slammed the door shut. The black and white sow lifted her head, sniffing the air and snorting in a low moan. Merton jumped from his seat.

"Why, that's Mona! I'd know that snort anywhere," he yelled, leaning over the seatback. "Open the door and I'll call her over. We'll fit her in somehow or other."

Truman peered through the windshield at the pig's massive bulk. Long-legged and humpbacked, she stared back at him as if expecting an invitation. He flipped open the glove box and pulled out a bag of unshelled peanuts, thrusting them at Nicolai.

"Keep an eye on the side mirror. When you see me at the back corner, throw a handful of these out front."

"Let me come with you."

"Not on your life. That pig would just as soon eat you as a few peanuts. You stay where you are and get ready to do your part."

He grabbed a rope from beneath the seat and eased open the door.

"What's that you got there?" Merton said, squinting at him. "Don't you hurt my pig."

"I saw an abandoned farmhouse a quarter mile back with a metal fence around it."

"That's the Meitner place," he said, nodding down the road. "The old woman died a year or so back. What about it?"

"I'll get this rope around her and we'll take her there for safe keeping until you get situated. That fence should hold her."

"The fence is not the problem," he snorted. "Don't you know you can't lasso a pig? They're smarter than any horse, and most people, if the truth be known."

""I'm not riding a pig in this van and you're too blind to help. Besides, she'll be so preoccupied with the nuts she won't notice the rope until it's too late. That is, unless you have a better plan."

He slipped out the door without waiting for an answer and rounded the van, careful to stay out of sight as he secured the rope to the rear bumper and tied a loop at the opposite end. Then he crept to the corner and peeked around it, nodding to Nicolai. He leaned out the window, shook the bag and tossed a dozen nuts in front of the van. The pig sniffed the air and quickly trotted to them.

Truman slid along the front fender and leaned past the grill, slinging the lasso through the air. As if hearing it, she looked up. For an instant the loop seemed certain to slip over her with ease. Then at the last moment she gave her head a graceful shake, ducking out of the way. The rope went skittering to the pavement.

Truman barely had time to take a breath before she pivoted, charging him, her jaws snapping. He scrambled up the bumper and pressed himself to the windshield, keeping his feet just out of reach. She stared up at him and snorted, looking as if she had no intention of moving. Nicolai tapped on the windshield.

"What's your plan now?"

Truman glared at him through the glass, saying nothing. Merton's voice drifted through the window.

"I told you she was too smart to lasso."

"If I had a gun, I'd shoot her," he yelled back.

"You'd probably miss," Merton quipped.

"Get her out of the way," he yelled to Merton through the windshield, "so I can get inside."

"She's dangerous even for me when she's mad," he answered, "and you got her hackles up good. I believe I'll stay right here."

"You two better think of something quick. I can't hang on forever."

"Just sit tight," Nicolai said. "I have an idea."

He scrambled over the seat, squeezing into the cramped rear of the van and swinging open the double door. Clinging to the frame, he leaned out and shook the bag of peanuts. Then he tossed a handful beyond the fender.

Mona snorted and stamped the ground with her hooves but stayed put. He shook the bag again. She took another look at Truman, snapped her jaws and then ambled to the rear, nosing through the dirt for the nuts.

"Get inside and drive us to that farm," Nicolai yelled. "I'll keep her interested enough to follow."

Truman scurried off the grill and climbed behind the steering wheel, easing the van in a semicircle and along the roadside before stopping next to the gate. Leaning out the passenger window, he lifted the latch and Nicolai tossed the bag inside. Mona trotted in after it. Merton leaned on the seatback, watching as Nicolai hurried to close the gate.

"Truman, that boy of yours is smarter than the both of us," he said, chuckling. "He's got a real future ahead of him."

Chapter Thirty-three

An hour later, they pulled away from the emergency shelter and back onto the blacktop. Nicolai watched as Merton's pale form slowly receded into the distance, vanishing behind the midday haze. His thoughts turned to the boarding house. With the radio stations back on the air, news of the storm was non-stop, grim and worrisome. The phones were still out.

Evidence of the storm appeared at every bend of the road, torn and uprooted trees, dead farm animals, missing roofs. A lone car stood upended in the middle of a flattened wheat field as if balancing on its hood. Mats of grass and broken tree limbs hung from sagging power lines.

They came to a low bridge littered with driftwood and crossed by skeins of mud, and Truman slowed the van, dodging the larger limbs and mounds of silt. Nicolai peered out the window, shocked by the devastation. The creek had been scoured to bedrock, smooth and bone-white beneath the noonday sun. Downstream, kitchen appliances, farm machinery and mounds of fallen trees lined the banks on both sides. Further on a four-poster bed sat perched in the branches of a towering cypress as if a sleeper might arise any moment.

Nicolai leaned out the window as the bridge vanished below the ridgeline. They followed the narrow farm road up through the meandering hills and along the watershed, passing in and out of thickets dark with shadow. From time to time the muddy river appeared through the trees like a dirty ribbon. Mourning doves streaked overhead, skimming the treetops as they vied for position within the flock.

Thunder thumped somewhere in the distance. Nicolai craned his neck to study the clouds looming over the road, the pit in his stomach growing. Memories of the previous night dogged him, morphing into an image of the boarding house reduced to a mangled heap of wood and glass. He turned his eyes back to the road, trying to think of nothing at all.

The van crested a rise and the outskirts of Hackney appeared in the valley below them. Like so many in the area, the once thriving boomtown had been reduced to a decaying shell. Dilapidated houses and weed-filled lots lined the main avenue. Truman pulled in front of a two story building with a granite archway framing the entrance. Built in 1902, the bank was now a coffee shop run by a local church seeking converts. Truman cut the engine and sat staring through the windshield.

"I don't do well on no sleep," he muttered. "I need coffee."

"I can drive."

"Not a chance," he grumbled. "Come on, then."

They pushed through the door and stepped into a narrow room cluttered with wooden crosses, Christmas ornaments and handmade signs reading 'Only God Knows' and 'Jesus is the Way'. Christian self-help books shared shelf space with cross-covered picture frames and Bibles, some huge, some no bigger than a man's wallet. At the far end of the room a young man stood behind a counter, humming to himself and smiling. Within seconds, Truman found his sunny mood annoying.

"A cup of coffee," he barked, "the largest you've got."

"Coming up right away, sir."

He filled a cup from a nearby pot and set it on the counter, his smile never waning. On the wall behind him, a certificate from New Life Bible College read 'Jimmy Swift, Licensed Pastor'.

"You sure are smiley." Reminded of Reverend Butts' humiliating treatment, Truman slapped a dollar and change on the counter.

"Every day is reason for celebration when you walk with Jesus," the man said.

"I don't see much to celebrate," he growled, "when half the countryside is torn all to hell."

Nicolai glanced at him. He had seen that look before and knew it meant trouble. Hoping to distract him, he grabbed a soda from a nearby cooler and set it on the counter.

"Pay him for this and let's go, Truman," he said. "We don't have time to visit."

"If you let Jesus into your heart you would understand," the man continued, his tone patronizing. "God and his love are in all things."

"You think so?" Truman squinted at him. "He sure managed to make himself scarce last night."

"As I tell my congregation, Jesus is always with us, even in the darkest hour."

"You've got a lot to learn about the real world, sonny."

"Don't do this," Nicolai said under his breath.

"His hand touches all," the man said.

"Are you telling me," Truman said, his voice rising as he pointed to the door, "Jesus ordered up all this mayhem and heartache? What about my dead friend, Julius? Where was your god when he…"

Unable to finish, he turned away, the memory bitter in his throat.

"No, he… he wouldn't…" the pastor stammered. "You must have Jesus confused with Satan."

"Is that right, parson?" he turned, sneering. "How in all your wisdom do you know which is which?"

Nicolai grabbed his arm and started steering him toward the door.

"Satan comes in many forms when he tests our faith," the parson answered, again sounding confident, "even those forms least expected."

"So, the devil could be anything or anyone, even someone like me?" Truman said, pulling away.

"I suppose so," he answered, stepping back from the counter and eyeing him. "Satan is always finding ways to tempt the weak-minded and lost, and sometimes even those strong in their belief."

"You could be right," Truman said, forcing a smile. "Now that I think about it, I've had an attraction to pitchforks and open flames lately."

"Stop goading him," Nicolai whispered, grabbing his arm again. "He might have a gun behind that counter. He wouldn't think twice about shooting Satan."

"What do you think that means?" he yelled as Nicolai pushed him out the door. "Will I grow horns next?"

The outskirts of Hackney vanished below the treetops like a sinking ship as the van strained to climb out of the valley. The narrow highway wound up and over the top of Caddo Peak, descending the slope before threading through the jagged hills and arroyos south of Clayton. They rode in silence, Nicolai's thoughts on Carlisle and Aiden, and the fate of the old house. Truman ruminated over the naïve but smug confidence from the likes of Reverend Butts and the young pastor.

Shadows thrown by the low sun stretched across blacktop in thinning lines. Below the horizon, light glinted off the lake, winking like an indecipherable Morse code. He imagined Kennis standing waist deep in the water, wearing nothing. Suddenly he wanted to see her.

In spite of their night together, he was unsure where they stood. He could not say, even to himself, what he wanted from her. One moment he had to be with her, the next he wanted escape. His feelings seemed to change from minute to minute, hour to hour. As much as he hated to admit it, he envied the naive certainty of Reverence Butts and his ilk, even if it concerned beliefs he himself could not accept. Disgusted with himself, his ambivalence, his disconnected life, he pressed the accelerator to the floor.

Pulled from his thoughts by the rattling engine, Nicolai glanced at him, gripping hold of his armrest to keep from falling. The roadside raced past in a blur.

Truman's troubled mood worried him. The van skidded around a curve and he grabbed the seatback, yelling above the engine noise.

"Why are you in such a dang hurry? You've about thrown me out of this seat twice already."

"Mind your own business," he growled.

"If I live or die *is* my dang business!" he yelled, making no effort to hide his anger. "Don't take it out on me and this old van just because you're mad about something. That's what kids do. You're supposed to be an adult."

Truman stared at the blacktop, his knuckles white against the steering wheel. Dark thoughts came at him from all directions. The van shuddered over a rough patch and he glanced at Nicolai, stung by the truth of his words, and then he eased off the accelerator. The engine dropped from pitched whine to low rumble.

Moments later, the landscape before them opened, the trees thinning and then falling away altogether. The earthen sides of a road cut, crimson and peppered with limestone, flashed by in a rush of color. Breaking from behind a cloud, a cloudless sky cast the hills in a golden light. He slowed and pulled off to the side of the road, lifting his aching hands from the steering wheel one at a time and working the joints loose. Nicolai took a breath and faced him.

"Are you alright, Truman?"

"I'm just tired is all."

"You're not mad at me?"

"No, I'm not mad at you. Why would you think that?"

"I don't know. Back there you just seemed…" he stopped, overwhelmed by all that had happened, by nearly losing his own life and, even more unthinkable, Truman's. He peered into this face. "I want you to like me, Truman."

"I do like you, Nicolai."

"My father hated me."

"I can't imagine why."

"You can't?"

263

"Whatever was wrong with your father, it wasn't about you. And what just happened back there wasn't about you."

"What got you so wound up then? I've never seen you that hard on anyone before, not even Mercer."

"That young preacher got under my skin, him peddling his religion along with his coffee. I don't like people pushing their ideas uninvited, as if you have no choice but to agree."

"I thought you believed in all that Jesus talk."

"What gave you that idea?"

"You work in a church, don't you?"

"I'm doing that because I have to, because I have a debt to pay."

"I thought you liked fixing up that church."

"I do like it. But just because I'm restoring a church doesn't mean I believe like the people that belong there."

"You don't believe any of what the parson was saying?"

"I can't say for sure just what I believe. All I know is it doesn't have much to do with a church, any church. Still, I was wrong to act like I did. I don't know what got into me. I'm tired but I won't make excuses. The way I treated the man was plain rude, no way to sugarcoat it. You were right to pull me out."

"I guess we both have reason to be tired."

"Once I see that the house is okay, I can rest."

"I wish we were there already. I don't think I can stand any more bad news."

As if answering his wish, the copper roof of the old hotel appeared above the hilltop, shining like a beacon. Minutes later, the broken down Clayton Oil and Gas building appeared on the left. Truman turned and started up the gravel street, passing between the dilapidated train station and the hotel, its brick walls glowing red in the afternoon light. The familiar hill loomed before them, the rutted and pockmarked road looking as it always had.

Truman angled up the slope, dodging potholes as the van strained to climb. Just before they reached the crest he came to a stop. As much as he wanted to see the old house he was hesitant, worried at what they might find. He glanced at Nicolai, seeing the same look in his eyes. Then he downshifted and the van lurched forward.

Chapter Thirty-four

The vacant lot and chain-link fence guarding
Throckmorton Hole passed to their left. Seconds later the
boarding house rooftop appeared above the road. Nicolai
leaned his elbows on the dashboard and peered through the
windshield in anticipation, murmuring a quick prayer of
hope under his breath just as they crested the hilltop and
the house came into view, looming above them, castle-like
and stately. He ran his gaze over the porch and walls, and
across the broad lawn. Though a shutter hung askew and an
armful of roofing tiles littered the yard, the place seemed
relatively intact, especially considering all they had just
seen. The old oak appeared as it always had, timeless and
grand.

He breathed a sigh of relief and then caught himself as
he spotted the sheriff's cruiser parked beyond the porch.
Truman saw the car an instant later. He slowed to a stop
and nodded toward the house.

"Looks like the sheriff has come for you again. We
can keep on going if you want to."

Nicolai peered at him. "You would do that for me?"

"I would. You deserve better."

Nicolai turned to the house, feeling as if he was
looking at an old friend, one patiently waiting for him to
arrive. At least the place had been a home, his home, for
awhile. If he had to leave, at least he would still have that.
He let his gaze drift over the house and sprawling oak,
memorizing a scene he hoped never to forget. His earlier
decision still stood. He would not go back to what he had
once been. That person was no more.

"I never thought anyone would help me like you all
have," he said, unable to face him for fear he would not
finish if he did, "you and Carlisle and Aiden, and most
surprising of all, Julius. For the first time in my life I had a
home, a real home here in this big house, this place of

spirits and sacred trees. But I'm through running away. I've got to face whatever comes next."

Tico stepped onto the porch and squinted into the waning light, waving them over as he climbed down the stairs. Carlisle and Aiden appeared in the doorway. Truman parked and reluctantly climbed out. Tico stood waiting under the oak.

"He's willing to go," Truman said, clasping Nicolai's shoulder. "Just give him a moment to say his goodbyes. I promise you he won't run."

"There's no need for all that," he announced as he waved off the idea. "I've brought good news for once."

Truman stared at him, reluctant to believe what he heard.

"What sort of news?"

"At the hearing," he said, pointing a finger at Nicolai, "Kennis argued that the usual foster family set-up doesn't work in your case. So, the judge decided you can stay here indefinitely as long as someone agrees to be responsible for you."

"There'll be no problem there, Tico," Truman said, glancing up the stairs. "Between the three of us, we should have it covered."

"That's just what I told him."

"The judge is letting me live here, like it's my real home?" he asked, unbelieving.

"He talked to Dr. Macallan about your mother and he understands the situation. He's hoping this arrangement is temporary and that eventually you'll be able to go live with her."

"What about that old witch from children's services? Will she stop chasing after me now?"

"The word is she's being reassigned to another region. I sure hope so. I've had about enough of her guff." He turned to Truman. "And that's not the half of it. Horace and Jerome Bell's brother flipped on each other like I figured they would, and then they turned on the Weeks."

"They've implicated the brothers in the murders?"

"Those Weeks boys will need a boatload of lawyers to skate on this one. I heard tell the district attorney is already bargaining a plea deal with their side, always a good sign. Now, I got a loose horse somewhere down the highway that I'd better find before an eighteen wheeler does. You all take care."

Tico's words roamed Nicolai's thoughts as he watched him hobble to the car and wedge himself behind the steering wheel. As much as he had hoped for a real home, he could not quite believe he finally had one. He climbed up the stairs and turned a circle, surveying the house and lawn, the hills beyond, violet in the waning light, and he felt a sudden and unfamiliar sense of belonging, as if the place held some part of him inside it.

The cruiser had just vanished below the hillside when another car crested the ridge, a plume of dust rising behind it like an omen. Moments later, Mercer's white Cadillac slid to a stop feet from the porch. Throwing open the door, he stumbled out, an unlit cigar clamped between his teeth. He squinted at Truman from the bottom of the stairs and jerked his thumb toward the street.

"That was the sheriff I just passed. What's he doing here? Are you people causing trouble again?"

"The sheriff's business with us is not your concern, Mercer," Truman said. "What do you want?"

"No need to be rude. I came to express my condolences for poor Rose. As much as he got on my nerves, I still respected the man, admired him even."

"You didn't come all the way up here just to tell us that."

"Well, I do have one other piece of business to tend to. I've had a change of heart in light of the unfortunate demise of Rose. I came to tell you I've decided not to sell the place after all."

"You decided this just out of the goodness of your heart, just because of your admiration for Julius?"

"Is that so damn hard to believe?" he grumbled.

Truman squinted down at him. "We know about the Weeks brothers and their legal troubles, Mercer."

"Oh… uh… right," he said, glancing down the road. "I guess the sheriff would've told you. They've reneged on the offer, the two-faced bastards."

Truman climbed down the stairs, stopping within inches of him.

"Do you have any idea what my name is, Mercer?"

"Why, it's Truman, of course. I've heard you called that on more than one occasion. Why on earth would you ask me that?"

"Truman is my first name. My last name is Birdsong."

The color drained from Mercer's face as he stared at them, speechless. Then he pivoted and started for his car.

"Well, it's an honest mistake, a mistake anyone could make," he jabbered as he hurried to leave, occasionally casting furtive glances in Truman's direction. "We dealt in cash only. I wrote no checks so I had no need for such details. Anyway, I need to… I'm going to be… I have an appointment in Abilene I have to get to."

"Surely you remember," Truman called after him, "the name of your ex-business partner, Royce Birdsong?"

He stopped and pulled a handkerchief from his pocket, wiping the sweat from his brow before turning to face Truman. Anger replaced the fear in his eyes.

"I've had business dealings with many individuals over the years," he said, his tone defiant. "I can't be expected to remember them all."

"You ought to remember the man you betrayed, the man you left responsible for debt he could never pay, the man whose life you ruined," he growled, barely able to contain his anger. "He lost the family ranch because of you."

"What's it to you how I conduct business? Not everyone has the knowhow to be successful."

"Royce was my father."

"Well, no one gets to choose their parents," he groused, unsurprised. "Some don't turn out so well."

"He was okay before you double-crossed him."

"That was years ago. I don't see that it matters now."

"I'll tell you how it matters, Mercer. The records Julius mentioned are financial statements showing you cheated the government out of thousands in tax dollars, money you still owe the feds not including interest... or jail, if you prefer. Those records might make their way to the authorities if you evict us."

"You wouldn't turn me in because of something that happened when you were still a kid, would you?"

"Sell this house out from under us and you're likely to find out."

"Why that's blackmail, exactly the kind of harebrained scheme Rose would concoct," he said, his voice shaking.

"It was his idea alright. I found a detailed plan in his desk, complete with papers drawn up by an attorney friend of his. The whole thing is airtight. You let us live here rent-free and the financial records stay where they are."

"That sounds like a threat."

"I call it a fair trade."

"I... I... it's a damn highway robbery!" he sputtered. "You Birdsongs are all alike, not to be trusted!"

He jerked open the Cadillac door and climbed in, scattering dust and gravel as he sped away. Truman watched the cloud rise into the air, disappearing above him like a pipe dream. Nicolai stood at the top of the stairs.

"That was sweet," he said, grinning.

"Now don't get any ideas. What I did was not smart. We may all end up homeless after all."

"But you didn't back down. That felt good, didn't it?"

Truman peered up at him, smiling in spite of himself.

"It did."

A dome of blue sky arched overhead as the van topped a sandstone ridge and began a slow descent onto an open plain studded with scrub brush and cacti. Waves of blonde grass stretched into the distance like an ivory sea, undulating before the coursing wind. The first real cold front of the season had sailed through overnight in a rush of thunder and rain, leaving in its wake a biting chill.

Nicolai glanced at Truman and turned back to the window, following the level horizon with his gaze. The scene seemed a stark contrast to the brush-crowded hills he had grown accustomed to. In his lap he cradled an unopened bottle of red wine. He could almost hear Julius nagging him to take care not to break the valuable cargo. He tightened his grip and peered through the windshield.

Clouds of red dust jumped from the roadside and vanished in the gale. Down the road a lone tree emerged from the haze, rising above the flat landscape like a compass needle. Truman slowed the van, pulling before a wrought iron fence that ran a quarter mile along the highway, a gate bisecting the near side. The sign over it read simply 'Rose'.

A gravel path led to the tree, a towering pine, and to a scattering of weathered headstones surrounding it in an irregular square. At one corner the ivory gleam of new stone marked the most recent grave. Without a word, Truman climbed from the van and began making his way toward the grave. Nicolai followed him through the gate and past the tree, the air beneath it filled with the acrid aroma of pine needles and resin. Wind hissed through the branches like rushing water.

They reached the marker and stood alongside the freshly spaded earth. The stone face stood brilliant in the autumn sunlight, the letters sharp as cut paper. Nicolai stared down at Julius' name etched in shadow. He still found it hard to believe he would not be back in his room when they returned, as if he had simply been away. The headstone seemed an impostor, a cruel joke, unnerving but without real meaning. Truman motioned toward the marker.

"Go ahead and leave the bottle," he said. "He's probably mad we took so long."

Nicolai set the wine at the base of the stone and stepped away.

"What do I do now?"

"If you have something to say, you can say it."

"I don't know what to say. Will you say something for both of us?"

Truman peered at him for a moment, nodded his agreement and turned back to the marker.

"We didn't always get along," he said, laying his hand on the smooth stone. "So, I thought you'd like this little peace offering. I owe you that much."

He stared at the grave, lost in thought. A burst of wind whipped past them, coursing through the iron fence in a low whistle. Nicolai shivered in the chill air.

"I never got to thank you for stepping in the way you did, Julius," Truman continued, "but I do thank you, we both do. You probably wouldn't see it this way, but you saved Nicolai. We'll never forget that."

He stood for a moment and stared at the mound of earth, and then he turned without another word and started back through the gravestones. Nicolai hesitated, peering out over the broad expanse of grass, the sky stretching horizon to horizon blue and infinite, scrubbed free of cloud. Above him a lone bird sailed on the buffeting wind. He watched it circle, marking a tight spiral, effortless, serene, rising as a spirit might choose to take flight.

Chapter Thirty-five

Silas' lilting voice drifted from Carlisle's room, followed by the cracking of pecan shells and the clinking of glasses. Nicolai stopped in the doorway and eyed the two men sitting opposite one another, tumblers cradled in their palms. Noticing him, Silas raised his glass and held it to the light.

"Take a look at the finest color this side of heaven, my boy. Come and have a dram with us."

"Not on your life," Carlisle barked, waving off the idea with flourish. "He's far too young..." he continued, a mischievous smile crossing his lips, "to appreciate a sublime twelve year old whisky such as we have here."

He took a sip and sat back, nodding his approval. Silas twisted the glass in his fingers, studying it.

"Perhaps you're right. Besides which," he added, setting the tumbler on the desk, "we have an errand to complete. We're due at the hospital shortly, so I'll need to save this beauty for after our return."

"We're going to see my mother?" Nicolai said, surprised.

"You don't remember? What happened to that exceptional memory I've been hearing about?"

"I do remember. I just thought Truman would take me. Anyway, Carlisle says my auditory memory is much better than my visual memory. When I hear something I remember it."

"Those are some fancy terms you're tossing around, son. Are you planning to take over for me? I'm not getting any younger, you know."

"Perhaps he will someday," Carlisle said. "There's no reason he couldn't be a doctor if he chose to. He's plenty smart enough. Besides, if you can do it, it can't be that hard."

"Oh, I'm just a lowly country doctor, not a fancy university don such as yourself." He stood and started for the door. "And don't drink my whisky while I'm gone."

Half an hour later, Nicolai followed Silas through the hospital entrance and down a brightly lit hallway, the polished floors water-like beneath the fluorescent glare. Nicolai watched as a woman in slippers and robe shuffled past, mumbling and crossing herself repeatedly in some sort of endless ritual. Two men dressed in white bolted from a nearby room, crossed the hall and vanished through a stairway door. Silas turned to him and shrugged.

They continued down the hallway, passing an adjacent corridor that ended in a glass and metal door edged with an elaborate set of security locks. Nicolai glanced through the wire-crossed window and jerked to a stop. Parfit was just inside. His eyes glassy, the stubble thick along his jaw, he paced the wall with deliberate, halting steps. Nicolai walked to the window and stood watching him for a moment before turning away.

Silas led him back to the hallway and pulled two pecans from his coat pocket, cracking them against each other and handing the nut to Nicolai. Tilting his palm, he let the shells drop to the floor. Nicolai stared down at the scattering of hulls.

"The nurse won't like that."

"I leave them just for her benefit. General Patton needs a bit of a reminder now and again."

"Who's General Patton?"

"That's what I call her, our friend the duty nurse. She likes giving orders."

"Oh," he said absently, glancing back toward the corridor.

"I'd have taken a different route if I'd had my head on straight, son. You weren't meant to see old Parfit like that."

"Is he really crazy?"

274

"Oh, I wouldn't put it that way, exactly. Old Parfit sees the word differently than you and me. He's a free thinker, a bit like you and Truman."

"We're going to end up like Parfit?" he said, his eyes wide.

"No, boy, what I mean is you and Truman, you don't let yourselves get hemmed in by someone else's idea of how the world works. You want to find your own way, see things as you see fit." He cracked open another pecan and popped it in his mouth. "Old Parfit has a bit of that. Unfortunately, he has a lot of something else and it messes about with his life something terrible. He knew a bad time was coming for him, but he did what he could for you while he could, before it overtook him."

"Like it did my mother," Nicolai said as he turned to the hallway.

"Ah, the world, she can be a cruel host. Your mother has had her share of troubles, true enough."

"Then I think I'd better go see her."

Truman waited on the steps of the small church, a chill autumn wind gusting about him in a swirl of leaves and dust. Tree-scattered specks of sunlight flickered at his feet. Though he had asked Kennis to meet him there, he was having second thoughts. They had seen each other nearly every day for a week. Was he rushing into another doomed relationship?

Before he could find an answer, her car rounded the curve. She slowed and angled across the parking lot toward him. At the sight of her a chill ran up the back of his neck, crowding out any misgivings. Moments later she stood before him. Sunlight glinted off her hair in eddies of light and dark.

"This is a surprise," she said, the hint of a smile crossing her lips. "Have you suddenly found religion?"

"Now that *would* be a surprise." He started toward the entrance. "I have something I want to show you."

275

Pulling open the heavy door, he led her into the musty stillness of the sanctuary, stopping just past the foyer. Multihued shafts of sunlight filled the air, stretching to the center aisle and beyond. Motes of dust drifted through the air like birds, tiny and directionless. Kennis turned a half-circle, her eyes moving from one window to the next.

"This stained glass is amazing. Who would ever guess a plain little church would have such beautiful windows."

"I suppose sometimes a bad start can have a good ending."

"What do you mean?"

"I asked you here because I wanted you to see them. I'll have to turn in my key tomorrow and it's not likely they'll allow a heathen like me inside during Sunday services."

"You had something to do with this?" she said, gesturing around the room.

"I designed them."

"You mean the windows? You're kidding, right?"

"They came out better than I expected."

"You're not kidding," she mumbled in disbelief. "Truman, you never mentioned on top of everything else you're an artist."

"I'm no artist, but in another life I was something close, an architect. Those days are gone. On the other hand, I've been asked to design the windows for a big Catholic church in Abilene, and this time I'll even get paid." He nodded down the aisle. "These windows I did for free, part of a probation deal I made before I came here."

"I think I'm ready to hear the rest of that story now. How about telling it over dinner? I'll probably get struck dead for saying this in here of all places," she whispered, drawing close, "but we can even have your favorite dessert… *before* dinner if you like."

"I like, alright, but I have something I need to finish first. It won't take long."

She leaned into him. "I'll be waiting."

He climbed the porch stairs and turned to survey the broken hills, shadow-strewn and violet beneath the low autumn sun. Thin clouds trailed over the horizon like smoke from distant fires. A chill breeze swept past him. All at once he felt a kinship with the wide land, the beauty he had once seen with a child's eyes once again before him.

Silhouetted against the turquoise sky, a flock of geese moved high overhead, their pitched calls mixed with the rustle of oak leaves. He shifted his gaze to the old tree, its massive limbs black in the dying light. They seemed to him to reach for the house as if to shield it, to protect it from the gusting wind.

Nicolai's voice drifted down the porch. He was reading *The Hobbit*. Truman turned and pushed through the front door, making his way down the hall and stopping in Carlisle's doorway. His eyes closed, Carlisle sat listening. Aiden stood nearby with his back against the wall, his eyes darting about as he followed the tale.

Nicolai glanced up at Truman without pausing, his voice slow and deliberate but clear. Truman thought he saw a hint of pride cross his face. Leaving the doorway, he retraced his steps and turned at the stairs, making his way to Julius' room.

Stepping inside, he pulled a chair to the desk and opened the top drawer, lifting out a folder with Nicolai's name on it and setting it aside. His book would remain unfinished, not unlike his young life. The short passage Truman had added about him would suffice for the time being.

He reached back into the drawer and pulled out a thin sheaf of papers, setting the blank pages on the desktop. Putting pen to paper, he scratched out Julius' name at the top of the page. Nicolai appeared at his shoulder. Truman turned, locking eyes with him.

"This is the book on Julius. How should it begin?"

Nicolai looked around the room, the strange figurines, the stacks of papers, the air still filled with Julius' presence, and at once knew how to answer. He nodded to Truman.

'Julius Rose was my friend.'